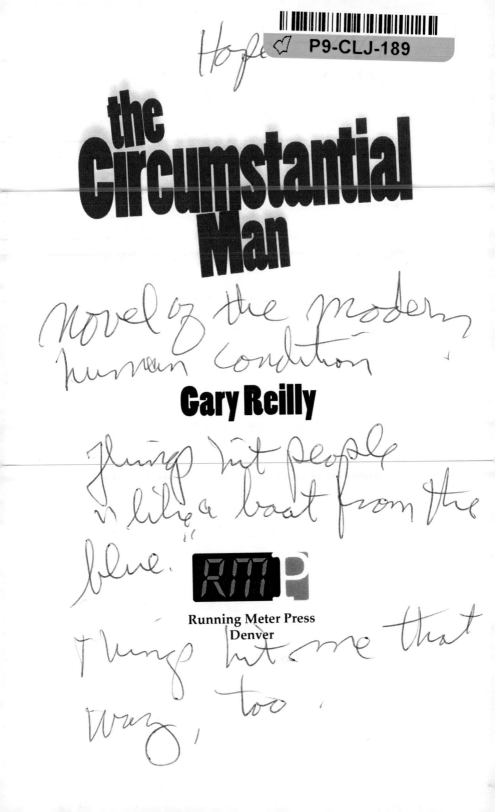

Hope

the Circumstantial Man

novel of the modern human condition

Gary Reilly

"Things hit people
'like a bolt from the
blue."

Running Meter Press
Denver

Things hit me that
way, too.

The Circumstantial Man

by Gary Reilly

Copyright 2018 by Running Meter Press

Published by

Running Meter Press
2509 Xanthia St., Denver, CO 80238

Publisher@RunningMeterPress.com
720-328-5488
Cover art and book design: Jody Chapel
Photography: Mark Stevens

ISBN: 978-0-9908666-7-1
Library of Congress Number: 2017959875
First edition, 2018

Printed in the United States of America

This book is a work of fiction. Any resemblance to actual persons, living or dead, business establishments, locales, or events is coincidental.

Also by Gary Reilly:

The Asphalt Warrior Series:
The Asphalt Warrior
Ticket to Hollywood
The Heart of Darkness Club
Home for the Holidays
Doctor Lovebeads
Dark Night of the Soul
Pickup At Union Station
Devil's Night

The Private Palmer Series:
The Enlisted Men's Club
The Detachment
The Discharge

Foreword

When Mike Keefe and I launched Running Meter Press in 2012 with the sole goal of publishing the vast trove of novels that Gary Reilly left behind, we really had no idea where the project was going or how long it would last. We made a quiet pledge, nothing too formal, to publish his books. That was it.

But how far would we make it into the stack of 25 unpublished novels? Which ones would we put out first? What if we didn't find Gary's audience? What then?

We need not have worried.

The Circumstantial Man is the twelfth title we have published since Gary's passing in March of 2011.

The response—your support—keeps us going. So have fabulous reviews from journals such as Booklist, stellar comments from literary lions like Stewart O'Nan and Ron Carlson, terrific reviews in *The Denver Post*, two rave mentions on National Public Radio, and a steady response from readers far and wide. Mike and I both knew Gary's writing was good. And we are thrilled that Gary's fans are eager to snap up the next title.

We are also indebted to the many individuals who are part of our growing, informal, erstwhile team. Thanks to Jody Chapel (my wife) for the cover, cover design, and interior design on this volume. Thanks to Canada's finest line editor, Karen Haverkamp, who poured in countless hours to make sure the copy was clean and consistent. Karen's keen eye never wavered and her level of precision should make atomic clocks feel as if they need to get their timing checked. Gary left clean manuscripts, but Karen's edits were impeccable.

Thanks also to The Tattered Cover for continuing to champion Gary's work. .

With *The Circumstantial Man* we say goodbye to Private Palmer, the protagonist of Gary's three Vietnam-era novels, which were based on Gary's experiences as an MP at Qui N'hon Air Field. We are also letting Murph, the star of eight novels in The Asphalt Warrior series to date, take an extended break from driving his cab around the humorous streets of Denver. Murph, we will get back to you soon. We know there are a couple more strange trips yet to take with your unique perspective on the world.

The Circumstantial Man is a suspense thriller. It's also stand-alone, as are many of the remaining novels in Gary's stash of stories. But of course a cab driver plays a key role. And there are cops. And yet again, like Palmer and Murph, there is a man who is up against the world and has lots of questions about the way that world works. His name is Pete Larkey. You won't soon forget his peculiar predicament and the forces that darken an otherwise routine day. But you'll always remember, when your car battery dies, to try wiggling the cables. Always, and I mean *always*, try that first.

Mark Stevens
November 2017

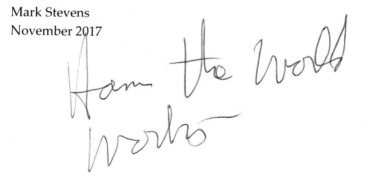

One

A winged creature the size of a fingernail fluttered past my face. I called these things "death moths." I didn't know what they were. There always seemed to be two or three in my house. I sometimes found their lifeless bodies on the kitchen counter or near the glass of water I kept on my bedside table at night. If a death moth flew past while I was getting ready for bed, I placed a paperback on top of the glass so the creature would not land in it and drown while I was sleeping. I was repulsed by the idea of feeling a soft fingernail sliding down my throat.

I was eating breakfast when the thing flew by. Cornflakes and a can of Coke. The moth interrupted my thoughts. I had a lot of things on my mind that morning. I had lost my job a week earlier, so it was time to start making the rounds. I had to get some money going, had to talk to strangers, put my thin roster of skills out there for employers to examine. In college I had been a liberal arts major but my degree never played a critical role in my hiring. I had always been a blue-collar worker, though not by design. I was once offered a teaching assistantship at a university through the influence of an English professor with whom I drank beer after classes, but I had no desire to teach grammar to pre-med students and slide-rule geeks. After I got my mitts on that degree, I said goodbye to learning.

The job I had lost was that of assistant maintenance man in a box factory. The maintenance man was a drunk who didn't show up for work half the time. My job was to follow him around and hand him tools, fasten pipes, change lightbulbs, push brooms, clean oil spills, do the things he was too weak or drunk to do. But he got fired, and since I had no one to assist, I got fired. I went straight to the state agency to see about a weekly unemployment check, but they told me that because I had quit a better job as a delivery driver six months earlier and had taken a cut in pay, I didn't qualify for benefits. Just the government messing with me. A judgment call on their part. Their definition of "better" did not coincide with mine. In my view, assisting a drunk who never showed up for work was better than driving a truck.

My Ford was parked on the driveway in front of the carport. The carport is simply a roof with four wooden posts supporting it. I don't have a garage. I don't own the house I live in. It costs me $450 a month in rent and is a bargain. It's located beyond the south edge of town where the woods begin. Nobody else wants to live out here. That's what I like about it. The nearest neighbor is a quarter mile away. We never communicate. That's what I like best about the place.

I tried to read the morning paper while I ate my cornflakes but the news bored me. It was all bloodshed. You get your fill of that. I read the comics, then closed the paper. I've never read a funny comic strip in my life. After I finished my cornflakes, I stared out the kitchen window at the landscape. I could see a section of Crestmoor Road. The two-lane blacktop wanders south out of town and passes by my house. No sidewalks. That's fine with me. If there were sidewalks people would just walk on them. But there is nothing out here. Broad fields and an asphalt road that meanders in sweeping curves toward town. It must have been a cow path in the olden days, which was eventually paved by the state. Roads intrigue me. Who plans roads?

I had to get on the road soon. Crestmoor was where the jobs were. I had to make the rounds. I was still wearing my slippers. I have carpeting in every square inch of my house, which means I don't have to wear shoes when I'm indoors. The people who built this house must have been morons. They put carpeting in both the kitchen and the bathroom. Christ knows what kinds of fungoid cities thrive beneath the bathroom carpet. I vacuum the bathroom once a week and spray it down with Lysol. But at least I don't have to put on my goddamn shoes when I get up in the morning. I feel like a king.

I put the breakfast crap away and decided not to do the dishes. I would be home by noon. I would get the breakfast and lunch dishes done in one swoop. I went into the bathroom to do all the things you have to do—shit, shower, and shave, as we used to say in the army. One two three. I stepped into the shower and let the spray hit me in the face. Hot thin needles. I cannot take a shower without thinking about Janet Leigh—ominous spigot blasting the camera. Only Hitchcock could make a terrifying object out of a bathroom fixture. I soaped, scrubbed, rinsed. Afterwards I brushed my teeth, flossed, gargled. The modern human body is like a boat held together with baling wire and spit. Constant maintenance, like the *African Queen*. Kick the carburetor, patch the hull, watch the fuel gauge, check the boiler. Christ. When was soap invented? Who took the bull by the horns and instituted hygiene? Monks? The Bible is filled with cleanliness tips. The Pentateuch. It's all in there. My mind drifts to thoughts like these when I'm in the shower.

I strolled out of the bathroom feeling like a new car

coasting out of a showroom, shiny and sparkling. I went into the bedroom and got dressed, picked up my keys from the chest of drawers. Another death moth fluttered past as I went about getting ready to go into town. I checked my billfold. Five twenty-dollar bills, some tens and ones. I would be needing more money soon. A steady cash flow. I was thirty-eight years old and had no job, no money, no wife, no friends, and no future. But I did have a past—a past thirty-eight years long, thirty-eight years wide, and thirty-eight years deep. It was filled to the brim with cravings and failure. Twenty years ago I was working as a janitor. Ten years ago I was delivering ice-cream. Death moths flew in and out of my past searching for something edible to sustain them, but there was nothing inside that box, not even a tiny particle of fleeting glory.

I peered through a rear window and studied the forest behind my house. I had never seen a deer, or even a squirrel, in the woods. I never hear birds. I don't know what lies beyond the far fringes of the woods. The trees probably peter out to farm fields where houses will be built someday. Dream castles. Young husbands and wives bloated with the excitement of manufacturing a future in the middle of nowhere. I did that once. Me and her.

I checked all the things you check before leaving the house. Lights. Locks. Billfold. Money. Keys. What else does a man need before going out into the world? The day was so nice I didn't need a coat. I stepped outside my cardboard castle and locked the door. I crossed the short sidewalk to the driveway. My car was an old pale green Ford. After our divorce, my ex-wife got the Plymouth. I opened the door to let the heat spill out, then climbed in and settled behind the steering wheel. I slid the key into the ignition and turned it. Nothing happened.

I lost all sense of being. It was as if a croquet mallet had knocked my brain a hundred yards into the deep grass. The battery was dead, this I knew. I twisted the key again and again like a bored baboon batting at a tire swing. I stopped and sat staring at the empty space of the carport. Why would my battery be dead? It had worked last night when I parked after coming home from the bar where I stopped off for a beer. Why do things cease to function, why do things die? There was no reason for it. No one had touched the battery in the past twelve hours. Batteries don't have moving parts. But somehow the electricity had escaped, dripped onto the driveway, and spilled into my lawn, executing ants before being absorbed into the body of mother earth.

I got out of the car and went back into the house and sat on a living room chair with my face in my hands to block out the daylight and allow my brain to calm down. I sat the way I always do when experiencing angst, like a Rodin statue. I remained this way for two or three minutes, then dragged my fingers down my face to wipe away the last residue of defeat before making a decision. It was a long walk into town, the equivalent of eight city blocks—the long blocks that go north and south, not the short blocks that go east and west. It would take a half hour to walk to the edge of town where the Crestmoor strip mall made its appearance. There was an auto-parts store in the mall, as well as the bar where I had stopped the previous evening before driving home with my perfectly working battery.

I glanced at my wristwatch. It was a few minutes after nine. I would walk to the mall, have a beer, and buy a battery. I needed the exercise anyway. But I would take a taxi home with the battery. An eight-block ride. The driver would be exasperated. Taxi drivers act like the world owes them a long trip. I would tip him three dollars just to keep him from hurling lightning bolts of mental disgust at me.

I walked outside and locked the door, then stepped over

to the driveway and took a look at the dead hunk of steel on wheels that made me feel impotent. How did the human race survive five thousand years without automobiles? How did Shakespeare write plays, how did Beethoven write symphonies, how did George Washington overthrow the British without a jalopy parked beside his tent?

I started walking. I crossed over to the side facing traffic, even though there was no traffic. Cars rarely seemed to come along the road. I live in the suburb of the suburbs. Very little traffic, a selling point if I was in the market to buy the box I live in, but isn't this how fate bushwhacks you? You grow so used to the vast emptiness of the road that your mind wanders and the next thing you know, a hot rod nails you from behind. Traffic is homeopathic. You need just enough of it to keep you alert. There is nothing to reflect the noise of approaching traffic. I can shout at the top of my voice and the sound dies five feet from my mouth.

A few weeks earlier I was driving on an interstate and saw a lone man playing the bagpipes. A man of knowledge, I told myself. He was centered in his private universe. He looked young, so he probably didn't have a wife to tell him to take that Christawful screeching out of the house. Parents maybe. But it didn't matter. He took it upon himself to stand alone in a field squeezing the plaid bag and making the music he loved. Why else would a man play bagpipes except out of love? But I was driving so fast I couldn't hear the music. My windows were rolled up. I saw him for only an instant, but he filled my heart with joy. He was a fellow who knew exactly what he was doing, why he was doing it, and where to do it with maximum verve and noninterference. I sensed all that as I watched him dwindle to nothing in my rearview mirror.

I tried not to think about my dead battery as I hiked along the road. Victimization gets my goat. But it's hard not to think

12

about why you're walking when you should be driving. It was only eight blocks though. Already on the horizon I could see the roofs of the Crestmoor strip mall and the fast-food joints that had sprouted near it like fungus around the drain of a bathtub. It was like seeing distant boats on a yellow ocean. The fields beyond my house are dry and fallow. They will be filled with castles one day. The human race is ever expanding. I laugh when I read alarmist science-fiction novels about an overcrowded world. They're written by nerds who live in megatropolises. They think the whole world is like New York City. They ought to visit Nebraska sometime. They will flee to the tenements of the Bronx and pray that the prairie will never creep east and get them.

The boats on the horizon changed into storefronts, and I saw the Apex Auto Parts store, which I immediately assumed would be closed. Worst-case scenarios infect my mind when I need something. But a couple cars were parked out front. One had a raised hood. People fix their cars outside the auto store. People do things for themselves as they did in the nineteenth century. Civilization peaked when the man who wore the big bright Texaco star was put out to pasture. The memory of pump jockeys is bizarre. When was the last time you said, "Fill 'er up," not to mention "Check the oil"? The great-grandchildren of America will not believe there was a time when uniformed men swarmed all over our cars with sponges and smiles.

I passed the T-intersection at Hawthorne Drive, a newish asphalt road one block south of the strip mall. It shot off to my left. There is nothing on either side of Hawthorne for a quarter mile, then there are new houses, the first wave of suburban castles that will creep toward my cracker box.

I had time to go to the bar for a morning beer. I had all day, in fact. The auto-parts store closed at five. I learned this the hard way. My patch of the earth shuts down at five o'clock.

The auto-parts store is at one end of the strip mall, and the bar is in the middle, next to a liquor store. There are other small businesses that I have never frequented. There was a head shop once but the outraged citizenry talked the city council into shutting it down. But that was long ago. The city outlawed drug paraphernalia, glass tubes, mirrors, the kinds of things dopers can buy at any drugstore. This town is overrun with morons.

I changed my angle of approach and headed for the bar with its discreet neon signage that says "Lemon Tree Lounge." When I first moved to town it was called the "Tip-Top." They might as well have called it "Who Gives A Damn Come In And Buy Our Booze." Words are stupid.

I crossed the asphalt parking lot. There wasn't a speck of dirt or windblown newspapers anywhere in sight. The strip mall is as clean and tidy as Holland. Everything in Crestmoor is clean and tidy, except the inner lives of people like me. The door to the Lemon is padded on the outside with a soft red material like Naugahyde. It's the stupidest door I have ever seen in my life.

"Oh, looky looky, look who's here. It's my friend Malarkey."

I was barely through the door, the sunlight at my back, when I heard the voice of the last man on earth I ever wanted to see. He recognized my silhouette framed in the doorway. He had seen it before. Height. Girth. Stoop-shouldered, that's me when the weight of the world has me down.

"Now get on over here and answer me a question," he said. His name was Morton. He used to be a mechanic at a place called Mac's Garage. He was seated on "his" stool at the far end of the bar. There were a couple other drinkers in the lounge, early boozers, businessmen sneaking in for a quick one before hitting the road with their satchels, briefcases, sales pitches, whatever white-collar commission men carry. The door thumped at my back, folding the fan of white light that was blinding the patrons. I couldn't see. That's daytime drinking for you. Bars are midnight places. Thick curtains on the windows. Ambience. My pupils adjusted. The colored lights of the silent jukebox made their appearance, then the beer signs behind the bar. I inhaled the pungent smoke and alcohol odor of airtight joints. Rudy, the bartender, was backlit by a sign advertising Carling Black Label. He was polishing a glass.

"Right here," Morton said, slapping his palm on the stool next to him. Patting it down. Preparing me for lectures. "Draw one for my man Malarkey."

Guys like Morton are hard to take at dawn, noon, early evening. You need three or four beers in you before you can tolerate guys like Morton. Part of me wanted to turn around and go back outside, walk to the auto-parts store, buy my battery, call a cab, go home, start my car, and look for a job. That's where *that* part of me ended. I had all day to look for a job. I had all my life. I would be looking for a job ten years from now.

I trudged with resignation toward the padded barstool. No point in sitting at the other end of the bar, he would just talk louder to me. No point in hiding in a booth. His voice was everywhere. No point in ruining the day of the commission men bolstering themselves to snatch the first buck and hang on tight. They had wives. Men who dress and drink like that at dawn have wives.

The bartender set a beer in front of the stool before I got mounted.

"Now you tell me," Morton said, raising a finger and crooking it like he was going to tap a doorbell. "Was I born for a purpose, or for no reason at all?"

I nodded and let him choose the answer he liked best.

"I mean to say," he continued, "if I was born for a purpose, why is my left knee worthless? And if I was born for no reason at all, why am I still alive?"

"Just lucky I guess," taking my first sip and feeling the clock race toward midnight. Every sip is a midnight sip. Doesn't matter what the clock says. It would spring back to 9:30 a.m. when I stepped outside. I had things to do, fix my car, find a job. I took a second sip to forget the first sip.

"I was born in 1953," Morton continued. "Billions of people lived on this planet before me, and then one day I came to consciousness inside a baby's brain, and I want to know why the universe held up my appearance until 1:30 a.m. on April 14, 1953, to place me in a maternity ward in Holyoke, Massachusetts."

"Luck of the draw," I said.

"She. It." He took a sip of his private midnight. "I don't buy it. Luck cannot possibly be involved. Trillions of years, hundreds of trillions, the black void, Big Bang, then one night I open my eyes after a doctor slaps my silly little pink ass." He took a sip. "Why?" he said. "Why was I born in 1953?"

Why was his leg crushed under a car? Why was he on permanent disability? Why did he have a compensation check coming in every month that gave him just enough money to stay alive until he died?

I set my beer down and looked at the complacent face of the bartender. It takes a special breed of man to endure people like Morton and me and commission men and late-night weeping women and testosterone bucks of the last-call fistfight. I could never be a bartender.

"Maybe the universe wanted your opinion of television," I said.

He faced front, rested his left elbow on the bar, and pinched his lower lip between thumb and forefinger. "I'll take that into consideration."

"What's up, Pete?" the bartender said. "You're in here early."

My name is Pete. My last name is Larkey. Morton grabbed hold of that fact the day he met me.

"It's a long story but I'll make it short," I said. "I tried to start my car this morning but it's dead. I had to walk here. I have to buy a battery at the auto-parts."

The bartender nodded. He approved of walking drinkers. He set the polished glass down and fished a new one out of a tub of water in front of him.

"Dead battery," Morton mused. I could hear the gears grinding in his brain. He would link that up with something else. He could make a connection between the temperature of the Arctic and the price of a Renoir, given enough time. He didn't even need beer to do it. I had seen him sober plenty of times. It was my car that crushed his left leg. That, and a defective jack. The jack was the property of the garage where he had worked, thank God.

"Did you check it?"

I looked over at Morton.

"The battery," he said. "Did you check it?"

"What's to check?" I said. "The car wouldn't start."

"But did you check it?"

I could see it coming. He had worked in a garage. He was drifting into the wan territory of his lost turf. The humor had gone out of his voice. He was in his element now. Cars. Garages. The technical aspects of internal combustion in conjunction with electrical wiring systems. The time to joke had passed. An amateur was seated next to him. The probing glare of the tried-and-true expert graced my face.

"I turned the ignition and it wouldn't start," I said with a snarl.

"But did you check it?"

"What's to fucking check?"

"Did it make a clicking sound?"

"It didn't make any sound at all," I said. "It was dead. No life. No juice. No click. No nothing. Like a boat out of the blue."

He flinched. I was toying with him. He once got into a psychotic argument with a barfly who insisted that Jiminy Cricket sang "Like a *boat* out of the blue, fate steps in," etc., and I was there to witness Morton trying to talk sense into a drunk. The drunk was insistent and Morton was pedantic. A volatile combination even when two men are sober. Who among us has never tried to talk sense into a drunk? Morton did not like to be reminded of that duel. He glanced at me and offered the dour look that says I know where you're coming from so let's drop it and get on with the real business at hand.

"Did you wiggle the cables? Did you examine the battery for corrosion?"

"What do I look like, a goddamn garage mechanic?" I said before I could stop myself. My car cracked his tibia when the jack collapsed. Bone sticking out. Ambulance. I stood speechless throughout the entire drama. A cop even showed up.

I sat on the barstool waiting for Morton to get angry. A wisecrack like mine could generate rancor. But he was too wrapped up in the dynamics of turf management, memories of the old days, tracing a problem back to its source. "Did you open the hood?" he said with a frown that demanded I say yes.

"No."

A puff of air shot off his tongue like a torpedo. He faced front and took a drink of beer. I had violated every precept he had lived by since the day he had graduated from shop class in 1971. Holyoke High. Destined for greatness, he would work only on American cars. The Japanese put an end to that dream. He had to learn how to repair Toyotas, Subarus. But the dream didn't die until I showed up with my pale green Ford. Dream Dasher. Bone Breaker. His wife later left him.

"If I was you, Malarkey, I'd walk back home and give your cables a wiggle. You're gonna spend upwards of sixty bucks on a battery you might not need."

"That's an expert talking, not a layman," I said. "When my car won't start, I clear the decks, buy a new battery, and start my life over again."

"That's what keeps the auto-parts industry in business," he said. "People like you."

I was finished drinking for the day. I could have quizzed him on his moves whenever his water heater blew, but that was midnight talk. One-upmanship. Get the bartender to referee. Call upon drunk strangers for backup. Divide the room into opposing teams. But I knew in my heart he was right. I could have popped the hood, wiggled the cables. I had done that before. It's the kind of thing you do so rarely that you forget to do it in the clutch. It made my head spin. What to do now? Walk back home and pop the hood, or just buy a battery and call a cab? But I knew what to do. Even if I brought the old battery back to life I would still end up buying a new battery. The gods had spoken. They give hints. They toy with mankind. Did I want to spend the next two weeks wondering if my car would start every morning? It's cowards like me that keep the auto-parts industry going.

"Why don't I come with you to your house and look at the battery?" Morton said.

I shook my head no. "I wouldn't want to put you to the trouble. I had to walk here."

19

"No trouble," he said. "We'll take a taxi. I'll buy and we'll fly."

I was annoyed by his offer. There was no rationale to my refusal. It's just that I do not like offers of help no matter how well intentioned. A childish posture, I will admit. But I can stumble through life on my own two clumsy feet, thank you.

I slapped three bucks onto the bar. "Keep it."

Bang. Conversation over. Morton and his death questions. He didn't want me to leave, go it alone, test my battery without the supervision of an expert. I could feel his invisible grip reaching out to drag me back to the barstool for one more beer before hitting the road. The bartender was indifferent to my leaving. You don't open a business because you're worried there won't be any customers.

I stepped outside into the nine-thirty sunlight. Not a cloud. It could have been May or September. It didn't matter. It wouldn't matter ten years from now when I stepped outside a factory door or a bakery where I would be delivering bread for a living. Between the bar and the auto-parts store stood a cluster of newspaper boxes, some steel, some molded plastic. The molded plastic stocked free real estate pamphlets and job guides. The metal boxes held the authentic news, local, national. I stopped in front of a molded green box and looked at the stack of untouched newspapers, tabloid size. I opened the lid and reached in and pulled out a paper and strolled along the sidewalk flipping through the pages. Accountant. That's always the first listing. What does it take to be an accountant? Two quarters and a box top and no reason to exist. I was out of box tops. I paused to scan the other ads. Same old shit. I always looked at the ads for "drivers." I wanted to work on the open road, no boss, no supervisor, just mountain highways that lead downhill to lost brakes and deadly pileups. I could never be a cross-country driver. One week of that and I would be going to accounting school. One week of that and I would be looking for a reason to exist. But I gave up on that long ago. What was it Morton had said? "Was I born for a purpose, or for no reason at all?" Here I was, looking to Morton for career guidance.

I stuffed the newspaper into a trash barrel. I walked on down to Apex, wondering what it took to work in an auto-parts store. An encyclopedic familiarity with inventory and stock numbers that would put a Burroughs Business Machine to shame. The dreams of auto-parts clerks must be bizarre. Roaming surreal stockrooms looking for parts that don't exist. An esoteric version of my own dreams. I still dream of the first job I ever had, a stock boy in a carpet warehouse. Again and again I return to that awful place in my dreams and get my old job back and practically weep for joy. Security. I was eighteen years old when they gave me that job and I couldn't believe my luck. Manual labor! I can do that!

I did it in the army. Two years. Thought I was going to be a fighting man. I swept floors. Made beds. Did that beat ducking bullets? Reason and intelligence would say yes. Jack Kerouac is quoted by Ann Charters about his brief term of service in a navy boot camp, mop pushing, bed making, KP, "As if they couldn't hire shits to do that." And what—I asked myself when I read his hilarious account of his minimal stretch in the service—did he think he was? His mother ironed his shirts and pants before he went to town to get wasted. An amusing guy. Funnier than he ever realized.

I stopped outside the parts store and looked off down the asphalt ribbon of Crestmoor Road, thinking about my car. I couldn't see my house from there. It was just over the horizon. I stared at the curve of the earth, thinking about Morton's warning. Sixty bucks for a battery that I might not need. What if it was just a cable problem? Could I get the battery tested and save money? When had I bought it?

I stood in the hot morning sunlight wracked with new indecision. That's what I got for interacting with the human race. If I hadn't gone in for a beer I would have simply bought a battery and been home already, and probably on my way to the employment agency. I should stop going into places. That was part of my indecision. Should I go into the auto store and buy a battery and call a cab? I decided to go in. What else could I do—make a 12-volt battery out of a tree stump the way the ancient Romans did? Maybe the parts clerk would let me borrow a shopping cart to push my battery home. Save the taxi fare. I thought this over. No. People will sell you shit, but they won't loan you shit.

A bell above the door rang as I stepped inside. There were no other customers now. It was like a mortuary. A passive racket, biding its time. A clerk was fiddling with the computerized cash register as I walked in. He looked up at me, smiled, nodded, looked back at his monitor. He didn't ask if he could help me find anything. People who walk into auto-parts stores know what they need in order to solve the problem ruining their lives, or they wouldn't be there. They would be down on their imploring knees in a garage.

I walked over to the aisle where the batteries were displayed. My eyes were drawn instantly to the sixty-dollar batteries. Morton knew his business. There were cheaper batteries, and batteries that ran to a hundred bucks, but the sixty-dollar model looked like my main man. Probably the bestseller in the store. I placed my hands on it, gave it a test heft. Heavy. Not something I could lug home on foot. The expense of a taxi added to the cost of the battery. Then it hit me. Walk home, wiggle the cables, see if my car would come to life, and if so, drive it back here and save the cost of a cab, plus avoid lightning bolts of mental disgust.

I walked farther along the aisle looking at all the auto gadgets that I would never buy. Baubles. Things to hang from your rearview mirror. Elastic covers for steering wheels. A Christmas store for grown-ups. I had a craving to buy something. The Big Boys know how to pry into a customer's brain like a safecracker and get at that money. Buy me. I'm new. Glue this tiny convex mirror to your side-view mirror and get The Big Picture. Safety first! When I was a kid, the neighborhood nutcase drove a purple 1956 Mercury with every rescue gadget known to mankind in his car. I'm talking shortwave radio, road flares, amber and red lights attached to the roof. He was a man with orange hair and a serrated voice who scared the hell out of us kids, but he was just a good-hearted guy who would take part in rescues whenever the National Guard or Highway Patrol needed civilian volunteers, the kind of fellow who would fill sandbags during a flood. He didn't seem to have a job. He drove the neighborhood with a microphone at his lips. God knows who he was talking to. Other members of his civilian nut corps, I supposed. You could see it in his eyes though. He wanted something bad to happen so he could help. Scared us kids. It was all one-sided of course, our side. My own wariness of him derived from knowing a person who was always prepared for any calamity. I couldn't wrap my eight-year-old brain around that. My parents were never prepared for anything. I am their offspring. If the rescue man saw someone changing a flat tire along the side of the road, he was Johnny-on-the-spot, hopping out of his purple Plymouth and wielding a jack handle and popping hubcaps. A crazed Batman. His life seemed otherwise purposeless.

I wandered through the auto-parts store looking at things that reeked of new-car smell, the way a man might browse through a hardware store when he didn't really need anything to keep his house properly groomed. Then I headed for the front door. The man at the cash register looked up at me, smiled, nodded, looked down at his computer. There was no grease on his uniform, a snappy gray affair. Morton was covered with grease the day my car broke his leg. Grease and blood. That's why I don't avoid him when I see him in the bar. I've seen him at his worst already, like a combat casualty. Permanent disability. He held nothing against me, yet it was my car that did it, my green Ford that brought his world crashing down around his left leg. I didn't feel guilty though. Just maudlin. If I hadn't shown up that day, he would still be a functioning garage mechanic. Luck of the draw.

I stepped outside and headed across the pristine parking lot. I needed the exercise. When I found a job, as I knew I would, I would never get any exercise again. I lived on a couch or a car seat. With luck, I would find a desk job. I've had a few. Shuffled papers, watched the clock chew the seconds off my life like a beaver gnawing bark. As Morton said, "Was I born for a purpose, or for no reason at all?" As good a pointless question as any.

I headed off down the road feeling as if I had made a decision. Maybe my car would start. Like pulling the handle on a slot machine. Small thrill. Something to look forward to.

After I crossed the Hawthorne intersection it occurred to me that I ought to have called a cab, ridden home, wiggled the cables, and if it didn't start, come back, buy a battery, and return home. Give the cabbie a three-way round-trip. I felt tired already. My feet could feel the hardness of the asphalt. I wasn't used to walking.

A car passed me from behind. I was walking on the left side of the road. I glanced over and saw a woman at the wheel. It made me think of my ex. I thought of sticking out my thumb. Maybe she would pick up a hitchhiker. We would drive to my

24

house. Offer her a drink to show my gratitude. Get to know each other. Fall in love, get married, descend into a hellish mess that would end three years from now. Another bone to chew on. My brain is ravenous. It will chew on anything. I had a dog like that when I was a boy. My mother bought it special-diet canned food, but when I took him for a walk the dog would pick up dead squirrels, rotted food, anything festering on a lawn and gulp it down. The animal food industry is a racket. Special diets for beasts one evolutionary step away from the wolf. But we fall for it. Americans love their dogs. I loved Elmer. That was my dog's name. I named him after Elmer Fudd. He was a mutt, mixed breed, the heartiest of animals they say. I'll take their word for it. He died of old age. I am barely six in dog years.

A car came over the horizon in my direction. I stepped off to the side of the road to make way for the machine. I don't duel with cars, demand right-of-way, display umbrage. Self-righteousness isn't worth the price. My Ford wasn't even moving when it hit Morton.

I watched the approach of the car. It had a familiar carriage. It came closer, and familiarity blossomed into recognition. I slowed.

Then I stopped.

Was that my car?

I stepped farther off to the side of the road and squinted at it. Could there be another green Ford in this county? It was traveling the speed limit, thirty-five, rolling toward me with every scratch and dent coming into familiar focus. My eyes were drawn to the windshield. Dark silhouette of a head. My Ford sailed past with someone else at the wheel. I was dumbstruck. I noted the blue work shirt worn by the driver, a tough-looking character, longish dark hair, staring straight ahead, didn't appear to see me.

I turned with its passing and watched my taillights dwindling down the road. I was drawn toward it as if invisible car hands were reaching out—save me, I'm being taken away! I yelled "Hey!" but the sound died on the prairie air. I began jogging after my car. My machine was alive. The battery worked. Manifest proof. My brain chewed on that as I ran toward the strip mall watching my car growing smaller and smaller in the distance.

It was instinctive, this run, as instinctive as running from danger. The body takes over. The mind is too rattled to make logical choices. The snake brain is activated—something belonging to me is going away. I saw the car turn left at the intersection of Hawthorne Drive and cruise toward the residential district. He wasn't speeding, this thief, just taking his leisurely time driving a car that didn't belong to him. The work shirt made me think he was a convict. Escaped. Was there a prison in the vicinity? I did not think so. He might have traveled for miles on foot in the night, then saw an opportunity to put fast distance between himself and whatever lockup or work farm he had fled—a car parked on a driveway in front of a house in the middle of nowhere. Surely he had come out of the woods. Might have lain in wait, might have witnessed my plight, dead car, dead battery, the fool who lives alone trudging off toward town leaving a window of opportunity to hot-wire an automobile.

I came to the intersection and looked off to my left and saw the faintest shadow of the rear of my automobile in the distance. It had stopped!

I made the left turn onto Hawthorne and picked up speed. The nearest house was two blocks farther along. I could phone from there. I hurried my pace and only then heard the whimpering of my lungs and lips. I had not run anywhere in ten years. It was catching up with me. I was forced to slow in spite of my desperation. Maybe the convict had stopped to pick up a cohort, someone on the outside, a dame who would hide him until the coast was clear. My analysis turned to fictive speculation, wishful thinking, hope—the duplicitous thing that yanks men out of bed every morning.

I slowed more as I got closer, my body faltering in the clutch. This is how it goes in dreams. You never seem to reach your goal. My car had stopped and my personal speed meant nothing. I was merely walking fast now and heaving tired breath. I justified it mentally. Save my strength for the moment when I arrived at my car and confronted the felon.

I imagined the scene. Yanking the door open, a snarl of anger, vindictiveness, a curled fist, the demand of an explanation. The movie heroics took a bad turn here. He leaps out and coldcocks me—or—he jams the shift into low and peels out, spinning me like a top. How many times in a wronged man's life is he granted the privilege of confronting a perpetrator? But you falter in the clutch. You don't know what to say. Adrenaline does battle with common sense. Call the police, that's what our system of justice was set up for, to let cooler heads prevail and allow the weak to defeat the strong.

Then it moved. The car lurched forward and began dwindling. Another whimper from my lips, I got back up to speed, my calves aching. My left hand reached out, stop, I almost caught you! But the car was moving, and I could see now that it was speeding. Fast exit. The dame probably had come running out of the house with a suitcase and dove in. Off to Vegas! Charles Starkweather and his moll back in action. I slowed to a fast walk. People were coming out of their houses. Had he burned rubber? Unusual sound in a placid suburb, mothers checking on children, fathers distracted from sports TV, what's going on out there on the normally quiet street?

People always converge. Herd instinct. Circle the wagons. Protect the tribe. By the time I was within hearing distance of conversations, I was moving at a trudging pace. At least I could phone from the home of a bystander. I would have to explain myself to these people. Yes, that was my car. Did you see the driver? Did he pick anyone up? I was rehearsing my lines for the moment when they would turn and see a lone man staggering along the asphalt and wonder what new strange thing was taking place in suburbia.

I was one block away when I saw the body lying at the side of the road. This brought me up short. I stopped and looked at three men who were kneeling by the body, peering closely but not touching it. My God, somebody had been knocked to the pavement. By my stolen car. A few faces turned my way. Why did this make me feel guilty? I began moving again, my lungs ballooning. I was in terrible shape. I did not think I would be able to speak when I got to the crowd.

I heard it then, the whine of a siren at my back. I turned and saw an ambulance coming my way. I stepped off to the side of the road and whispered a prayer of gratitude for the window of opportunity granted me to stop this maniacal and irrational run and catch my breath. The authorities were arriving. A stratum of care was lifted from everyone's shoulders. Men who knew their business were coming to take charge of things. I stood gasping and swallowing as the ambulance rolled by, its moderate speed incongruent with the soaring whine of the siren that made it sound like a meteor. A thought passed through my mind. What sort of men became medics? Was it a part-time job? They are not doctors, so what are they? One notch above a purple Plymouth man, trained in first aid, like soldiers in the army, medics on a battlefield, stop the bleeding, protect the wound. I had known two men in my youth who had gotten jobs as medics, assistants technically,

28

lugging bodies on stretchers down to ambulances and taking them to hospitals where the high-paid help plugged them into respirators, heart monitors, insurance systems. One of them was a student, the other had simply been unemployed. Twenty-two, twenty-three years old. Those were the sorts of people who became medics. Same people who clerk all-nite food marts. People like me, yet not like me—you have to harden your mind to deal with suffering. The day Morton was injured I felt as useless as an expired coupon.

It passed by. I watched it slow down, bright red brake lights, people parting to make way. Herd instinct. Large dangerous thing approaching. I stood gasping and panting for breath, fists on hips, torso leaning forward, the Rodin stance of the exhausted man. I watched the medics leap out white-coated and all business. The prone body was in front of the ambulance, so I could not see the medics kneeling to their work. I looked behind me and marveled at the distance I had made from the moment I had seen my car pass by. An L shape on the landscape, back along the road and to the south where the surprising sight of my car had interrupted my thoughts.

My breathing slowed. My health was returning. I looked at the ambulance and felt the compulsion of the good citizen to march toward these men and report the facts. I would now be speaking to authority figures, but it was inevitable—it was my car that had done this. When would my car stop harming people? I thought of Morton when my Ford pounced on him like a bear, the howl of surprise and pain. Everyone came running. I could not count the volunteers who grabbed my Ford by the slats and lifted it while mechanics placed red triangular safety supports beneath the frame so the medics could get at him as soon as they arrived, which was not long after.

My God, could these be the same medics?

It was not beyond the realm of possibility. What would these medics think if I showed up to report that—once again—I was a key player in a disaster? This altered my thoughts.

The frown that settled on my brow might have been mistaken by a rubbernecker as the frown of a man wondering what in blazes was going on here. However, it was, in reality, the frown of a man wondering to what extent his involvement in a hit-and-run ought to be reported to men of medicine as opposed to a cop. Did these men have a need to know? And what of the people standing around with expressions of shock, dismay, even anger? They would overhear me, the word would get out fast. It was *his* car that did it. "Again?" one of the medics might say with a stab of inappropriate black humor directed at me, a medic whose mind had been hardened to the suffering he dealt with daily, a remark like a friendly, tough, obnoxious elbow to the ribs in jest. "You again?" The crowd would turn slowly, "Niagara Faaalllls," and size me up with fresh eyes. "Your car? What was your car doing speeding on our street?"

I began to redirect my train of thought. Best to wait for the police to show up and make my report in private. This I told myself as I came to the fringes of the crowd of sightseers watching the medics expertly placing the man on the stretcher. One of the medics was saying something to the victim, and a curtain of relief was swept aside within my heart revealing a living being and not a fatality. I had closed my mind to that possibility. I did not want to think about it, my delinquent car graduating to the status of killer.

So I became a face in the crowd, one among many dressed casually this morning, strangers bonded by disaster, the way most strangers bond. Faces turned briefly toward me as I edged forward to get a better look. Yes. Blood on the asphalt. Not a minor thing. The victim's body was covered with a blanket. His head had bled. Some sort of temporary bandage had been placed on his forehead, hiding his eyes, obscuring the features of his face. God knows what kinds of gimcrack medical devices had been invented since the days of Civil War handsaws and a bottle of Jack Daniels to ease the pain. Plastic things. Neck braces. Splints. It's a cottage industry. Nobody goes broke investing in the medical racket.

The urge to tell all was still in me, it had the quality of confession. My car did this. But I was not the perpetrator. People would squint at me, "Say again . . . *your* car?"

The medics slid the stretcher into the rear of the ambulance. Volunteers held onto the doors, which were swept as wide as condor wings. Everything was taken care of with a speed and efficiency most people have little contact with. One two three.

"Did any of you see what happened?" a medic said loudly.

I could sense the hesitation of the crowd. I was its fountainhead. I said nothing. After all, I had not been close enough to see what had happened, I had noted only that my car had stopped while my mind spun scenarios of eager dames and flight to avoid prosecution.

"I didn't see it but I heard it," a man said. He was dressed for outdoor gardening, wearing green-stained cloth gloves and holding hedge shears. His world had been interrupted, perhaps a squeal of brakes, a hideous thud, perhaps glancing around as he trimmed his leaves to see a man lying on the street, a car stopped, only to become a hit-and-run.

"You need to wait for the police to show up. Tell them what you saw. We have to go."

I looked at the faces surrounding me and sensed a desire by some people to articulate their role in this scenario, let the medic know what they had been doing when their own worlds had been interrupted. But no one else spoke. Perhaps there had been a true eyewitness, perhaps he was saving his role like a surprise package to offer to the police and not to a mere medic.

I felt anger at what had happened. I was not the only one violated now, the thief had knocked a man to the road. I looked farther along the asphalt in the direction my car had gone, and I made a decision. I would continue my search. Things had been resolved here, the victim was alive and being taken care of, and the ordinary rubberneckers certainly had no need to learn of my connection with the matter. I would get in touch with the police after I quit my search. Tell them what I knew. A direct line to the authorities, they had already been called to the scene anyway. This decision was not grounded entirely in reason. Adrenaline was running neck-and-neck with my thought processes, shading them and bending neural twigs.

I stepped out on the right foot and continued down the road, sick with the desperate feeling of wanting to collar the perpetrator. Indignation, outrage, vindictiveness drove me onward, the righteousness of the vigilante who cannot wait for the authorities to set things right. Get on the stick, pal. Don't wait around for the bureaucrats to solve the problem. Isn't this the cry of Modern Man trapped in the morass of lawyers and hair-splitting? I would walk to the far edge of this suburban development and look down the road, peer across the undeveloped landscape that was waiting for castles, and if I did not see any sign of my car, which was probably halfway to Nevada by now, I would come back and do my civic duty, contact the police, fill in the blanks. I felt noble. Knight in shining armor heading into the wilderness alone and unaided, armed only with a special knowledge: it was my car that did this. I was compelled to see my run through to the end.

The end was not long in coming. I made a half mile and was nearing the last of the houses in the development, some of which did not have lawns they were so new. I glanced to my right as I crossed a quiet intersection. I looked up a short block that ended at a field and saw my car parked at the curb.

I froze.

I squinted to see if a dark head might be inside the car, the felon at the steering wheel. But the car appeared to be empty. This meant he could be anywhere. Perhaps he had run into a dame's house after all. Or perhaps he was lying in a field catching his breath and could see me standing at the crossroads staring at my car. Maybe he would recognize me as the lone man who had been heading in the direction of the house where he had stolen the car. Would he have the brains to put two and two together and surmise that the lone man had been walking homeward, the man whom he may have observed from his perch in the woods? Had he noted the way I was dressed as I got into and out of my car and began the trek toward the strip mall? And more significantly, when he had passed me along the road did he in fact recognize me as the owner of the car and thus deliberately not look me in the eye as he drove by?

This I remembered distinctly. When my car had come toward me, my eyes were drawn to the windshield, and the driver did not turn his head, did not look at me with recognition—but that may have been due to the fact that he had already seen me from a distance, recognized me, and pretended not to notice me. I knew the move. How many people had I walked past pretending non-recognition? Legion. A human trait. We all do that to avoid confrontations, arguments, simple conversation—I have places to go and things to do, I have no time or desire to shoot the breeze. Everybody does that.

I stood at the intersection and scanned the silent houses. Could he be inside one of them, peeking past a curtain at me? He knew he had struck a man with the car. Surely he would not have remained in the vicinity for the cops to arrive, cordon off the neighborhood, make a house-to-house search. This may or may not have been entirely rational but it served to motivate me to walk toward my car. My poor Ford. Stolen, bruised, a dupe of human duplicity, as innocent as a large animal put to bad use.

As I approached my car I pretended I was merely a man out for a stroll. I did not look directly at the car as I came at it from the rear. I did not want anybody in the neighborhood to suspect that it was my car. I looked at my watch. It was ten thirty. How long had it been parked here? Mere minutes?

I instinctively touched the right-hand pocket of my pants as I always do when approaching my car, heard the jingle of keys against keys, some of which no longer had locks to match the teeth. We all collect keys that lose their purpose. The sorting and disposal of useless keys is a minor chore that grinds Americans down. I reached into my pocket and pulled out the ring to have it at the ready in case the felon appeared out of nowhere, as I imagined felons habitually did.

I arrived at the car and dragged an extended finger along the sheet metal as if to lay claim to the fender like a dog marking its territory. I glanced through the rear window to see if the thief might be crouched on the floor in pathetic concealment, but there was no one in the backseat. No one in front either. I yanked the driver's door open and slid behind the steering wheel in high dudgeon, this was my car, and if any neighbors wondered what a stranger was doing climbing into a car parked by another stranger, that was their problem.

I inserted the key with a fleeting sense of trepidation, uncertain the engine would start, moving fast like ripping off a Band-Aid, and heard the purr of the ignition, the roar of the pistons. The pedal was to the metal, a nervous tic of importunity begging this thing to work. I let up on the gas and felt a flood of relief. Victory belonged to me. I reached over and pressed the door lock shut, sealing my mobile castle, giving me total control over my world.

I looked at the gas gauge. Three-quarters full. I looked across the shotgun seat to see if the felon might have left contraband, a gun, an empty sack of bank dough, a bloody shirt, evidence for the police to pick through. It occurred to me that his fingerprints would be on the steering wheel. Had I touched it, smeared the fine evidence? You do things unconsciously, small moves you don't think about until it is too late. But I was glad I had thought of this. An image came to me—the felon's hand had been holding the top arc of the steering wheel as he had passed me by, the cocky grip of the smarmy punk. Like a man under hypnosis I closed my eyes and scoured my mind for the full photographic image of what I had seen during his quick passing in order to tell the police everything. Dark hair. Light blue work shirt. Seated erect, right fist on top of the steering wheel. But no good look at the features of his face, other than the sense that he was a tough customer. I imagined unshaven cheeks, mottled skin, images from prison movies. Perhaps a scar. I heard a knock on my window and opened my eyes. A cop was standing two feet back from the door, leaning down and peering in. He was pointing a pistol at me.

"Shut off the engine and get out of the car," he said.

He backed away to allow me to open the door and to avoid danger of attack. I had seen this in real-life shows on TV. Cops watch those too, training videos pour into police stations from across the country, updating the dangers of mistakes made by less fortunate policemen.

I gently shut off the engine. I slowly opened the door and climbed out with hands tentatively raised, a TV viewer well trained. Americans are notably cooperative fast learners.

"Step to the rear of the vehicle," he said.

I was familiar with this dance step. I knew what he was doing, knew enough not to speak, to babble explanations, just let him do his job. He ordered me to place my hands on the trunk in a spread-eagled position. I obeyed.

"Is this your car?" he said.

"Yes, sir."

"Did you strike a pedestrian with this car some time during the past thirty minutes?"

"No, sir."

"Place your right hand behind your back," he said.

I heard the jingle of cuffs, felt a thin icy grip snap my wrist. My left wrist was then cuffed. It was over in a few well-practiced seconds. I found myself standing erect and helpless, arms bound at my back, the ideal suspect.

"Stay right there," he said. He walked backwards along my car with the pistol drawn, walked until he came to the hood, where he bent his head and peered at the grill, bumper, etc.

He came back to me. "There is blood on your bumper, sir, and your left-front headlight is broken."

I nodded as if to say I knew that, although it was news to me. "My car was stolen," I said. "I just now found it parked here."

He glanced at the house perpendicular to my car and said, "Do you live here?"

I gave him my address. He asked for my name. Peter Larkey.

"Have you been drinking alcohol?" he said. He was standing close enough to smell my breath. A cop technique? Possibly. Or maybe a standard operating question.

"I had a beer at the Lemon Tree Lounge about an hour ago," I said.

Morton would be my witness. And Rudy, the bartender. Was I on safe ground now? They knew about my battery. I had a load of alibis, as well as a nodding auto-parts clerk. I was positioning myself for an innocent plea. Except my battery now appeared to be in excellent running condition. A multitude of disparate thoughts strafed my mind because I understood fully that I was the prime suspect in a hit-and-run accident involving alcohol.

"Sir, why were you sitting in the car with the engine running?" he said.

I opened my mouth to reply and found myself searching for the beginning of that answer. The dead battery at dawn? The sight of my car rolling past me? The traffic accident? The stunned delight at seeing my car parked on this short block? I had not really expected to catch up with my car, my jog had become a journey of blind will, the determination that drives a hopeless cause. How many times does a man succeed in his lifetime? The shock of success can be as visceral and long-lasting as the agony of defeat. A delight that one never quite gets over.

"I started the engine to see . . . if . . . it . . . would start." Like that, nervous babble sprang from my lips. But as I uttered this redundant statement I could not help but feel it would work to my benefit. Cops learn from experience, are quick judges of lies spoken by the guilty, and clumsy truths spoken by the frightened innocent. Psychologists could learn a thing or two from men who go to work each day uncertain they will come home alive. "My battery was dead when I woke up this morning," I added with a flourish so awkward that it surely bolstered my cause. "My car was stolen about a half hour ago." I threw in the word "about" deliberately, emulating the soft precision of a man trying hard to cooperate with an inquisitor. Not quite a half hour. Perhaps a few minutes more than a half hour. Do you see how earnestly and amateurishly I am trying to give you a timeline that will help you run the perpetrator to ground?

"Uh-huh," he replied. "Sir, why were your eyes closed when I approached your car?"

This unexpected and seemingly irrelevant question brought me up short. I licked my lips. How to explain? You see, Officer, I was envisioning the felon so that I could give the police an accurate description when I offered my witness statement.

But instead I said, "I was just so relieved to find my car that I was . . . you know . . . I closed my eyes with relief."

Redundancy again. I now doubted its effectiveness.

He glanced toward the front of my car, then pointed at his own car with the muzzle of his pistol. "Sir, I'm going to have to place you in the backseat of my vehicle."

This was acceptable. Chaos dominated the square feet of asphalt where we were standing. He had no idea if I was telling the truth, and I understood that fully. As I was escorted toward the rear door of his vehicle it occurred to me that a truly skilled felon might have the wits and experience to behave like a frightened, babbling innocent. I was navigating uncharted waters. Reality TV can take you only so far. I thought it best to remain silent until other cops joined to sort things out. The cuffs would come off posthaste, they would send out an APB, would scour the woods, drag the river.

As I ducked expertly so as not to bump my head, thus alleviating him of the necessity of a verbal warning, I saw a police vehicle round the corner with lights flashing, though there was no siren. I slid into the backseat and sat awkwardly erect, unlike slouched villains who glance with sallow-eyed derision at reality cameras.

When he shut the door I felt the pressure of tightly

sealed air squeeze my body. Trapped. A clear plastic screen separated the backseat from the front. There were no door handles, no handles to wind down the windows. Two cops stepped from the newly arrived vehicle, and the three men held a conference. Thumbs pointed here and there. I glanced casually at them and then away so as not to appear nervous. I looked straight ahead. I could not make out what they were saying. Sealed in a vacuum. The three of them strolled to the front of my car, and one of the cops squatted to examine the damage.

I raised my eyes and looked out across the field that began where the road ended. An odd sensation of disconnectedness began to engulf me. What a strange morning. The distant landscape had no character. I could have been in Connecticut, or Mill Valley, or Phoenix. I have lived in all those places. The squatting man stood up, and the three remained at the front of my car talking. I began to grow impatient. Was my story being doubted? What further questions might they ask me? I tried to compose myself for the grilling. I would take them step-by-step from the time I opened my eyes in bed until I was seated in my car with my eyes closed.

They came for me. I saw it in their stride, a determination that sank my soul. The officer in whose car I was sitting opened the door and told me to step out. I emerged clumsily, thinking how difficult life must be for people who had lost their arms, then stood up and looked at the two new officers who studied me with blank, level gazes. A learned thing, I was certain. Express no emotion. Treat suspects with the respect due to men whose innocence has not been disproven. My officer went around behind my back and proceeded to remove my cuffs. A relief filled my heart. The situation had been resolved in my favor. Perhaps the felon already had been run to ground. My life had been put on hiatus for perhaps five minutes, but now my arms were free, preamble to my entire being, I presumed wrongly.

"Sir, I am required by law to give you a sobriety test," my officer said. At this point I looked at his nameplate: *Wilson*. I had known a sergeant in the army named Wilson. He was twenty-six years old and had the mind of a child.

"I would like you to close your eyes, hold your arms outspread, and bring the tips of your index fingers together."

I felt foolish. I was in the principal's office, a boy wrongly swept up in a rebellion of student troublemakers. But I played along. I knew the score. I take the law seriously. For some reason, I shook my hands at my sides as if shaking off water before closing my eyes. Remove the kinks. Maximize the coordination. I closed my eyes and outstretched my arms, then slowly brought them together with my fingertips meeting in perfect sync.

Bingo.

I opened my eyes.

"Hold your arms out and walk ten feet in that direction touching your heels to your toes as you walk. Then turn around and walk back." He was pointing to the middle of the street. The other officers had strolled apart as if prepared to tackle me should I make a strategic blunder. I did as I was told. I made the journey there and back again without losing my balance. I felt proud.

Officer Wilson said, "Sir, I am placing you under arrest on suspicion of drunk driving."

My heart dropped like a chandelier. I had been *had*. Taken for a ride. A victim of police procedure, a mere formality, and by-the-book. I had confessed to having drunk a beer within the past hour and had been found seated behind the steering wheel of a running automobile. Perry Mason would have laughed me out of his office.

"May I say something?" I said, shaken to the core of my being.

At that point he advised me of my rights, including the one to remain silent. Miranda is as well known to Americans as the Pledge of Allegiance. But it must be stated by a policeman. Any American who pleads ignorance of his rights is flat-out lying. Let's be honest about that.

"I still want to say something," I said.

"All right, sir."

"When I went out to my car this morning the battery was dead so I walked to Apex Auto Parts to buy a new battery. I stopped off at the Lemon Tree and had a beer with a friend, then decided to walk back home to see if I could make the battery work before spending money on a new one, and while I was walking toward my house, my car came past driven by a stranger. He stole it. I followed it and found it here. That's why I was sitting in it when you drove up. I wasn't driving it. I didn't hit that man."

"What man?" the policeman said.

Was he toying with me? He had already mentioned the accident. But I knew from television that asking the same question over and over in different ways was a police technique.

"I passed the scene of the accident back along Hawthorne Drive," I said. "I saw the ambulance take the victim away. Then I came here and found my car."

The cops looked at each other.

"Why didn't you wait at the scene for the police to show up?" Wilson said.

"Because I wanted to find my car."

"Did you have any reason to believe that your car might be parked here?" he said, apparently taking advantage of my dismissal of my right to remain silent.

41

"No, sir. I just felt compelled to keep on looking for it. The ambulance took the victim away and there was nothing I could do, there were no police around, so I just kept on going, hoping I might see my car."

They looked at each other again. I did not doubt that there was a bit of mind reading taking place among the cops, although not a mystical phenomenon but an ability to size up facts and draw conclusions without spoken words, the legacy of long experience. I'm sure this ability is shared by janitors as well as computer geeks in the presence of rank amateurs.

"This man who stole your car, can you describe him?"

I did the best I could. My heart sank a bit more as I gave my meager description. I left out the tough customer part. I could have been describing half the men in the state.

"Do you have anything else to say?" Wilson said.

"Just that I didn't hit the victim with my car."

"All right, sir, we'll take a written statement from you after I transport you to headquarters. I'm going to place the handcuffs on you again."

As soon as I was back inside the pressure chamber, as I now thought of the backseat, the sense of disconnectedness began to return. The police car made a U-turn on the block and headed toward Hawthorne Drive, hauling me like so much luggage toward a train terminal. I began to feel disembodied. Phoenix. Mill Valley. Connecticut. I was floating through the dull, familiar, redundant landscape of my past, a ghost, rootless, helpless, blown by cosmic winds. What was I doing in the rear of a police car?

A large vehicle was coming down the road in our direction. I fixed my sights on it, then recognized it as a tow truck.

"Is my car going to be towed?" I said.

"That's correct, sir," Wilson said. "We're going to take it in and hold it for inspection. We'll examine it and see if we can match the blood with that of the victim."

My God. My car was gone for good. Evidence. It would be hauled into court piecemeal during my trial.

"Are . . . are the police going to look for the man who stole my car?" I said.

He paused a few uncomfortable seconds before answering, uncomfortable for me. "Yes sir, we are going to keep a lookout for anyone who fits the description."

"He's probably on foot," I said.

Wilson nodded. An amateur was trying to help out. He was probably used to it. The police knew how to keep an eye out for furtive suspects on foot, in cafes, bars, bus stations. I felt foolish, but a noble foolishness born of desperation. In spite of the histrionic past of detective films, life was now just like the movies. Follow up every lead. Make no judgment calls, stick to prescribed procedure, police work is legwork, tedious checking of facts, interviews with reticent witnesses. Television had made that clear. I sat back resigned. Goddamn me, I thought to myself. Goddamn me for not wiggling the battery cables at dawn.

We arrived at police headquarters. It was a blonde-brick building, looked like a grade school, flat-roofed, with an American flag idly fluttering on a pole. I was escorted through the front door and booked on suspicion of drunk driving. They gave me a choice: I could either take a Breathalyzer test or be chauffeured to County General, where my blood would be drawn to determine the alcohol content. Whether or not I had been the driver of the car that hit the man, I had still been apprehended sitting in a car with beer under my belt. What was it the experts said? It took an hour for the liver to process

43

an ounce of alcohol? This meant my biological functions had probably already discarded the evidence against me, but there might still be a tincture of incriminating C_2H_5OH in my blood. Was the legal limit still .01 percent for DUI? I seemed to remember reading that the limit had been lowered to .008 percent. There were sixteen pints of blood cascading through my system. Astonishing what a few molecules of a foreign substance can do to the human body, the brain, the mind. A whisper, a speck, a pinprick of pharmaceuticals can ravage reason. It's a wonder the human animal is not born deranged. Germs, bacteria, devastating infection, we are paper lanterns in the eye of a hurricane.

I agreed to a Breathalyzer test. Continuous exhalation into a small device that captured my sins for analysis. I once read of a bar where a Breathalyzer machine was installed to allow people to check their blood-alcohol content before driving home, but it backfired as do most good intentions. The barflies tried to set records for the highest readings. Americans love competition, duels, one-upmanship. The underdog is passé.

I was not told the results of my test. I was moved along the conveyor belt, fingerprinted, photographed, and held in a slammer for what seemed like an hour but I was not certain. My wristwatch and billfold had been taken away. I learned what so many sad cases have learned in their lives, that Time slows down behind bars. Then I was taken into a small room where I was allowed to give my version of the truth. I had not written anything official since college. I found myself composing the statement in my mind, afraid of producing an erroneous sentence that would have to be awkwardly scratched out, although I realized the police would be used to the hideous syntax, grammar, and thought processes of the average rattled witness. Americans abandon writing as soon as they can, usually after they get that diploma in their mitts.

I took a moment to think about what had happened. This would be a mental reenactment. Audie Murphy had reenacted his life in *To Hell and Back* but that was ten years after the fact. This was barely two hours. I tried to recall my state of mind and physical being. I had been exhausted by my quixotic jog. Was I slump-shouldered? But the sight of my car had perked me up. What is it the pharmacologists say? It is not the cocaine, the heroin, the LSD that affects you, it is neurons within your brain responding to the drug, creating the physical pleasures, the mental trips. Drugs are mere catalysts. The body does it all to itself. We are walking opium dens waiting for a speck of chemical crud to ring our doorbells.

I tried to keep it focused on relevant facts. Dead battery. Hike. Admission to the beer. Names of people I had spoken with. The walk toward home. Stolen car, the chase, the accident, the dead-end street. I now wished I had talked to the ambulance men, made my presence known, waited for a traffic-accident investigator to arrive rather than continue my jog. What had made me think it was important to track down my car? The police would have done that anyway. Green Ford. Ugly and obsolete. If the car had been spotted moving along a country road it would have been chased and seized immediately. But why do I do anything I do? I could fill volumes of police reports on that speculation. I stuck to the facts.

After they took my statement away I was sent into an office where Wilson and his supervisor were waiting, another uniformed man. I didn't know what rank. Army ranks I could decipher, but civilian paramilitary ranks baffle me. His name tag said *Roberts*. Wilson returned my billfold and wristwatch, then told me that because my car had been involved in a hit-and-run accident, and because the suspect that I had described had not been found, my car would be held in the impound lot

45

until the situation was resolved. The problem was that alcohol was still in my system. Not enough for DWI or even DUI. I would face a court hearing due to the nature of the accident, face a judge, but I was not going to be held in jail. I would be released on my own recognizance. Yes, they were looking for the man whom I had described, but they volunteered no more information. Close to the vest. I understood, and was relieved that I would be going home, even though an undercurrent of pique like a subterranean stream flowed in my gut. I had done nothing wrong. Is there anything worse than being innocent? I was now just an ordinary suspect, like the faces of wanted men on post office walls. The Law is blind in all ways. Everybody is treated equally, everybody is suspect, everybody is innocent until proven guilty beyond a doubt. The police must maintain an air of indifference because, after all, I may have been as guilty as hell and they knew it. Rules of the game.

"Can you tell me if the victim of the accident was hurt very badly?" I said.

"He received a concussion," Wilson replied in the level tone of a doctor.

"There was blood," I said. "I mean, did the man get hit in the head by the headlight of my car?"

Why does redundancy plague me when I am trying to be precise? Head. Headlight. I felt like I just got off the boat.

"Apparently the man's left hip was struck by the headlight and the back of his hand sustained severe cuts. His head struck the pavement when he went down. He was knocked unconscious."

"Is he going to be all right?"

"He's alive," was all Wilson said. But that's all anybody can say for any of us. I sensed that he did not want an in-depth discussion of the details of the collision with a prime suspect, and I was probably right. It would be difficult, I supposed, for the police to gauge my sympathies for a man whom I was suspected of having run down. I let the matter drop. A part of me wanted to ask what hospital the man had been transported to, so that I might visit him and offer my sympathies, but another part of me was constricted by guilt due to the fact that I had not stayed at the scene of the accident and made a fast report to the police when they arrived. Who knows? By continuing on my journey I may have squelched an opportunity for the police to run my car to ground before the perpetrator had abandoned the vehicle.

I was shaken by this admission to myself. The police could already have booked the man, incarcerated him, and released me from that shadow of doubt. I might never have been brought in for questioning, booking, photographing. My quixotic umbrage had bollixed everything, this I was forced to concede.

As I walked out the door of the police station I had a sour feeling, like a man who had been called "out" by an umpire when he knew damn well he had touched first base before the opponent's glove brushed his shoulder. So different from television where injustices have no effect on the viewer except a mild sense of delicious irritation. I was free though. I was clutching papers that I would have to take to court with me. Things were up in the air. The stolen car business was not resolved. They were still looking for the tough customer. But I was free. A moment prior to my release from the office, I had felt that Wilson and his overseer were sympathetic to me but were still forced to maintain the objectivity concomitant with the majesty of the law. Wilson had offered to drive me home, but I thanked him and told him I would call a taxi. This was not an inverted form of noblesse oblige. I had no intention of going home. I was headed straight for the Lemon

Tree Lounge. I wanted to bare my soul to the only friend I had in town, a man whose left leg I had destroyed by dint of my existence on earth.

TWO

I walked into the bar. The door thumped at my back, folding the fan of white light that was blinding the patrons. I couldn't see. This was how it always was. A return to the womb, to the last moment in time when you left this place or places like this. The clock stops and the outside world ceases to exist, a liquor industry tactic going back to the invention of refuges, haunts, drinking establishments in every country, like the language of music, universal. I paused to let my eyes again adjust to the darkness, seeing the colored lights emerging like rare, luminous, aquatic creatures. There were no other customers in the bar. I crossed the room and smiled at the bartender as I slipped onto the stool.

"Mr. Larkey," he said, nodding at me.

I nodded back. I knew his name was Rudy but I never called him by his first name. I was not that sort. I did not glad hand people, speak their names, cry out like drunks in the night, "Hey, Rudy, my glass is empty again!"

"What'll it be?" he said.

I glanced at Morton's stool. If Morton wasn't on the premises I didn't want to get into a conversation with Rudy. So instead of a beer I asked for a shot of bar liquor, make it a quick one, cut the potential conversation short and get out.

There was a dancing grace to the way he poured, the manner by which he brought an abrupt halt to the spill of liquor, raising it at the precise moment to keep the liquid from topping the lip of the rim. Give the customer an honest pour.

"Did you get the word?" he said as he capped the bottle.

I glanced at him with my eyebrows raised.

"What word?"

He turned away and set the bottle on the counter in front of the wall mirror, then turned back. "Morton was hit by a car in front of his house."

My blood turned to ice.

"When did this happen?"

"Couple hours ago. I got a call from the police. Said they would be coming by to ask me a few questions. They want to know where he was and what he was doing before the accident. He talked to them at County General and said he had been here at the Lemon Tree."

The police were coming here.

Wilson!

I didn't know what to do. Make a polite show of inquiring into Morton's health, or get the hell out. I had told Officer Wilson I was taking a taxi home, and now here I was, after being arrested for drunk driving and having my blood-alcohol content checked by a Breathalyzer, sipping scotch in a local dive. Fear gripped my heart.

"This is terrible," I said.

Rudy nodded.

I could not slide off the barstool and make a run for the door. There was a full drink in front of me. It was ringing like a bell. I answered it, drank it off.

"My God," I said. "Morton. Maybe I ought to run over to the hospital and see him."

"Might cheer him up," Rudy said. He was already polishing

a beer glass.

"Thanks for the information," I said. "My God. Morton. I hate to make this a quick one, Rudy, but I want to get to the hospital."

Did I see a flicker in his eye, a questioning? Did he find it odd that I referred to him by his first name for the first time ever? The look in his eye was like the look in the eye of a cop when you say something that may or may not be true. Slitted. He wasn't smiling, but there was nothing to smile about. His best customer was flat on his back in the ICU.

"Give him my regards," Rudy said as I laid a couple bucks on the bar and began my slide off the stool. I was terrified that the front door would open spraying blinding light into the joint like a searchlight scanning the wide earth for yours truly.

I stepped outside. The parking lot was deserted. No cars anywhere, no police vehicle coming toward the bar. I looked across the road where the field began that led toward the distant strip of Hawthorne Drive and wondered how Morton had gotten from the bar to his house. He could not walk well. Had he taken a cab? But this was a fleeting thought. I turned to my left and began walking in the direction of Apex Auto Parts. As I put distance between myself and the Lemon Tree I felt a lessening of the connection between myself and the bar. Should Officer Wilson suddenly pull into the lot he would have no way of knowing I had just left the lounge.

The farther away I got, the less connected I felt, as if guilt was being assuaged. I would appear to be an ordinary pedestrian strolling along the sunblasted sidewalk, although I will admit that I was moving faster than a stroll. I had the urge to duck into Apex and watch for the police car to pull into the parking lot, to see if Wilson were still on the job, to wait until he went inside, then duck out and hurry home.

As I passed the picture-window I saw the same clerk leaning into his computer, toying with stock numbers, prices. What would he make of my second appearance? I had not bought anything the first time I was there. His store was like a revolving door. I would feel obligated to say something to explain my reappearance, my inexplicable wanderings.

I took a chance and bypassed Apex, continued on to the end of the sidewalk, and stepped down to the asphalt where, at any moment, Wilson might pull in and wonder what I was doing at the strip mall when theoretically I was at home. I crossed the asphalt lot to the street and began heading south, feeling myself becoming disconnected from the strip-mall itself. Should Wilson come along, he would have no way of knowing that I had been there. Then I realized Rudy might reveal the fact that I had come in for a quick snort. The police were tracking Morton's moves. Rudy might casually mention that I had been inside his establishment at nine thirty and that I had come back during the past fifteen minutes. I looked at my watch. It was a few minutes before one. As I crossed to the far side of the boulevard that would take me back to my house I tried to gauge the implications of this possibility.

"Mr. Larkey was just in here?" Wilson might say.

"That's correct, Officer," Rudy might reply as he worked a gleam into another empty glass.

"Strange," Wilson might say. "I would have expected Pete Larkey to be at home by now."

But would he really say that? Close to the vest, that's how lawmen play it. He might not say anything at all to Rudy, just gather the facts and sort them out later, not unlike I was doing as I hiked down the empty country road with a frown on my face battling the blazing sunlight.

Pete Larkey had been picked up on suspicion of hit-and-run and was subsequently arrested on suspicion of drunk driving—and less than a half hour after being released on his own recognizance he was downing a shot of scotch in a bar. Wilson would ponder these facts and fabricate conclusions. Was Pete Larkey a chronic lush oblivious to the unwritten code of civilized behavior?

Something new to add to my wish list: I wished I had not gone back to the Lemon Tree. But I had been motivated by lonesome fear, a victim of bewildering circumstance, I wanted to connect with someone, tell my tale, diffuse the vile emotions that come from false accusation, and garner absolution's little brother: reassurance. Morton would have sympathized. People who are made privy to stories of injustice are thrilled and honored to hear the inside scoop, the lowdown, delighted to play the role of a juror asked to sort out and pass judgment on stated facts. They tend to take the side of the speaker. But Morton was the victim here. How did he come to be struck down by my car?

My frown grew deeper as I hiked along the road, glancing back surreptitiously to see if a police car might be silently racing toward me from the mall. Perhaps Morton had seen my car coming along Hawthorne Drive and recognized it, waved at the driver whom he thought was me, even stepped off the curb to flag me down. Perhaps he had crossed toward the middle of the road expecting me to stop, only to be struck by the headlight, the driver surprised at the sudden appearance of a man on the asphalt. Car-thievery aside, is this not how most accidents occur? Drivers do not run people down, they are taken by surprise, children chasing balls bouncing into the street, distracted joggers loping between parked cars, the elderly misjudging their ability to expeditiously cross an intersection. The newspapers are filled with redundant quotes: "He ran right in front of me—I didn't even have time to hit the brakes."

I glanced back at the wide sweep of the bare landscape bisected by the road. No traffic. I looked toward my house. I was three blocks away, although there are no blocks out where I live. One long uninterrupted strip of asphalt with inexplicable gentle sweeping curves meandering across the fallow countryside toward the woods behind my house. I wanted to get inside as quickly as possible, climb into bed, pull the covers over my head, and block out the harsh light of day and the thoughts ricocheting around inside my skull, half fact and half surmise laminated with shock and fear.

I then remembered I had told Rudy that I intended to go to the hospital and visit Morton. Would he pass this tidbit along to Officer Wilson? Would Wilson make a detour to the hospital to see if I had arrived at the ICU for a visit? And if he did, what would he make of the fact that I had not shown up? As I hiked the last block toward my house I found myself concocting alibis that might prevent Officer Wilson from cocking his head to one side and gazing at me with slitted eyes. I became balled up in arranging facts to explain crimes that had not been committed. I was exhausting myself.

The sight of my house wiped all that from my mind. Home. Castle. Sanctuary. I dropped my frantic calculations, reached into my pocket, and pulled out the keys to the front door.

As I stood there fiddling with the lock I felt the absence of my car at my back. Always on the driveway, always ready for sudden trips to town to buy food, liquor, laundry detergent, the rental of movies, all the things people do with cars, it was like a tooth missing from my gum. This was what had been truly stolen from me—the immediate gratification of mobility. I might as well have been living in a log cabin during the colonial days, minus a swayback nag to trot me to the village. Christ but I felt bleak.

I opened the door and stepped inside, closed it tight,

locked it, and crossed to my bedroom where I lay down and stared at the ceiling. I closed my eyes and emptied my mind, a technique I had become adept at as a result of living in America. Let undefined impatience learn its rightful place in the hierarchy of my life. I had not accomplished a thing that morning, and now I was burdened with new things, including a pending court date, which magnified my impatience. I wanted to get it over with, clear out the new crap from my life. The slightest obligation made me impatient, and this was what I blocked temporarily from my mind, because there is no end of obligations right up to the grave. Build a barricade. Let the problems simmer. They would always be waiting at the door like stray cats or bill collectors. Allow the body to relax, the mind to grow empty, take refuge in that most ridiculous of all illusions until worries begin to creep back like water through the cracks in a poorly constructed dam built by the lowest bidder.

I made ten minutes before a death moth batted my forehead. I opened my eyes and saw it flutter away, fade into the background of the wallpaper. Sometimes I do find the little bastards in the glass of water I keep on the table next to my bed. They are always drowned. I do not doubt that I have drunk the things in the dark, awakening dry-mouthed and taking a sip before falling back to sleep. I once read that the average human being swallows seven spiders during his lifetime while asleep. As soon as the moth faded from view, a thought sprouted in my mind: Morton. Of all the things I knew I would have to do, that seemed the most immediate. Call a taxi, get over to County General and make an appearance. But don't get me wrong. This was not an attempt to rid my mind of an unbearable obligation, like a plastic bag filled with rotted fish. I truly was concerned about Morton, although I will admit that making a guest appearance was a small part of looked at my watch. 1:35.

Suddenly I was in a race with the cops. If Rudy had told Wilson I was going to the hospital, I had to get there before Wilson. If I arrived after Wilson did, he might wonder where I had been? What was the holdup? Why had it taken me so long to get to County if I had left the bar and climbed right into a taxi? As I looked up the number of the taxi company I concocted answers to these questions. Easiest answer? It took forever for the taxi to arrive at the strip mall. The sight of the taxi ad in the Yellow Pages thrust this alibi into my mind.

I dialed and gave the dispatcher my address. I had done it before but not often enough to remember the number. In some cities I had lived in they had a one-number pattern, 888-8888 or 444-4444, etc. Clever marketing. Make it easy on people whose personal problems forced them to do the unusual, take a taxi, meet unexpected needs, emergency runs, trips to hospitals, jails, morgues, name the vexation, a quick dial is at your fingertips. But not in this burg.

"We'll have a cab there as soon as possible," he said. He did not give me a time. Twenty minutes tops in most cities. But I did not mind. It aided my alibi. The cops would not be questioning a cabbie.

I was hungry. The patina of scotch on my tongue was not as pleasant as it usually is. Nor was the slight high from having downed a shot and then making a fast eight-block walk. It merely agitated me. I went into the kitchen and pulled the bread out of the box, fielded three slices of lunch meat, made a quick cold-cut meal, and opened a can of soda pop. I shoved the sack of bread back into the breadbox. A horn honked outside. What the hell?

I hurried into the living room and peered out the front window. A taxicab was parked in my driveway. Good God. I stood holding the uneaten sandwich and full can of pop and wondered if it was legal to eat food in a taxi. We live in a world of laws, federal, state, local, business, school, country club, who knows what the damn rules are? But I was hungry. If necessary I would stand outside the goddamn cab and let the driver run the meter while I broke my fast.

I went outside, locked the front door, and approached the cab.

"Is it okay if I eat this during the ride?"

"No problem, sir," the driver said, grinning at me through a circle of dark beard, a round Vandyke. He was a character from *Mad Magazine*, baseball cap, T-shirt, perhaps thirty. I noted food wrappers strewn on his shotgun seat. I opened the rear door and hustled in with my lunch, made myself comfortable, and said, "County General Hospital."

He nodded and put the cab into gear, backed out, and headed up the asphalt highway.

"You got here fast," I said.

"Business is slow," he replied.

I wondered how many taxicabs worked a small town like this. Ten? Twenty? Perhaps only three? There are worlds unexplored, we visit them briefly but never inquire as to the customs, traditions, logistics, stats. How could a man earn a living driving a taxi in a small town like this? Our airport is something Lindbergh might have built, accommodating light planes, charter jets, but no 727s, no passengers fighting tooth-and-nail for a cab at the terminal. But I did not inquire. I concentrated on my sandwich and hoped the driver would not engineer friendly chatter to increase the size of his tip. I made a large show of raising the pop to my lips, placing my elbow in direct line of his rearview mirror. I hate being watched by taxi drivers. They must suspect everybody. Dangerous business, letting a stranger take a seat at your back. I could never drive a cab for a living. My thoughts would ricochet endlessly.

It took fifteen minutes to get across town to County General. It was located way out in the countryside, not unlike my house. A slick, new, modern place built to be surrounded by castles someday, the encroachment of wounded civilization.

Nine bucks on the meter, I rounded it up to ten and climbed out. I thought of asking him to wait, but business was slow. Perhaps the cabbie would be prowling this side of town and I would see him again. I had never seen a cabbie twice in my life.

I entered the hospital and was immediately infused with the odd reverence you feel upon entering a church. "People go to hospitals to die," my grandmother used to say. Elderly women say the damnedest things to children.

I inquired at the front desk, listened closely to the instructions on how to find Morton's room. He was on the second floor. I stepped into an elevator and felt hesitant reaching out to touch the button for Floor 2. It made me queasy. My grandmother had also told me that hospitals were the filthiest places on earth—but that made sense. God knows what sorts of viruses float in hospital air, what germs crawl the walls. Nature of the beast, there's no getting around it. Janitors are ubiquitous in hospitals, those constant moppers. How do doctors, nurses, orderlies tolerate working in such filthy places that look so pristine and antiseptic, the appearance of cleanliness only an illusion. But some illusions are necessary. Maybe all of them. If illusions didn't exist, Man would invent them. A self-evident truth.

I stepped out of the elevator and approached the desk. The nurse directed me down a hallway. I had no trouble finding his room: 222. This made me laugh to myself inappropriately. I will not dwell on that. Trepidation overcame me as I approached the door. Doctors and nurses were moving up and down the hallway, the whisper of shuffling in the air along with the viruses. I was unable to take comfort from the presence of other people. I was about to face true tragedy, a man who had bled, had known recent fierce pain. I had never been hurt in my life, although I once experienced a half hour of what a doctor later told me was a mild form of food poisoning that I had apparently contracted from a can of chicken soup. It was like an ice pick lodged beneath the washboard of my right rib-section. That had taught me everything I ever wanted to know about pain. You are alone in the universe. Ambitions, hopes, dreams, they do not take a mere backseat, they are exiled from the car entirely.

I stepped into Morton's room as one might step into a confessional, silent, apprehensive, even when absolution is guaranteed. But there is something about confronting your own sins that makes a mockery of self-worth. You are not alone in that universe—the confessor is waiting.

Morton was lying on the bed with a bandage on his forehead, but it did not hide his face. His left arm was taped, pierced with a rubber tube. I saw the tiniest stain of blood where the tube disappeared between strips of gauze. His eyes were closed.

They opened.

"Malarkey," he whispered.

How did he recognize me? Drugged, in a stupor, this was what I expected of all people laid up in hospitals. But his recognition was immediate. I felt exposed, unmasked, I had fashioned a scenario in my mind involving a slow coming-into-focus as he blinked and finally recognized the familiar visitor standing beside his bed with a compassionate smile of pity and concern. I fashion scenarios quickly, possibly as a result of spending most of my life watching TV. It's as much a part of me, I suppose, as an accent defining the section of the country that a man hails from—the South, the Midwest, New England.

"Rudy told me what happened," I said, sidling up close to the bed and looking down the lumpy length of his body beneath the stark white sheet. "I came here as soon as I could."

He drew his head back a fraction of an inch insofar as his head sank deeper into the pillow. He gazed at my face with searching eyes.

"Rudy?" he said with an undertone of a growl. "What do you mean? You know what happened. You did this to me."

A frosted sheet closed across my heart like the drawing of a curtain.

"No, Morton," I said, a quick jitter entering my voice. "I was not driving the car."

"Why did you hit me?" he said, his eyes rounded and bright blue with clarity.

"No, Morton, listen. My car was stolen. I wasn't at the wheel."

My God. Did he tell the police he had seen me? Had he given them my name, my address?

"Listen, Morton, let me tell you what happened. After I left the lounge I decided to take your advice and go back home and wiggle the battery cables. I was walking along the road when I saw my car go by. Someone stole it from my driveway. I chased after it. I wasn't at the wheel when it hit you."

He closed his eyes the way people close their eyes to the Truth in favor of Belief. I intuitively understood that I was confronting a wall that would have to be breached. But belief is virtually indestructible in comparison with truth, the most fragile substance known to man. This I understood as I stared down at the pillow where Morton's head had rotated so that his face was perpendicular to the ceiling.

"The police are on the lookout for the man who stole my

car," I said, snatching desperately at straws. "I already talked
to them. I gave them a statement and a description of the man.
They put out an APB." They're scouring the woods, dragging
the river, racing down country roads with sirens howling and
red lights blazing.

"Mister Larkey," a familiar voice said.

I looked around and saw Officer Wilson standing in the
doorway. He was holding his hat in his hands. It was the type
of hat described by truckers as a "Smokey Bear" hat. My drill
sergeants wore them in basic training. Flat-brimmed, severe,
stiff as starched canvas, heavy with authority. Civilians do
not wear hats like that.

"Officer Wilson," I said. It took all my willpower not to
glance around at Morton's face. I felt trapped, though not so
much between a rock and a hard place as between a truth
and a lie, except it was not a lie, it was a Third Thing. It was
Morton's misconception of what he had seen earlier in the
day. It was an untrue thing, but it could also be a witness
statement. I realized at that moment that witness statements
are not what I had always thought them to be, the truth
anchored in the bedrock of the majesty of the law. Who
would lie on a witness statement except a madman? But there
was also misconception. Witness statements were so much
smoke. Police and lawyers surely knew what I had only just
now learned. Words on paper must be interpreted, translated,
read with a jaundiced eye. Words were worse than stupid.
They could be malevolent, spinning webs tighter than your
garden-variety tangle of lies.

"How is Mr. Morton?" Wilson said quietly.

I glanced at Morton as if to assess his condition and render
judgment, and was shocked to see a dribble of spittle coming
from his partially opened lips. His eyes were half-lidded. His
flesh seemed to have changed hue. Ashen. I glanced at Wilson,

my eyes wide of their own accord, my mouth a startled O.

"I think there's something wrong with him."

He crossed the room quickly and looked down at Morton, then reached out and grabbed a plastic device at the side of the bed, a call button, and began pressing it. A nurse was there instantly. Another nurse entered the room, and I was told to leave. Stunned, I backed into the hallway and saw medical personnel hurrying toward the room. A voice from a muted loudspeaker began saying "Code Blue, Code Blue." A doctor hurried past me and entered Room 222.

Officer Wilson came out of the room. He placed his hat squarely on top of his head—to have his hands free, I felt—and riveted me to the spot with his eyes. He raised a beckoning finger. "Come with me."

He walked at my side. I was speechless. A police officer had been standing right there *when it happened*, whatever it was. Could an innocent man find himself in a worse position? It would take some deep thought to add items to that list, and I did not even try.

He pointed toward a waiting room. It was empty. I entered. He followed but stopped at the doorway, blocking it with his uniformed, badged, and bulky armed body.

"What happened in there?" he said.

"I . . . I . . . I don't know. I went in to say hello and . . . and . . . and then you arrived. I mean, I was only in there for a minute."

"Did the two of you converse?"

Oh God. I knew exactly what this was—a moment when a man had to think fast. The truth would not fully serve justice. I could not lie, but at the same time I knew I had to describe things with an exactitude that would vindicate me from any suspicion of wrongdoing. But how could I do that? I had no experience with impromptu verbal gymnastics, the deft juggling of words like rubber balls that never fall, bounce, roll off the stage. I am not an expert at anything.

"Yes," I said.

"What did you talk about?"

Oh Lord. How could I repeat what Morton had said—that he saw me hit him with my car? I could not possibly say that. And if I did, would it be admissible in court? Or could it be dismissed as hearsay—an accused man accusing himself falsely? A snake swallowing itself? Time to plead the Fifth, I told myself. This scene was untenable. I felt sick. I sat down on the nearest chair and felt my skin go pale.

"Are you all right, Mr. Larkey?" Wilson said.

"I feel faint," I said, sticking to my program of not lying. It seemed that perhaps another Third Way had come into play: neither tell a lie nor tell the asked-for truth, but rather make an end-run around the matter by changing the subject.

He handed me a glass of water. Where had he gotten it? Had he left the room briefly? I was too dizzy to notice. At any rate, he probably mistook the source of my sickness as my presence in the room when Morton took a bad turn. But it went beyond that. I swallowed the contents of the glass, thinking of viruses.

"Better?" he said.

I nodded.

"How long were you in Mr. Morton's room before I arrived?" he said, picking up where he had left off.

The water helped. It bolstered me. The sickness faded. To hell with it, I told myself. I am an innocent man.

I cleared my throat, coughed in preamble, and said, "I walked in and said hello to Morton. I told him that I had heard that he had been hit by a car and was in the ICU." I looked up at Officer Wilson as I said this. I was coming clean. But goddamnit, I had done nothing wrong that day—except not wiggle the battery cables. That was my crime, the only crime I had ever committed, the crime of stupidity, and it was against my own person. I had already flagellated myself thoroughly for that one.

Wilson's eyes were boxed in by a faint squint, as if he was sizing up my words, weighing them. It was obvious to me that he had visited the Lemon Tree. I had no secrets. He was testing me, that was it, waiting silently to see if my story veered from the facts as he knew them—yes—*knew* them to be.

"After I left the police station I went to the Lemon Tree Lounge to talk with Morton and to tell him about my stolen car." As I said this a hardness, a confidence entered my voice. "I ordered a shot of scotch, then the bartender told me that Morton had been involved in the hit-and-run accident." I paused to let the shame generated by the truth of what I was about to say run its course. "After I left the Lemon Tree I walked home and lay down for a few minutes. Then I took a taxi to the hospital."

"Why did you go home?" he said. "Why didn't you go straight to the hospital?"

"I was bushed," I said. "I've been through a lot today."

He nodded. "I spoke with Mr. Flanagan," he said.

I glanced up at him with raised eyebrows.

"Rudy Flanagan, the bartender," he said.

I had never known Rudy's last name. Doubtless the prosecutor would use this fact to send me to the gallows.

"He told me you had come by and ordered a shot of whiskey."

I nodded.

"He told me you left in a hurry because you wanted to get to the hospital to visit your friend."

I nodded again. My God, was I a child, was my every move

to be observed, inspected, sliced and diced by Big Brother from here to eternity?

"I needed to lie down for a bit," I said, clinging by the tips of my fingers to the fragile wings of a struggling death moth. "Afterwards I called a taxi and came straight here to Country General. I was in the room for only a minute before you showed up."

"That's what the nurses at the desk told me," he said.

Witnesses! I was an open book.

"What did you and Mr. Morton talk about?" Wilson said.

So much for my elation. There was still the business of the false accusation, the stickiest business of all. My enthusiasm for spilling my guts waned. But what else could I do? If and when Morton regained consciousness, he would simply repeat our conversation. No use hoping it would slip his mind. Who was I to stake my fate on luck? When had luck ever done me one goddamn favor?

I took a deep breath and sighed. "He seemed to be under the misapprehension that I was driving the car when it hit him," I said, trying to put the best light on the situation without appearing disingenuous. "He knows my car. He's worked on it before." I didn't mention that he also knew how much my car weighed.

Officer Wilson nodded. "We'll be taking a statement from Mr. Morton as soon as he has recovered."

What if he didn't recover? This thought passed through my mind. I felt ashamed thinking it. If Morton didn't make it, that would be one less witness I would have to worry about. How human was I to have thought such a thing? I was one evolutionary step away from the wolf.

"Thank you for your cooperation, Mr. Larkey," Wilson said. "I'm going to head back up the hallway and see how Mr. Morton is doing."

"Do you need me to stay here?" I said.

"Not at all, Mr. Larkey. You can leave any time you want."

"All right, thank you," I said, then immediately wondered what I was thanking him for. I had been in situations where I had said, "Fine," even though the person I encountered did not ask me how I was doing. It's as if I have a file of stock phrases that erupt from my mouth at peculiar moments, sometimes when I am taken by surprise, sometimes when I have no desire to engage in further conversation. It can be embarrassing. People may not be certain that I hear well or that I possess all my marbles. But it occurred to me that I was thanking Wilson for giving me a reprieve. Perhaps he would interpret it that way. I worry about how people interpret things I say, especially cops. But I put it out of my mind. I was sure that the cops had more strangeness to deal with than conversations with inarticulate, innocent, rattled men. Perhaps they joked about it in their locker rooms during shift-change. "You should have heard the witness I scared half to death this morning . . ." That sort of banter. But they earn it. They put their lives on the line. The famous thin blue line. I could never be a cop or a criminal, the opposite edges of the circle that borders civilization. It takes a certain type to live on any edge.

I waited until Wilson's footsteps faded down the hallway, then I got up and peered out the door. The hallway was empty. Should I wait to find out how Morton was doing? Had my surprise presence in his room sent him into cardiac arrest? Had I killed him? I wondered that on the day my car dropped flat on top of him while I was sipping a Coke outside the garage where he worked. He was checking a brake-fluid leak. There were two cars on the lifts, so he simply jacked up the front end of my Ford and slid beneath it on a rolling dolly for a look. The jack was defective, as was later determined by his lawyers. He was fortunate in that sense. The weak jack wasn't his fault. The opponent lawyers asserted that he should have waited until a lift was clear, but that argument faded into the mists of legal back-and-forth. He won. Some win. I followed the case closely both in the papers and in occasional conversations with other garage mechanics. Did I do that because I was concerned about Morton or because I was afraid that I myself might be drawn into the mists of legal back-and-forth? After he won his financial compensation I closed the casebook on that question.

I stepped into the hallway and looked up toward Morton's room. I finally surrendered to my uneasiness, but it was a battle. I walked to the desk where a nurse was peering at the screen of a computer. "Excuse me, ma'am, can you tell me how Mr. Morton is doing?"

"His condition has been stabilized."

I nodded, pursed my lips. That's all I wanted to know. I softly thanked her and eased my way toward the exit feeling less like a coward than if I had simply made a dash to the outside world and phoned in my query. Poor Morton. It would have been best overall if we had never met. I had never said such words to myself before, but I had felt them in the past, usually generated by other guilts. This partially explained my reclusive behavior, the fact that I lived alone and had made no attempt to move to another part of the country after my wife split.

I lived so far away from the rest of America now that it seemed best to remain rooted to the least dangerous spot. I had no intention of remarrying, and as far as making new friendships, that option wasn't even on the table. Morton had simply stumbled into my life, so to speak, and we had become drinking friends at the Lemon Tree. He had never been to my house, and I certainly had not known where he lived, until my car ran him down. "Why did you hit me?" he said. I thought about this as I made my way to the lobby. What had he said to me earlier in the day? "And if I was born for no reason at all, why am I still alive?" I seemed to recall answering, "Luck of the draw."

I stood at the big glass doors of the lobby peering out at the landscape and wondering how much of it was owned by the corporation that operated the hospital, and how much of the land was owned by real estate developers crouched like spiders in their webs waiting to snag customers, young married couples, elderly people looking for property to build retirement homes. There were signs here and there on the landscape, small billboards that I had never taken much notice of, announcing the construction of gated communities scheduled to erupt from the earth. Castles aplenty, get in on the ground floor, lock in that mortgage rate!

I decided it was too far to hike to town. The thought had occurred to me. Walk all this off. Cool down and collect my thoughts. Instead I crossed the lobby to a phone and dialed the cab company again. I hoped for a different driver. Was beard-boy prowling the suburbs waiting for my call? Money in the bank, a man visiting a friend in the hospital. I tended to doubt it. He told me business was slow. He was probably taking everything he could get off the radio. It didn't matter, but I did not want to see him again and answer awkward questions as he hauled me back to my house. I feel childish sitting in the backseats of taxis.

I made the call, told them I was at County General, and gave them the address of my home, then went outside and sat on a low flagstone wall to wait for the cab to arrive. A hot, cloudless afternoon. Silent. After five minutes I reached to the top of my head and felt my hair. It was hot. I thought about going back into the lobby, which was air-conditioned. But there was something comforting about being baked alive on the flagstone that bordered the concrete apron accessible to wheelchairs. I felt as if viruses were being burned away from my body. I made a small O with my lips and blew a silent whistle, imagining residual viruses being ejected from my lungs. I know that makes me sound hypochondriacal, but I am not one of those people. It was just my limpid imagination combined with the grotesque memories of my grandmother. I could tell you things that would disgust you, warnings articulated by that woman, who was first-generation Swedish, born on the East Coast and raised by true immigrants. Admonitions having to do with bodily functions, but I will not tell you those things. In all probability everybody has an earthy ancestor tucked away in their memories who said the sorts of things in polite company that made hearts sink. Her parents had been farmers whose lives were immersed in the raw facts of animal reproduction, excrement, mucous, flatulence, birth, disease, death, my God, she made my hair stand on end when she got going.

"Mr. Larkey?"

I looked around.

Officer Wilson was behind me.

"Sir?" I said.

"Do you need a ride home?"

I quickly scanned the road for sight of the taxicab but saw no vehicles at all. I had lost track of time. "I'm waiting for a cab," I said.

He raised his chin and peered out at the bleak landscape. His eyes were darkened by an effective shadow cast by the brim of his Smokey hat. A full circle around his head like a ring of Saturn. It occurred to me that the only people who did wear hats with full-circle brims were cops and ladies.

"When did you call them?" he said.

I did not really know. I looked at my watch. It was a quarter after two. I made up a time. "Twenty minutes ago," I said.

He nodded. "Well, they might be busy. There might not be a taxi available for a while. I don't know if you are aware of this, sir, but drivers are not sent to an address, they make the decision on their own whether to take a call off the radio. What I'm getting at is that you could get stranded out here."

I looked back at the road. Stranded at the front door of a virus factory. Was this what I wanted? I hated to cheat a driver out of a fare but my body was burning up on the portico.

"Maybe I'll take you up on that," I said.

I did not want to ride in a police car again but my body was playing a key role in decision-making, as it does when I am hungry or tired or my bladder is full. I hope that does not sound grotesque, but we are virtual slaves to this talking water-balloon that bears our souls from the cradle to the grave—65 percent water according to the science books. The rest is carbon, iron, riboflavin.

"No need for you to accompany me to the parking lot," Wilson said. "I'll go get my vehicle and swing by here."

"All right, sir. Thank you."

He touched the brim of his hat with one finger. Had he learned that on TV or did they teach it at the police academy? Perhaps his uniform generated a certain level of behavior modification unknown to civilians. I had not been saluted since I was in the army. During the first day of basic training, we practiced walking back and forth saluting a sergeant in order to prepare ourselves for the gut-wrenching moment when we would have to salute an officer for real. I still remember my first salute. It was directed at a lieutenant. He came around the corner of a barracks unexpectedly and my right hand flopped toward my forehead like the boneless tentacle of a squid. I felt like an idiot, but I had survived the crucible. First blood. I wanted to run back to the barracks and tell my new buddies what had happened. Youth is strange. Mine was anyway.

Wilson disappeared around a corner of the building. I turned back and faced the road. It was empty. But for how long? Suddenly I worried that the cab driver would show up. It would be awkward telling him that I no longer needed a cab. I had been offered a free ride, and I wanted it. I was unemployed. God only knew what this drunk-driving charge would incur financially. A fine and court costs. I had found myself thrust into the world of counting pennies, even though I did have some money in the bank. But bank money dwindles quickly when you are unemployed, this I had learned in my youth.

I grew edgy and began glancing to the corner of the building, hoping Wilson would arrive quickly. Perhaps I should call the cab company and cancel the ride. I was indecisive. I kept looking off toward town, then at the corner. How was it that I continually found myself in untenable situations? Should I have said no to Officer Wilson and taken my chances with being stranded? Like my body, my cheapness was now in control of my decisions. I suddenly felt annoyed at the cabbie. Why hadn't he shown up as quickly as beard-boy? There is no consistency, no steadfastness in this world. It is my burden, my bête noire, to be forced to rely on others. If only I had my car.

Wilson's vehicle came around the corner. To move things along quickly, I began walking toward it and felt an odd sense of security knowing that even if the taxi arrived now, the driver would see me and realize that, due to forces beyond his control, his fare was evaporating. Arrested. Hauled off to the slammer. It made me feel good to reside within this cone of protection. The cab driver would be shocked, possibly even relieved to know that a criminal, a deadly felon, would not be taking a seat at his back. Of course this had nothing to do with reality. The taxi man might be infuriated. But what did I care? I had the aegis of a cop to ward off his lightning bolts.

I reached for the back door but Wilson pointed at the shotgun seat. I had never sat in the front seat of a cop car or a taxi, so my mistake did not make me feel foolish. I was a tyro at this. A professional would understand.

I climbed in and felt as if I was sliding into the cockpit of a jet plane. There were gadgets on the dashboard, the controls of sirens, lights, radio. It was baffling, and I did not make any effort to discern what was what. Sit back in the bucket seat and take the ride. A man could find no better refuge in this world than the front seat of a cop car. Pinnacle. Zenith. Valhalla. I felt safe.

"It looks like your friend Mr. Morton is going to pull through okay," Wilson said as he turned onto the main road and headed toward town.

"I'm glad to hear that," I said, instantly pretending ignorance of Morton's stable condition. People, even cops, like to be the bearers of good news, especially if the good news is linked with a bad situation. But then I regretted it. My ignorance of his condition might indicate to Wilson that I had made no inquiry, which would put me in a bad light. Did I not care about the man who had been struck by my car?

Wilson glanced over at me. "I'm sorry we had to put you through so much trouble today," he said. "I'm afraid we are going to have to keep your car at the impound. I know that creates a burden for you."

Perhaps not. It was an effective excuse to avoid looking for work, although there was nobody demanding explanations. Thank God my wife had left me. She would have thrown a fit and made me take taxis to the employment agencies, the job

72

interviews, etc.

"I'll get along okay," I said.

He made a "tsk" sound and gave his head a twist. I supposed he was showing sympathy for a man who had been victimized. I had the urge to ask about the drunk-driving charge, but kept mum. Leave it alone, as my grandmother would say of scabs, mosquito bites, poison-oak rashes, the minor annoyances of life. Don't pick at it, scratch it, or irritate it in any way because you will only make it worse. This was one bit of wisdom I had hauled like a survival kit out of my childhood—do not do anything that will make it worse.

We bypassed central downtown, skirting the south side along an east-west highway that had been built a few years earlier, precursor to the castles and projected expansion of the town. It would eventually arrive. Cities expand toward the equatorial sun, yuppies and retirees looking for refuge from urban strife. My own house had been built in the mid-1960s when the frantic flight from crime and riots had only just begun. A lone wolf of pedestrian design, a bland carport adjacent to a cardboard box of a house, but it served its purpose. I estimated that it had cost between $15,000 and $18,000 to build at the time. Conceivably, my landlord could make as much as a quarter million off the structure and property when the building boom finally took off, but by then I fully expected to have moved away from this burg. I never seemed to be where the money was. My wife had made a few inquiries about buying the property five years back, a move that I had vociferously opposed. Given my spotty job history, I did not wish to be tied down to a mortgage on the off chance that someday the property would increase exponentially in value. I am not the long-range planner that she turned out to be. Her decision to leave me apparently had been in the works for some time, possibly after our tiff about home ownership.

73

As we came within view of the Crestmoor strip mall Wilson slowed the cruiser a bit and looked over at me. "I assume you want to be dropped off at your house."

His question had an implied accusation: perhaps I wanted to be dropped off at the Lemon Tree Lounge. It had not occurred to me until this moment, and I must admit that the idea had its appeal, which faded rapidly. As much as I would have enjoyed a mid-afternoon snort in the comfort of an aquatic womb, I did not wish to face Rudy Flanagan and answer inquiries about the health of Morton.

"Yes," I said.

"Listen, if you need to pick up some groceries or anything I can run you past the IGA store," Wilson said.

I looked over at him. "I appreciate that," I said, "but I'm fine." I did not know this for a fact, but I did not want to go shopping in a cop car. It was too peculiar, too intrusive. This was not a taxi service. I felt it would somehow diminish the majesty of the law to dash in for eggs and celery. "My larder is well stocked," I said.

He gave up one brief, tight chuckle. "Larder," he said. "There's a word you never hear anymore."

As we sailed down Crestmoor Road toward my house I began thinking about my larder. Was it well stocked? What if I found I had to go to the store after all and took a taxi? How would I feel if Wilson spotted me shopping an hour from now? Maybe I should have accepted his offer. Why can I not take advantage of largesse? That was the sort of question my ex might have posed. She accused me more than once of not being aggressive enough when it came time to seize the moment. Behind every failed man there stands a furious woman.

But my choice had been made. My carport came into view. I would be taking taxis for a while. If Wilson saw me shopping later in the day, I would concoct another larder quip and let the cards fall where they may. Current events had made it abundantly clear that I was not in control of anything.

Wilson wheeled into my driveway and stopped. "I'll keep you apprised of the situation, Mr. Larkey," he said, looking at me with sympathetic eyes.

"Thank you, Officer Wilson." I climbed out and stood in the driveway and watched Wilson back onto the empty road and cruise up toward town. As the sound of his car faded, it was as if all sounds were being sucked out of the air in its wake. Utter silence descended upon me, the next best thing to a blanket. I stood in the hot afternoon sunlight gazing at the ribbon of asphalt that meandered toward town, then I turned and looked beyond my house toward the woods. When we first moved in, my wife and I imagined taking long walks in the woods. Commune with nature. Lug a picnic basket. Perhaps take up bird-watching. We took exactly one walk between the trees, stepping over brambles and kicking through bushes and worrying about the presence of ticks. End of idyll. Eden abandoned. After she left me I did take a walk through the forest alone but finally admitted to myself that it was more of a romantic posture than a source of solace. I kept tripping over tree roots.

I walked up the empty driveway and pulled out the key to my front door, unlocked it, and stepped inside, but when I closed the door I felt no sense of sanctuary. My car was not parked in my driveway, and I had to deal with the court date. I felt as if the front door was not locked at all, that I was vulnerable, my house invaded by obligations.

I tried to assess the situation. How long could I go without looking for a job? I looked at my wristwatch. Two thirty. Should I resign myself to doing nothing for the next two days, possibly three, until the bullshit ran its course? I felt the way I had felt during my time in the military. Put my life, my brain, my hopes and dreams on hold until the day I was handed a discharge. I had also felt this about jobs that I knew would not last. Punch the clock, put in the time, and wait for the day I decided to quit. I had been fired twice, but when it came to quitting, there was an extrasensory mechanism at work, like that of animals who anticipate the coming of an earthquake, bovine stampeding from the epicenter, birds taking flight, the insect world going silent. I could always feel the end of a job coming on. It was accompanied not by fear but by relief.

I put it all out of my mind. Trying to assess my life was as pointless as planning it. I walked through the living room into the kitchen and realized I had left the bread on the counter. One end of the wrapper was open. Moisture was evaporating, the end-piece was doubtless dry. I washed my viral hands at the sink before manhandling the cellophane and shoving it back into the breadbox. But then I stopped. I distinctly remembered doing this before the arrival of the taxi that had taken me to County General. The physical sensation of wrapping the end before shoving it into the box brought it back to me. A redundancy. I was certain I had put the bread away. The extended logic of this deduction indicated that someone had been in my house. To take the construct further, someone might still be in my house.

I started to close the cover of the breadbox. The cover was constructed like the slatted wood of a rolltop desk. It made noise. I stopped. I looked around the kitchen to discern whether anything else was out of place. Next to the kitchen sink stood a small wooden cube containing four carving knives. I crossed the floor and pulled one of the knives out of the slot and turned around to face the doorway that led into the living room. Directly opposite was the kitchen door that led to the backyard. I thought it might be best to ease out the back door and work my way around to the driveway, where my goddamn Ford was missing. This exacerbated my sense of helplessness. Missing wheels. Empty gums. No teeth.

I gripped the knife tighter in my fist and decided I ought to dial 911. If there was someone in my house, I would need the aid of the police. I was not prepared to engage in a frantic knife-fight in the backyard, but neither did I want to be chased across the living room by someone who might have a gun. Scenarios rang like bells in my brain. I had never been in such a situation. This was a peaceful community. There had been times when I had wondered what we were paying taxes for, since the police seemed to have so little to do, the sort of disingenuous thought that taxpayers indulge in when everything is copacetic. But the police have plenty to do. The average citizen does not live near the thin blue line and see the petty crimes that never make the papers.

I eased myself out the back door. Square one. Give myself plenty of room to run and/or think. I closed the door gently, heard the latch click, and stood peering through the glass expecting to see a face peek around the corner from the living room. I began to calculate. If I were to have been assaulted inside my house, the criminal would have done it while I was wrapping the bread. I was trying to append logic to the mind of a sociopath, doubtless a wasted exercise, but I was new at this. I had never been mugged, robbed, burglarized. I was playing it by ear. Perhaps a transient had passed by, stopped in to make a quick sandwich, and was already gone, a man who had less of an appetite for violence than I did. The alarmists of our nation give too much credit to the homeless, the hobos, the needy who hit rock bottom and are forced to violate the social contract just to get something in their gut.

The knife felt good in my grip, a necessary illusion, though one which would not ward off bullets. But it was an attitude adjustment that calmed me. I possessed a tooth. A fang. A claw. I edged around to the side of the house and peered into the master bedroom. Empty. There was a small bedroom on the opposite side of the house, my room during the final days before the divorce. No dining room. Four large rooms in toto with a fifth counting the bathroom, which had a frosted window. At night it was possible to see fragmented shapes moving about in the bathroom if the plastic curtain was not drawn and the light was on, images as diffuse as a cubist painting. A bad hiding place for any but a desperate man. I edged around to the opposite side of the house and took a peek into my former bedroom. Empty. I edged around to the front yard and looked through the living room window. Empty. If an intruder was in the bathroom I might be able to enter the living room, make a 911 call, and exit before he came at me. But was it worth it? Goddamn me to hell. Why didn't I wiggle the battery cables at dawn?

I turned and looked at the road. Someone might come along. I could flag them down and ask for help to search my house. But I doubted I could draft anyone into acting as a posse. Who wants to dive into danger? You are driving to the IGA when a pedestrian wielding a knife begs you to corral a housebreaker. A ludicrous proposition viewed from any angle. But still, they might have a cell phone, or might be willing to give me a quick lift to town. My mental machinations added up to nothing, of course, because the road was as empty as always. Traffic was exceptionally light on this road. No cars would be coming by. I grew frustrated, angry. I wanted to open my front door and holler—but there might be gunplay. Then the phone rang. I heard the muted bells through the window. Wilson? I could see the telephone across the living room next to the couch. Lifeline. I had to do it. He who hesitates. Seize the moment.

I opened the door silently and hurried across the wall-to-wall carpet and plucked the receiver from the cradle with finger and thumb to minimize the rattling noise.

"Hello," I said in a harsh whisper.

"Mr. Larkey?" a woman said.

"Yes."

"This is Ace Taxi."

"Who?"

"This is the Ace Taxicab Service. Did you call for a cab at County General Hospital?"

My God. What was this? I glanced around at the short hallway that led to the bathroom. My heart was pounding. "What about it?" I said in a vicious stage whisper.

"Mr. Larkey, the driver contacted us and reported a no-show."

"Pardon me?"

"You were not there when the taxi arrived, so the driver contacted us to find out if you had canceled the trip."

I stood with my jaw hanging open, my life dangling by a thread, guilt leaking through the pores of my skin like sweat.

"I . . . I'm sorry but I got a ride home with someone else."

"Mr. Larkey, if you found another ride it would have been courteous to call and cancel the taxi. Our driver waited outside the hospital for fifteen minutes."

"I . . . I'm sorry."

"In the future we ask that you phone the taxi company to let us know about any change of plans. It is costly to our drivers when people cancel without notice."

"Yes, I understand."

Lifeline!

"Wait a minute, listen, if you can send the driver to this address I will pay him for the canceled trip."

"That is not necessary, Mr. Larkey. All we ask is your consideration in the future."

"Wait, what I mean is, I need a taxi. I have to go shopping. I don't have a car."

There was a moment of silence, a rattle, a shuffle, then her voice. "You would like us to send a taxi to your address?"

"Yes, I would."

"And what is your destination?"

My mind reached for a name, an address, grabbed it like fruit off a tree. "The Lemon Tree Lounge at the Crestmoor Shopping Mall."

"All right, sir."

"And if you could send the driver who came for me at County General I would appreciate it."

We rang off. I was outside and hurrying across the lawn before I realized it. Fear, anticipation, they blocked motion from my mind. I gripped my knife in my fist and turned to face the house, waiting for the front door to slam open, a charging bull of a hobo dashing at me with snarling features, gnashing teeth, shoulders bulging from sledgehammer work in a lockup. Was this not the universal image of the criminal? *I Am a Fugitive from a Chain Gang*. Brutal stuff. I waited in silence for death to mow me down.

I was standing near the edge of the road when I heard the distant sound of a car coming from the direction of town. At this point I realized I was still holding the carving knife in my fist. Not a good posture for a taxi customer. I looked around for a place to stash it. My lawn ended at the edge of the road, demarcated by a two-foot-wide ditch approximately four inches deep, standard suburban ditch. It was partially overgrown with grass. I tossed the knife down into the ditch, then stuffed it further into the grass with my foot.

The taxi came along the road, not sailing like Wilson's vehicle but cruising at a moderate speed. Now I would have to deal with this. Apologies, perhaps an exchange of cash, then a request that he come into my house and confront a deranged Paul Muni. Again I was playing it by ear. Should I tell him the truth and ask him to accompany me inside? But what was the truth? How far back to the early hours of the day would I have to go to convince him to aid another human being? My stolen car? The accident, my arrest, the open wrapper of bread? Maybe I could ask him to come into my house and carry some luggage out to the taxi. Drivers had done this for me before. But not empty luggage. Still, cab drivers probably encountered as many nutty people as the cops did. I could tell him I wanted to buy some clothing at the mall before going to the airport. Maybe I should just take the taxi straight to the airport, get on a plane, and fly to Canada. To hell with my court date. I would live among the fugitive kind.

Thoughts like these sprout and evolve in my mind with frequency, and I have learned to ignore them. Again, too much television combined with awkward situations. I have tried hard to live a normal life, but perhaps not hard enough.

The taxi slowed as it approached my house. Beard-boy was at the wheel. His eyes were fixed on mine. His cab came parallel, his head turning toward me as if a long steel pole were welded to our faces. He stopped on the road but said nothing. Dangerous place to stop, theoretically, but there was no traffic. He did not look happy.

"Hello again," I said as I crossed the road. "Your company called and told me about the mix-up at the hospital."

"What mix-up?" he said in a voice devoid of inflection.

"A no-show, the lady called it."

"Was that a mix-up?" he replied. This was sarcasm. The vibes were thick. It was obvious I was trying to contrive a scenario of Marx Brothers proportions, missed cues, missed taxis, disappearing customers, oh my heavens, chaos reigns!

"I got a ride home with a policeman," I said, succumbing to

shame and honesty. Strangely, my mention of the policeman broke some ice.

"Why a cop?" he said.

I snatched at this crack in the frozen wall between us. "I was visiting a friend who was involved in a hit-and-run accident this morning, and the policeman was there to check on him. He offered me a ride home. I guess I should have called and told your boss I didn't need a taxi."

"I don't have a boss," he said. "I'm an independent contractor." He put the taxi into gear and wheeled onto my driveway. I interpreted this gesture as a form of absolution. The taxi rocked to a halt and he looked at me with either a smile or a squint, there wasn't much difference. "You say you knew the guy that got hit on Hawthorne Drive?" he said.

I was momentarily taken aback by his knowledge of the incident, then realized that as a driver he probably had been made aware of the situation. In a small town like this, maybe Ace Taxi sent missives on the radio to keep an eye out for problems on the road, like a spy-in-the-sky traffic reporter.

"He's a friend of mine," I said, walking up to the cab.

"Is he going to die?"

"Oh no," I said. "His condition is stable." Maybe Ace Taxi didn't provide details—dead or alive, a party is down on Hawthorne so keep your eye out for emergency vehicles.

"Did they catch the guy?" he said.

"They've got an APB out," I said. I fell into cop jargon the way a man might fall off a log. I was talking to a blue-collar worker. I have an uncontrollable tendency to talk the way I imagine people I am conversing with talk. I concluded long ago that I have no center, but my conclusion did nothing to stop me from ingratiating myself with people who were in a position to help. I would consider this a vice, except it also helped me to distance myself from everyone else.

"Sorry sonofabitch to leave a man lying in the road like that," he said. "Hanging's too good."

"I hear you, man," I said. "Listen. I'm sorry I left you high and dry at the hospital," reaching for my billfold. "I want to make up for that."

"Forget it," he said. "No-shows come with the territory. It's all a part of the game." He glanced at my house, then looked back at me. "Tell ya what, man, I got caught short after dropping off my last fare. Any chance I could use your bathroom?"

I slowly slid my billfold into my back pocket. My God. This was what I had been hoping for. No beseeching. No explanations—please accompany me into my house to check the bathroom. How many times in a man's life does hope ripen to fruition? I looked at the front door with a squint, as if debating whether to trust a stranger in my home. I felt that my moment of hesitation, my cautious behavior, and my ultimate acquiescence would be interpreted by the driver as a positive assessment of his character, my approval equivalent to the dubbing of a knight by a king at the drawbridge of his castle.

"Why certainly," I said with a whimsical smile. I stood back as he swung the door open and climbed out. He was a strapping fellow, bit of a beer gut, an inch taller than myself. I had drunk with men like him in blue-collar bars. I had worked next to them on loading docks. Quick to anger high-school grads who listened to Jim Croce records. All I had to do was stand back and let the scene unfold. But as he began walking up the drive something raced ahead of him: my conscience— what if the driver was assaulted? The man deserved an explanation, this was what my conscience barked, turning and backpedaling and cupping its hands around its mouth. I hurried up behind the driver wondering if I ought to place a palm on his shoulder, whoa fellow, I have something to tell you, there may be a stranger in my house. But if I did that now, he might frown with wonderment: What the hell are you talking about?

The thing to do was stay close on his heels, enter the house, and look over his shoulder. I would have to give him directions, and if a charging bull exited the bathroom at full fury speed we would both be taken by surprise. After all— how could I possibly have known that would happen? The intruder had been lying in wait. These thoughts ricocheted around inside my skull as we entered the living room.

My conscience faded as an infusion of adrenaline fragmented my line of thinking. It left a single shard which told me that the man who had opened my bread wrapper had hightailed it out of there before I ever got home. I felt both melodramatic and foolish. This ameliorated my sense of guilt as I pointed at the hallway and said, "In there."

He nodded and went along the hallway. I stood in the living room feeling strangely hollow.

"Shit." The driver dashed into the living room. "There's a fucking body in there!"

He didn't stop. Shot past me and out the door.

Body? I looked at the hallway, then turned and ran out the front door. The driver was sitting on the front seat, but his car door was open and one foot was on the driveway. He was talking into his microphone.

I hurried down the drive, speaking before I knew what I was saying, my words fluttering ahead of me like confetti, "What do you mean. Body? What what what . . . ?"

"Check." He slammed the mike onto the dashboard, pulled his foot into the cab, and yanked the door shut.

"There's a fucking dead body slumped over the *toilet*," he said in falsetto pitch. "What the fuck's going on here?"

84

"Listen," I said. "Listen." But to what? A confession? An explanation? What explanation? I had knowingly let him walk into a possible assault.

"Back off, jackoff," he said, and started the engine. He threw the cab into reverse.

I stopped abruptly as his tires squealed. He rolled onto the road, turned, and drove backwards thirty feet, hit the brakes, and opened the door. He stood up and leaned across the roof, pointed a long arm at me, and shouted, "The cops are coming, man! You stay right the fuck there!"

I started to take a step forward but the all-powerful word "fuck" held me steady.

"Let me explain!" I hollered.

"Sit the fuck down on the grass and don't move until the cops get here," he barked.

I heard a siren in the distance.

I lowered myself to the lawn, which was warm from the overheated day. From this perspective the landscape looked different, the worldview of a child. I could feel at my back the presence of a body in the bathroom. My God. My fears had been proven true. Only now did I acknowledge that I had not for one moment believed anyone was in my house.

But it was the evidence of the intrusion, the opened wrapper of bread, which had fed my inflated caution. This gave me a glimmer of hope. I could feel invisible wings fluttering around my face like death moths, harpies of explanation who would materialize when the police arrived and began asking questions. The questions were myriad, legion, but summed up best by the cabbie—what the fuck's going on here? I would be responsible for the answer to each and every one of those questions and the subsidiary questions sprouting like leaves from the single vine of the thickest question of all—why did you let the cab driver enter the bathroom unforewarned?

A police vehicle came in sight, racing, red lights flashing, siren howling. God only knew what the cab driver had said over the radio. I glanced at the motionless taxi and saw the silhouette of his head behind the steering wheel, as dim and unidentifiable as the thief who had driven past in my car. The police cruiser came to a halt, the siren descending to a low whir, which was supplemented by a second siren coming from town. But I did not feel any panic. Wilson and I had a connection from our brief encounters, and I knew that the impending tumultuous moments would be smoothed over when he recognized me and told everyone to hold steady. It's only Pete Larkey.

As the first cop climbed out, the taxi driver jumped from his vehicle and jogged toward him, both arms raised high, pointing in my direction with a tapping finger. The second police car was there in half a moment. This would be Wilson. I felt encased in a cone of aegis. But Wilson did not exit the vehicle. I did not recognize either of the cops. The cabbie was babbling at the first cop, who was peering in my direction, hand touching his holstered weapon. The second cop joined them and they conferred as had the three policemen who had arrested me that morning. My sense of sanctuary evaporated as both cops drew their pistols.

"Lie face-down on the lawn with your hands behind your neck!" one of them barked.

I complied. Where was Wilson? How many policemen patrolled this small burg? My face sank momentarily into the stiff blades of sun-dried grass. I lifted my head and held it above the bristles. A third siren wailed in the distance, and I was certain it was Wilson. The mix-up would be resolved. I would be allowed to rise from this awkward position, a crude but effective method of control over a suspect, mother earth cuffing me through the magic of gravity.

An ambulance pulled up behind the police vehicles. It was not Wilson, not a reprieve, and I resigned myself to experiencing the same anonymity of the morning. This day was beyond belief. I gave one last thought to the battery cables that I had not wiggled, then lowered my face to the scourging prickles of grass.

The cuffs were applied quickly. Rough hands lifted me to a standing position. "Is this your house?"

"Yes, sir."

"Your name?"

"Peter Larkey."

"The body is in the bathroom," the taxi driver said.

I glanced at him, then looked away. Either of two erroneous scenarios made me bow my head: I had murdered a man in my bathroom, or I had allowed the driver to go into the bathroom knowing full well that he would see a body. But who except a psychopath would be guilty of the latter charge? My heart sank at the prospect of spelling out the truth. But I had been rattled, was new at this, good God, my home had been invaded, I couldn't think clearly! Would they buy that? They would have to, although it would not serve to put me in a good light. I felt ashamed as a policeman led me toward one of the cruisers. The truth would come out.

I was placed in the backseat and felt a compression of air as the door closed. Handcuffed, sealed in, I was free only to swivel my head and watch the scene unfold as if I was watching a television show, the side window acting as my video screen.

A policeman entered the house carrying a camera with a flash attachment. The medics wheeled a dolly up the driveway and along the short sidewalk to the porch, and worked it through the doorway. The procedure went smoothly. Another gadget of medicine. I wondered how many industries got together to consult each other on the efficacy of design, the width of doorways, of couches, stoves. What sort of cloakroom consultations took place between engineers of disparate structures? The medics disappeared into the darkness of my living room. The cabbie stood on the driveway with his arms folded, staring at me, our faces linked by that steel pole. I looked away. My heart sank further. The worst of two possibilities would come out: No, sir, I did not murder a man, but yes I had suspected there was someone inside my house. Why did I not say anything to the driver before he went in?

A fourth vehicle arrived. I heard it coming. The road was blocked so I twisted around, fearing a rear-end collision. The road was impassable in both directions. The citizenry would have to make impromptu detours. The car was black. I could see on the dashboard a portable red light that I had seen in movies, the type that a plainclothesman whips out and places on a roof by hand as he jams his cruiser into gear and launches himself along the streets of New York City in pursuit of drug dealers. The black car slowed and crept around the parked vehicles, pulled halfway into my driveway, and stopped. A man dressed in civilian clothes climbed out. Conservative suit. Crew cut. I knew what he was. I had never considered the idea that the town of Crestmoor had plainclothesmen. But this was not a lone village in the midst of nowhere. There were nearby communities, Belmont, Salisburg. Crestmoor was the hub, you might say. Perhaps jurisdictions overlapped. At any rate, where there were people there were violent deaths, and I could not help but think that this man was called in to examine bodies in the company of coroners: homicide detective.

He adjusted the pleat of his coat and touched the knot of his tie, then took a long, studied look at the landscape surrounding my house. He looked at myself seated in the rear of the police car. He looked at a policeman standing guard outside the car. He raised a finger as if to say, "I will be with you presently," then he strode slowly toward my front door, where the other policeman was waiting for him with fists planted on his hips.

They went inside.

I waited.

They came back outside and crossed the lawn toward me. There was a minor flurry of activity as I was released from the car but not from my handcuffs.

"This is Detective Coleman," the cop said.

"Hello," I said. Why did I feel that he was wearing sunglasses? His face was naked but there was nothing in the eyes or behind them. They were gray, expressionless, though crow's feet sketched the corners. He looked a couple years older than me, much bigger, like a former college fullback. His suit was well tailored. He would have looked comfortable in a Marine tunic. He nodded at me but said nothing. The uniformed policeman took me by the left elbow and guided me toward the shallow ditch, across the knife buried in the grass, and up to the front door where we entered the living room.

The stretcher was near the hallway but not blocking it. I was escorted toward the bathroom, where a medic was standing over the corpse. Now it was my turn to say "Shit," but I didn't. The body was kneeling in front of the unlidded toilet. Khaki shirt, gray chinos. The neck was twisted toward the frosted window, I could not see the face. There was a crumpled attitude in the posture, the left calf splayed unnaturally outward as if the man had died in throes. I don't care what anybody says. Every man is an island. When you die, you die alone. John Donne was an idiot.

"Do you know this person?" Detective Coleman said.

I glanced quickly at Coleman. Deep voice, interrogation soft. I shook my head no.

"Would you please take a look at his face?"

The medic edged around us and left the bathroom. The uniformed policeman helped me step to the far side of the toilet near the bathtub. I bent at the waist and took a look. The face was purple in death. Eyes open. I stood upright and looked at the detective. "I have never seen this man before in my life." There was a cop-melodrama quality to my statement but I wanted to make it perfectly clear that this was a new one on me.

He nodded, and the policeman took me back outside. No words exchanged. It had a rehearsed quality. They may have discussed it before I was brought in: "I will ask him if he recognizes the man, and after his reply, you can take him out to your vehicle."

The sun was blinding after that dark purple moment. I closed my eyes. My lashes felt wet. I had never been that close to a dead man before. A wave of sadness hung in my chest. How can a man die? What is death? What is the life force? Morton said things like that when we drank. Maybe I was taking refuge in his words because I had none of my own. I felt very bad for the intruder.

Again air pressure clutched my body. I sat in the rear of the police car. Time passed. My thoughts dwindled. Handcuffed, imprisoned, other men were taking care of the business of the world.

I peered out my TV window and saw white shapes working their way through the living room toward the front door. The bed of the stretcher had been low to the ground when it went inside, but now it was raised on cantilevered supports that allowed the medics to guide it while walking erect. They wheeled it along the short sidewalk to the driveway, where the cabbie began edging backwards, his eyes fixed on the lengthy lump of body beneath the cover, my victim, the man I had slaughtered and left to rot on the toilet. This was in the mind of the cabbie, I was sure. Perhaps he thought I had intended to kill him too. Leave a pile of corpses beneath the cubist window—the Crestmoor Killer the latest draw at Madame Tussauds. This dark humor sprang unbeckoned from my smoldering heart. Screw that blue-collar bastard for calling the cops on me, fingering me, hollering orders, "fuck! fuck! fuck!" when Peter Larkey was the injured party here.

I calmed myself down. Deep breaths. Wilson would be my character witness. A brief oral statement and the cuffs would come off, mild apologies would be passed around, followed by levelheaded questions, and answers that were continuing to evolve in my mind. I would get out of this. I hadn't known there was a body in the bathroom, even though I had thought perhaps someone might be in there. Fuck the cabbie. I would do whatever it took to finesse my own shame.

I heard the static of a police radio. The back door opened and the policeman standing guard helped me out. "Detective Coleman would like to speak with you," he said. I debated whether to nod. What difference would it make? But still, I was an innocent man, and the decorum of innocence should be maintained.

"All right, sir," I said. I had nothing to hide. There was a truth or two that may have to be hidden in the future, but right now I was not guilty of bushwhacking a stranger in my bathroom.

I rolled my shoulders as if working out kinks, raised my chin, and walked alongside the officer who took me up to the house. Detective Coleman was talking quietly with the other policeman when we entered. Again the static of a police radio broke the quietude. The policeman reached to his left shoulder and shut off a receiving device.

"Please remove his handcuffs," Detective Coleman said, and they were off in an instant.

"Why don't you have a seat on the couch, Mr. Larkey," the detective said.

I sat down at the end farthest from the telephone. The detective and the two policemen remained standing. Here I was again, three-to-one, minions hovering like outfielders waiting for the first pitch. Coleman was standing with his head slightly cocked to one side as if he was examining a peculiar tool on a shelf at a hardware store.

"How long have you lived here, Mr. Larkey?"

"Nine years."

"Are you married?"

"Divorced."

"Mr. Larkey, can you tell me what happened here today?"

I was thrown off-kilter by this sudden shift from personal stats to current events. I cleared my throat. "I don't know what happened here," I said. "I don't know how that man got into my bathroom or how he died. He wasn't here earlier this afternoon."

"What time would that be?"

"When he wasn't here?"

"Yes."

I glanced at my watch. I began mumbling to myself, a quiet throaty buzz, "Got to the hospital maybe one thirty, two thirty got home." Coleman did not tell me to speak up. Maybe he understood that I was thinking out loud. Maybe he had seen it all, every sort of witness and suspect, every posture and attitude, every gaffe and mumble. I looked up at him. "I would say that he was not here at one thirty."

"Why do you say that?"

"Because I left here around one thirty. That's when I put

the bread in the breadbox."

Without asking me to elaborate on that statement, he said, "Where did you go?"

"To County General Hospital."

"Why?"

"To visit a friend who was involved in a hit-and-run accident this morning."

I paused as if expecting a gasp of surprise from the audience, heads turning, voices buzzing. But the sunshades were on Coleman's face again. Nothing. I didn't dare look around at the other cops. Criminal suspects always swivel their heads in movies, seeking signs of belief in the eyes of their interrogators—I didn't do it, ya gotta believe me, Louie, you and me went to St. Benedict's together, you *know* me, I couldn't have done it. That sort of beseeching.

"Mr. Morton," Coleman said.

"Pardon me?" I said.

"You went to visit Mr. Morton."

This tweaked my equilibrium. He knew. He knew everything. A hit-and-run takes place on his turf and he is among the first to get the lowdown—a man almost died on my watch and now Peter Larkey's name is back in the blotter for the second time today. Let's have a talk with this Larkey fellow. Coleman probably already had a talk with Officer Wilson. I was an understudy oblivious to the vast machinations taking place backstage at Minsky's, the invisible gritty netherworld of ropes and sandbags and painted flats.

"Yes. I visited Mr. Morton at the hospital. After I got home I discovered a loaf of bread on the countertop in the kitchen that had been left open. I did not leave it open."

"How did you get home?"

"Pardon me?"

"How did you get home from County General?"

"A police officer named Wilson drove me home in his car."

"What time did you get home?"

"Two thirty."

"How did you know it was two thirty?"

"I looked at my wristwatch."

I felt like a man being backed into a corner by a fencing master wielding a rapier.

"Was it important that you be back by two thirty?"

"No. Not at all."

"How did you get to County General?"

"I took a taxi."

"Why didn't you take a taxi home?"

The master was plucking buttons from my shirt with the tip of his blade. One by one. Humiliation prior to the fatal thrust.

"It never showed up."

"So you did call for a taxi, but it did not arrive."

I started to say yes, then realized that the very driver who did not show up was now standing on my driveway.

"There was a bit of a mix-up," I said, and regretted it immediately.

"How so?" he said.

I closed my eyes and held up a palm. "All I meant to say was that I had been waiting twenty minutes for the taxi to show up, and then Officer Wilson came outside and saw me waiting."

"Did you request a ride home?"

"No, he offered it to me."

"Did you explain that you were waiting for a taxi?"

"Yes."

"And then he offered you a ride home?"

"Yes. It seemed to me that he was merely being courteous. He said sometimes taxis did not show up at all and that I could get stranded, so he offered me a ride."

"Were you in a hurry to get home?"

"No. I just . . . wanted . . . to get home." I shrugged. What could I do but shrug? What did he expect of my explanation? Did he think that if he peeled away enough layers of the onion he would find a meaty kernel, a confession, a contradiction? Damnit, I lived here. When I got home I wanted to plant my weary ass in bed and pull the covers over my head!

"When did you discover the body?"

"I didn't," I said. "I never saw the body until you took me into the bathroom just now and showed it to me."

"And you did not recognize the man."

"No."

"You had never seen him before."

No. No. No. I don't think so. His face was purple, his features distorted, he would have been unrecognizable even if I knew him. Then I thought of the man who had stolen my car. It took that long to connect. My thoughts were linear. I did not have a holistic godlike view of life on earth. Could that have been the man who stole my car? But why would he come back? And who killed him? Or did the man who stole my car kill himself? When was the last time I was in my bathroom?

"When was the last time you were in your bathroom?" Coleman said.

Perhaps I am holistic—the synchronicity was mystical, but of course we were both trying to peel away the layers of the same onion.

"The last time I was in my bathroom was nine o'clock," I said. "I took a shower. I got dressed and left the house about ten minutes later."

"Where did you go?"

Oh God. I had been through all this. I had lived it and I

had told it and I had written it down. Had Coleman read my witness statement? Was he toying with me? Was he seeking the contradiction that would convict me of hit-and-run? Was this about something other than the body in the bathroom? Were the events of the entire day about to be fashioned into a slipknot on a noose?

I took a deep breath and let it out slowly. Time to square the deck. I would not be toyed with even if I understood his motive: everyone is a suspect.

"I was going to Apex Auto Parts because my car wouldn't start. I wanted to buy a new battery. While I was gone my car was stolen. It's a long . . . but I found my car, and a few minutes later I was arrested by Officer Wilson on suspicion of drunk driving and hit-and-run. I was taken down to police headquarters and booked."

"I know."

His interruption disconcerted me. I wanted to lay all my cards on the table in neat rank-and-file and then proclaim my innocence of all charges, drunk driving, hit-and-run, murder, Jesus Christ, why weren't these bastards scouring the woods!

"I gave them a written statement," I said. "They told me I would have to make a court appearance because my car was involved in the hit-and-run. After they let me go I went to a bar called the Lemon Tree Lounge. I drank a shot of scotch. From there I walked home and lay down on my bed for a few minutes."

"Did you sleep?"

"For a few minutes. But I couldn't sleep very well."

"Why not?"

I decided not to mention the death moth. I did not want him to think I lived in a pest-house. This seemed a minor lie of omission.

"Because I was thinking about my friend Morton lying in

the hospital, so I called a taxi."

"How long were you in your house?"

"Maybe ten minutes."

"Did you use the bathroom?"

"No." Quick question, quick answer. He would not trip me up. The truth is man's best friend, the all-seeing guide dog through the forest of suspicion to the land of innocence.

Detective Coleman raised his head and looked toward the hallway, then looked down at me. "So you left your house around nine thirty this morning. You got back home around one thirty, but you did not enter the bathroom."

"Correct."

"You came home again at two thirty and did not enter the bathroom."

"Yes."

"So at some point between nine thirty this morning and two thirty this afternoon a man died in your bathroom."

I paused before answering. We were dealing with numerals here, clockfaces, the elusive details of rotating hour hands. I thought about it, then nodded. "Yes. I left here at nine thirty and did not enter my bathroom again until you escorted me in there."

"When the taxi driver saw the body, did you go into the bathroom and look at it?"

"No, sir."

"Why not?"

I raised my hands, shook my head, shrugged. "I didn't know what was going on. He scared me. He ran right out of the house, so I ran after him. I didn't know what was happening."

Detective Coleman again looked toward the bathroom. This was followed by a long silence, perhaps ten seconds. Ten seconds is not long relative to the birth and death of a star, but it was the longest silence of my life.

"Do you have any enemies, Mr. Larkey?"

Enemies? Nations had enemies. Mobsters. Politicians. At the opposite end of that well-heeled spectrum I supposed poor people had enemies too, but I lived in the bland center.

"No."

"What about your divorce?"

"Sir?"

"Any conflicts with other men, jealous husbands, lovers, anything along that line?"

"No. My divorce had to do with financial problems. My ex lives with her sister and brother-in-law in Albany."

"Do you communicate with her?"

"Rarely. Things come up once in a while. I mostly communicate through her lawyer."

"What's your ex-wife's name?"

"Her maiden name was Laura Collins."

She was not a maiden when I married her. Not by a long shot.

"What's your brother-in-law's name?"

"Leonard P. Dexter. Certified Public Accountant."

Why don't you study to be a CPA like Leonard? my wife used to say. She might as well have asked me why I didn't hunt griz for a living.

"I'm going to have to ask you to come with me to the station and make out a witness statement," Coleman said. His eyes were hawk-like, peering, studious—it seemed every muscle of my face was being examined for a ripple, a twitch. Would a citizen under suspicion object to a sudden trip to the police station?

"That's fine," I said.

"Good," he replied. "Right now your house is going to be cordoned off until we get some people in here to investigate."

"Am I under arrest?"

"Nossir."

His answer did not mollify me. I felt as hollow as I had felt when I let the taxi driver enter the bathroom alone and unaided.

"Should I get my coat?" I said.

"No," Coleman said. "I want you to leave everything exactly the way it is, including fingerprints."

When I left the house this time I was not in cuffs, but I took note of the fact that the uniformed policemen stayed close on my heels. I took note of the fact that the cab driver was no longer standing on the driveway with his arms folded in blue-collar acrimony. Strange posture of aggression, when you think about it. A man prepared to brawl should hold his arms away from his sides like a tightly wound gunslinger. But perhaps it is the animal instinct, like a cat making itself large through arched back and raised tail. Bulge those pecs with your forearms, bulge those biceps with your fists. Fake out the enemy. Do the Viking dance. Go primitive. I hate horseshit people.

The taxi was nowhere in sight.

"Did the cab driver go back on duty?" I said, glancing casually at Detective Coleman.

"I'm afraid he's off duty for the rest of the day. He's already down at headquarters."

I wished I had not asked. By then I couldn't have cared less where beard-boy went. I was glad I had not given him money for the no-show. He had scared the hell out of me when he ran from the bathroom. He would be talking about this for years. He would have something to bore his drunk friends with at the dive where he wasted his weekend nights. I once knew a warehouse worker in Phoenix who told everyone he met that he would be playing pro baseball if he hadn't fucked up his ankle in an industrial accident. He was thirty-eight. The same age I was when Detective Coleman opened the door of his unmarked cruiser.

After he closed the door, which did have an interior handle, I noticed one of the patrolmen digging through the trunk of a black-and-white. He pulled out a roll of yellow tape the size of a duct tape roll. Crime-scene tape. I knew what a crime scene was. Everybody knows what a crime scene is. It's where they nail you. It's where they bring in the experts to scrape together the incontrovertible. Okay, fine, let them scour my house for the bludgeon that killed the toilet corpse, and then, when they were satisfied that I was not a serial killer, perhaps they might get around to scouring the woods, dragging the river, and capturing the prick who stole my Ford. That's what I paid taxes for.

It was 4 p.m. when Detective Coleman and I arrived at police headquarters. He parked around back and took me inside, down a corridor, and into an office.

"I'll have to ask you to wait here," he said. He seemed more of a businessman than a cop, had a politeness I associated with executives. I'd had a few jobs that involved office work. CEOs. Presidents. Human Resource Managers. The whole schmeer. He left. A few minutes later Officer Wilson entered the room.

"Good afternoon, Mr. Larkey," he said with a smile. "How are you doing?"

Was this rhetorical? I debated which level of sociability I should rise to. Self-effacing humor? Sullen honesty. If I did have a center, it held. I was in no condition to emulate the persona of a law enforcement officer. "A stranger died in my house this afternoon," I said in a level tone of voice. "The police are examining the scene for clues."

He nodded. "Detective Coleman filled me in on that."

By any chance did Coleman bring up the subject of "innocence" I wanted to ask but knew not to. I would have no trouble emulating a frantic suspect, but I decided to rely on the truth to see me through this mess. Falling cards and wheat straws, that's all I had.

"He asked me to take care of you while he attends to business," Wilson said. "This could take some time. Would you please accompany me down the hallway?"

The decks had been cleared for my mind to begin fixating on what I expected would be an inevitable confrontation with the taxi driver. My head remained motionless as my eyes quickly scanned the hallway in the manner of a boy in junior high scanning faces in search of a bully to dodge, a girl he likes, a teacher he wants to avoid like the plague— "Why didn't you hand in your homework assignment this afternoon, Mr. Larkey?" Teachers called me "Mister" when the shit storms erupted.

I glanced through an open doorway into a small room and saw the taxi driver sitting at a table with his arms folded. A few sheets of paper lay in front of him along with a ballpoint pen. His head turned and he looked right at me. Beard-boy making his witness statement, I assumed. A sensation of dread tickled my spine. Should I nod, utter a soft salutation, perhaps smile? I gave up a slight nod as if acknowledging his existence but did not smile or give a friendly flap of the hand in greeting. I casually walked out of his line of sight. What was he thinking? Was he entertaining the slightest suspicion that I had intentionally led him into a dangerous situation? Why had I not told him the truth when he arrived at my house? Why had I not wiggled my battery cables at dawn?

Wilson escorted me into a small room similar to the one

where I had written my first witness statement.

"I'll need you to wait here until Detective Coleman is ready to talk to you," Wilson said. "Would you like something to drink, Mr. Larkey? Coffee? Iced tea? I can get you a can of cold soda."

"No. No. I don't want anything to drink. I just want to go home."

"I'm sorry, but you will have to speak with Detective Coleman first. Then you will have to make out a witness statement."

"I know. I was just thinking out loud."

"We'll try to move this along as quickly as possible," Wilson said. "After we have finished with you here, I will drive you back to your house."

"Will they be finished with the . . . the yellow tape?" I said. Christ but I was exhausted. I couldn't put together a coherent sentence. I wanted my bed. Darkness. Sleep.

"They should be finished by the time I get you home," Wilson said. He glanced at his wristwatch. "This may take an hour or more."

I was fragmenting. A nap. A meal. A can of cold beer. I saw it all spread out before me like a map, a battle plan, a surrender ceremony. I wanted to kill my battery cables. Why was I unemployed? Why was I broke? Why was my life like this?

Wilson walked out of the room and closed the door. At least I wasn't behind bars, but I knew there would be a guard posted somewhere in the hallway. The curtain was rising at Minsky's. I began to feel edgy. Were my muscles tightening? I walked back and forth to loosen up. There was a stack of papers and a pen on a table. I sat down and looked at the stack, preparing myself mentally to do the thing I had done this morning. I was no longer a tyro. How many people do something unusual twice on the same day?

I glanced at my watch. Four fifteen. At nine everything was fine. Now my life was down the tubes. This was the price I paid for seeking employment. Forget wiggling the battery cables, I wished I had never left the house at all. Who made me do that? My wife was long gone, so I had made myself do it. I hadn't had anything else to do. Might as well set into motion the horrendous chore of looking for work. Now Morton was half-dead and a corpse had been removed from my bathroom. The gods had been thumbing through my files recently. Time to fuck with Pete Larkey again.

Forty-five minutes passed, and then the door opened. Wilson looked in. "Would you please come with me, sir?"

We went back down the hallway to his supervisor's office. I was offered a chair but I declined. I preferred to stand. It was the preference of a tired man too edgy to sit.

"In connection with the traffic accident, we are still looking for a man on the run, Mr. Larkey," his supervisor said. "However, there is the matter of the corpse in your bathroom."

"Well, I assure you that I did *not* murder anybody in my house today and you can plug a goddamn lie detector up my *ass* if it suits you." This staggering soliloquy erupted from my throat before I could stop it. I felt possessed by the spirits of Paul Muni, John Garfield, and fucking Edward G.

The cops couldn't handle it. Smiles cracked their faces. I wouldn't have been surprised to see truncheons come out.

"Take it easy, Mr. Larkey," the supervisor said. "The county coroner is currently performing an autopsy on the dead man, and until the results are in, things are on hold."

God was I embarrassed. Who talks that way to cops? Cagney, yes—but me? It was like an out-of-body experience. "I'm sorry I spoke to you like that," I said. "It's been a rough day."

"We understand, Mr. Larkey," the supervisor said.

Wilson then led me down the hallway toward Coleman's office. One-story, tiled, the building really was very much like a school. Echo halls. Intense silence. Not the sort of place where they work over suspects. Is it hard on cops not to beat the truth out of murderers, rapists, vile men of obvious guilt? Is it hard for police academies to weed out sociopaths who crave legal authorization to shoot people? 007. Licensed to kill. Of course, ordinary citizen/soldiers are authorized to kill at preordained moments. I myself was taught to use a rifle, but the army did not teach me to kill. Growing up in America taught me to kill. It took twenty years.

"He'll be with you in a moment," Wilson said, directing me into a room cluttered with filing cabinets, a metal desk, an interesting wooden chair, old-fashioned, roller-wheeled, dark brown wood with the varnish rubbed away on the arms. A Coleman family heirloom steeped in sentimental value perhaps, or else just a sweet deal picked up at a flea market. It looked inviting. I took a seat on an ordinary metal-framed chair in front of the desk. I did not have long to wait. Detective Coleman entered the room carrying a manila folder. He set it on the desk.

"How are you doing, sir?" he said with the affable abruptness of Rip Torn.

I nodded, wordless. His question seemed strange. I was not doing very well. Perhaps the manila folder would fill me in on how well I was really doing.

He sat down and took a deep breath and looked directly into my eyes.

"I have a preliminary coroner's report right here," he said, reaching out and tapping the manila with his index finger. "The man who died in your bathroom apparently choked to death. A piece of bread was found lodged in his windpipe."

He sat back. The chair creaked.

"It would appear that the man tried to swallow an entire slice of bread in one gulp rather than chewing it. The bread stuck in his throat. We surmise that he ran to the bathroom and made a vain attempt to vomit up the bread. There were two definite impressions in the bread which indicated that he had tried to stick his fingers down his throat to dig out the obstruction or to induce vomiting. The man suffocated to death."

The blood drained from my face. My body flushed hot with spreading physical horror. Dying moments. Last thoughts. An understanding of what is happening followed by darkness. This was something not communicated by television. I suppose nothing can truly communicate such a thing. Words are only catalysts, the mind does the rest to itself.

"How terrible," I softly said.

He nodded. "Death by misadventure."

I was familiar with that one.

He grabbed his nose between thumb and forefinger and gave it a few thoughtful pulls. He lowered his hand and looked directly at me. "Mr. Larkey, during our investigation at your house our people found something."

My eyebrows went up. Cat-arched. End the sentence, they were saying.

He unlocked a desk drawer, opened it, and withdrew a plastic bag. He held it delicately by one corner and raised it so the light from a window backlit the object contained therein: a knife.

"Do you recognize this?" he said.

I leaned forward. I wanted to take it, heft it, feel its weight, examine the dark handle, the ribbed saw-teeth. But I knew not to do that.

"Yes," I said.

"When did you last see it?"

I sighed. "The last . . . I . . . my . . ." I was trying to say more than two things at once. Three or four. I settled down and said, "I dropped it into the shallow ditch that runs along the front yard of my house. I tamped it down underneath the grass with my shoe. That's the last I saw of it."

He nodded and set the bag into the drawer, slid it slowly closed.

"Why did you do that, Mr. Larkey?"

How could this be? I was certain that the episode involving beard-boy had faded away. How could Detective Coleman be sitting there conjuring up that which had ceased to exist when my innocence in the toilet incident had been proclaimed by the majesty of the law? What were the odds? Of the hundreds, the thousands of subjects he might have focused on, he was bringing the cabbie back onstage. But I had done it to myself, this I knew. Goddamn me for skulking through my house with a knife in my hand. Who did I think I was? Rambo? An unemployed chump steeped in TV was what I was. If a criminal had dashed from the bathroom like a bull, I would have shit my pants. Me and my fucking tooth, claw, fang.

"Let me explain," I said, as if he expected anything else. No. He sat calmly as I cleared my throat and collected my thoughts. He was patient. Interested. Hanging on my every word. Not a whiff of equivocation would drift past his notice. "When I saw the loaf of bread open on my counter I took the knife from a wooden holder. I was afraid that someone was inside my house. I went out the back door and looked through all the windows except the bathroom, which is frosted and difficult to see through. I went around to the front yard and heard the phone ringing in my living room, so I hurried inside thinking it would be Officer Wilson, but it was the Ace Taxicab Service."

I paused.

"Why did they call you?" he said.

I explained about the no-show. That was as far as I could take it before my narrative began to grow difficult. The time had come. Now the truth would out. It seemed only proper that I would be the one to hang myself. But when had that never been true?

"I asked the dispatcher to send a taxi to my address."

"Why?"

There were two possible answers, both plausible: the truth, or a lie. I went with the lie. "Because I didn't have a car and I wanted to get away from there."

He nodded, turned his head slightly, and scratched at a spot behind his ear. He lowered his hand slowly to the desk as if it were a coffee cup. "Why didn't you ask the dispatcher to send a policeman?"

I gazed at him blankly. What was my status here? Victim or suspect? Was he getting at something beyond my comprehension, seeking answers to unarticulated questions? There were no lines between which I could read.

"I was so surprised to get a call from a taxi company that I asked for a taxi. I panicked. I'm not used to being in situations like that. It seemed logical. I thought a man was hiding in my bathroom."

"Why did you think that?"

My face went blank again. Now we were getting down to it. Why do I ever think any of the thoughts I have? "Look, I found an open loaf of bread on the counter. The bathroom was the only room I could not see into."

"So you entered your house even though you were afraid that someone might be in there."

"Yes. The phone was my lifeline. I was alone out there in the suburbs. I have no car." My voice was rising in pitch. Did he not grasp the spot I had been in? "I thought it might be Officer Wilson." Last ditch effort. It was *war*, you bastard. Men run toward machine-gun nests. Nobody says *why*!

"Why did you bury the knife under the grass?" he said.

He was getting ahead of my story. I took a deep breath. "After I hung up the phone, I left my house and ran down to the road to wait for the cab. When I realized I was holding the knife, I got rid of it . . . I mean I dropped it into the ditch and covered it with grass. I didn't want the taxi driver to see me standing there with a knife in my hand. He might not have stopped to pick me up."

All the bases were covered.

Coleman nodded and rubbed his nose with a knuckle. He looked down at the autopsy report, then looked up at me. "Is there any possibility in your mind that the man who choked to death in your bathroom was the same man who stole your car?"

In my mind? What did my mind have to do with any of the events that had taken place since I woke up at dawn? I might as well have left my mind in the womb for all the good it had ever done me.

"I thought of that," I said.

His irises seemed to sharpen. "And?"

"I don't think so," I said.

"Why is that?"

"Because the man who drove past me in my car appeared to be wearing a blue work shirt. The dead man was wearing a khaki shirt."

"Suppose he changed shirts?"

Possible. Laundry kiped from a clothesline. Movie fugitives did that. I shrugged.

"If you were to take another look at the man, do you think you might be able to draw a fresh conclusion?" he said.

"Oh God no," I said. "Please. I don't want to look at that again. The man who stole my car drove by so fast that all I saw was . . . his hair. It was black. Like a criminal's hair."

"How do you mean?"

I closed my eyes and shook my head. "It just seemed like the longish hair of a man who . . . I don't know . . . that was my impression. I thought of him as an escaped convict."

Coleman nodded. "The dead man had short hair, brown, recently cropped."

"I don't want to see that again. Please. I didn't see the car thief's face. I wouldn't be able to discern the faces. I was too shocked at seeing my car go by."

"All right, Mr. Larkey. I just wanted to touch on that. We're still looking for the thief and trying to contact anybody who might have seen him on foot."

Great. Goodbye. Leave me alone. My life is shit. Keep my car. Cube it in a junkyard. Give it to Goldfinger. I'm moving to Scottsdale.

Detective Coleman opened the manila folder and picked up three sheets of paper. Handwritten words. "I have read the cab driver's statement and I have a couple of points I would like you to clarify."

Back to that. It had the quality of a gelatinous waterfall cascading onto my head. Buster Keaton trapped in a caramel factory. Chaos. Reigns. Eternal.

"According to his statement, he asked if he might be allowed to use your bathroom. It says here he intended to go 'number one.' You told him that he could."

He lowered the fan of paper to the desk but kept a firm hold with thumb and forefinger. An urge to ask to see the statement flickered like sheet lightning in my heart.

"That's true," I said.

He opened his mouth, took a whiff of air, and sat up a bit

straighter on his fine antique chair. "If you thought someone was inside your bathroom, why didn't you tell the cabbie?"

My soul dwindled to the size of a child, a mouse, a flea.

This, then, was the crime being investigated that day. Not a murder, not a hit-and-run, but a moral failure.

Our eyes locked.

The world ceased to turn.

The clock ceased to tick.

That would not do, of course. The world was turning, the clock was ticking, I had to say something.

Here's the thing though. I did not know the real answer. Why would anybody show such reckless disregard for the life of another man? Why would I say nothing when I assumed the cabbie might be walking into a death trap? By "real" answer I am getting into the realm of metaphysics. The surface reason was because he was a big guy so I figured he would make a damn good shield. But could I say that to a cop? Why had I not simply blurted out my fears to the cabbie when he drove up? This is what I am getting at. Letting him walk into the house was not the crux of the matter. The crux was my hesitation to explain the situation that had generated the current mess I was in, this verbal jousting, this inquiry into the nature of my character.

"Did you in fact already know that there was a body in the bathroom?" Coleman said.

My reflective thoughts popped like a balloon in a cartoon. "Pardon me?"

"Did you in fact want the cab driver to discover the body?"

My God. I was right. The detective was getting at something beyond my comprehension, seeking answers to unarticulated questions, following a line of reasoning as hidden from me as Nazis skulking behind French hedgerows.

"I'm sorry," I said. "I don't know what you mean."

110

His right hand was splayed on the desk. He lifted two fingers and lowered them while simultaneously cocking his head to one side and bringing it back upright, like a man conceding a possible point in a negotiation.

"It strikes me that if you wanted a person to find a body in your bathroom, you would tell him to go into the bathroom."

"The driver *asked* me if he could use the bathroom. I didn't ask him if he needed to use the bathroom."

"For the sake of argument, let us suppose that you knew the body was in the bathroom and you wanted him to go in there and see the body. Is it possible that you might have come up with some sort of ruse to get him inside your house?"

Like luggage you mean, you bastard, oh Jesus.

"Detective Coleman, I did not know there was a body in my bathroom. You seem to be accusing me of something."

"Not at all. I am simply trying to find some congruity that ties together all of today's coincidental events. The only common thread that ties them together seems to be you."

He let that hang in the air for a moment.

"I understand that your Ford was involved in a mishap awhile back. It fell from a jack and broke the left leg of the hit-and-run victim, Mr. Morton."

"That's right. It happened six months ago."

"And today a man driving your car ran Mr. Morton down and almost killed him."

"That's correct," I said, taking courage from fact.

"We can't seem to find the man," he said.

I shrugged. "I suppose you'll have to keep looking."

He smiled. "I can assure you we will. The law never sleeps."

"You wouldn't know it by me," I wanted to say but did not. Are your people scouring the woods, dragging the river, demanding ID cards from sullen men on cross-country busses? Are we done here? Can I go now? I am an *innocent*

Gary Reilly

man.

But I kept a tight leash on all that. Courage can take you only so far, then it stops to watch you step off the cliff.

"You said something about a dead battery," he said, glancing at the folder and leaning back on his creaking chair. "We tested the battery and it works just fine. The car seems to be in perfect running condition."

I laughed. This I did in his presence. It was as if a TV commercial for Delco had popped up. "I tried to start my car this morning but it wouldn't start. So I walked to Apex to buy a new battery."

"Prior to that did you make any attempt to correct the problem?"

"No. I'm not a mechanic. It didn't even occur to me. I threw in the towel and set out for Apex."

"You didn't wiggle the battery cables or anything?"

The smile that had remained on my face throughout my short narrative faded. Did he know something? Had he spoken with Morton? But maybe battery wiggling was an intuitive action common to the male species, something that would occur to any ordinary man, even a cop.

"Didn't even think of it," I said. I wanted badly to tell him that Morton himself had suggested this solution. Morton was, after all, a mechanic. But I wanted to ease Morton out of the picture.

Detective Coleman nodded. He closed the manila folder on the paperwork and smiled at me.

"Mr. Larkey, I am going to have you make a written statement describing everything you did from the moment you got up this morning until the moment that the cab driver discovered the body in your house. When you have finished making your statement, you will be free to leave."

The End

I say that only to underscore the monumental nature of the undertaking. A true and full accounting would fill a book. But I understood. The trail was hot, it had not yet cooled. He wanted me to get it down on paper before the first wave of short-term memory loss kicked in. Write it in a white heat like Jack Kerouac, Thomas Wolfe, the mad lyricists who eschewed the anal rules of syntax in favor of visionary overload. The critics could sort it out later, and the ordinary reader just did not count.

As I said, I had been a liberal arts major in college. A lot of good that did me. One of my former roommates has already retired a rich man. He majored in computer programming. I get the alumni newsletter.

"Do you want me to include the information I gave about the hit-and-run accident?" I said.

"Yessir," he said. "That statement goes into the files of the traffic division. I realize I'm asking you to go over old ground, but I would like a full accounting of everything you did today for the homicide division."

I nodded. I glanced at my watch, then wished I hadn't. It seemed rude, like snapping a wet towel at someone's ass. The implication was there. My time is valuable, I have better things to do. A curse on small gestures. But then, I was in the presence of a person who had probably experienced every small gesture known to mankind, the sneer, the rolling eyeballs, the finger, the reactionary crude moves of collared culprits. I pictured angry hookers sticking out their tongues, spitting, stomping spiked heels as they were stuffed shrieking into paddy wagons.

"Okay."

"Just stick with the facts," Coleman said. "Your actions and conversations. No need to draw conclusions. Just describe exactly what you did, the things you saw, and include the time element if you feel you are certain of the time that the events took place."

"Yes, sir."

He escorted me down the hall past the room where beard-boy had given me the silent eye. I was led into the same room where I had waited earlier. There was plenty of paper. It took only half an hour to describe my day from nine to five. I enjoyed that particular little irony. Most of the shit jobs I had held in my life were from eight to four thirty, with a half hour off for lunch. It was only after I completed the paperwork that I realized I had not felt a pang of hunger since gulping down that lunch meat and Coke in the cab. I had been running on unalloyed adrenaline, the drug Mother Nature put inside of me to handle the tests the gods put in front of me.

I signed my name at the bottom of the statement.

I dated it.

I laid it face-down on the table and sat back on the chair, folded my arms, bulged my pecs, bulged my biceps with my fists, and waited for Detective Coleman to return. Of course I knew what Coleman was up to. Compare and contrast my witness statement with the one I had written in the morning. Search for contradictions, lapses of memory-fact, perhaps subtle alterations in the timeline to cover up my guilt. The criminal element of the world has ruined it for the innocent. The cops don't trust anyone. But of course, we pay them to not do that.

Three

The sun was below the horizon when Officer Wilson drove me home and parked his vehicle in my driveway. He asked if I wanted him to accompany me inside my house to check the place out one last time. Why not? Now that I was safe, now that all was right with the world, now that the victims were being cared for by appropriate agencies, why not let a cop run interference for me? "Sure," I said. After all, I had nothing to gain. It was too late for that, as usual.

He checked out the interior of the house. That took ten seconds. The life and death of a star. "I'll let you know as soon as possible if there is any news on the hit-and-run driver," he said. "You'll probably get your car back tomorrow."

I thanked him. He left. I watched through the picture-window as he drove away. I suddenly wished I had my car so I could drive to the video store and find something good to take my mind off reality. Perhaps *Rashomon*. Kurosawa capitalized on a universal truth there, multiple points of view, honest contradictions, a virtual cliché, a celluloid niche that he carved for himself. But I was tired. My nerves were shot, frazzled, yet I felt I would not be able to go to sleep. I had sometimes experienced this after a hard day's work on a loading dock when I was younger, coming home and finding myself unable to sit down and relax, keeping busy in a daze, doing dishes, vacuuming, unable to sleep. I interpreted it as my body revolting against the fact that it worked on a loading dock. Do something fun, for Christ's sake. But it was probably just the coffee I gulped all day long to help me lift those boxes. My poor body. It had been worked half to death for twenty years and it was still broke.

I looked at my watch. Not yet eight o'clock. Early to go to bed. I went into the kitchen to look for something to eat. Get the belly churning, drain the brain of blood. Siesta time. Maybe sip some milk. I decided against alcohol. If things worked out the way they usually didn't, I might find myself tomorrow picking up where I had left off at nine this morning and start looking for a job again. I didn't want to throw in the towel, succumb to drink, and find myself sleeping in when I had so many things to do. Bail my car. Buy a new battery—I was determined to do that regardless. Play it safe. Then go to the employment agency. Get that hopeless tactic out of the way before I began knocking on doors to ask people if I could mow their goddamn lawns.

I opened the refrigerator and checked my larder. Milk, Coke, lunch meat, vegetables, the things bachelors stuff in their fridges and let rot. There was a half pint of chocolate ice-cream in the icebox. There was a plastic tub of macaroni salad, there was peanut butter in the cupboard above the sink, canned spaghetti, chili, fruit salad, and pears. I was living as I had lived before I got married. Old habit or the natural state of man? A woman once joked on TV that men get married so they will have someone to cook and clean for them. Ha! Obviously, she had never visited bachelor digs. Boys dial takeout for dinner, food means nothing to studs on the make. Laundry day comes when there is absolutely nothing on the hangers.

I pulled out the tub of store-bought prefab macaroni salad and opened it, scooped two cups onto a plate. Simple dinner, quicker than takeout. I opened a can of peas and dumped half of it onto the macaroni. Grabbed a Coke and went into the living room, where my wife never let me eat. By "let" I mean hounded me to eat at the kitchen table. The living room was for guests, not living. Whenever she went to visit her sister in Albany, I reverted quicker than a junkie in the presence of free horse. I drew closed the curtains on the picture-window, then turned on the TV and watched part of an old movie while I ate. Cary Grant. I didn't recognize the film. Didn't matter. Cary was Cary. Master of suave befuddlement. I was ten years old when I first saw *Bringing Up Baby*. I nearly choked to death with laughter when he sailed past the hedgerow standing on the running board of the flivver. How could a grown-up be so goofy? Total absence of dignity. Hard to believe Howard Hawks had directed it. But I found most things hard to believe as I grew older.

I finished my meal, turned off the TV, and went into the kitchen. I decided to do the dishes, then read myself to sleep. I was washing a plate when an odd feeling came over me. I paused and pictured the tub of macaroni in my mind. Now that I thought about it, it seemed to me that there had been less macaroni in the tub than the last time I had scooped noodles from it a few days earlier. I set the plate in the sink and went back to the fridge, pulled out the tub and opened it, looked down at the swirl of half-moons and mayonnaise and bits of vegetable. A sick feeling came over me. Had someone been eating my macaroni?

I closed the lid and set it on the countertop. I looked around the kitchen as I had done earlier in the day, searching for things out of place. I opened the silverware drawer, opened the doors beneath the sink, peered, studied, opened the cupboard and gazed at my tin cans. My eyes fell on the jar of peanut butter. "Aw jeez," I said aloud. It had been moved, of this I was certain.

I did not want to touch it. I knew who had moved it. The corpse. I improvised. I ripped two sheets of paper towel off the rack and took hold of the peanut butter jar. I unscrewed the lid with the trepidation of a man who knew that cloth-covered snakes were waiting to spring out at him. Gag gift. Friends tried to pull that on me in my youth but it never worked. "Here, open this can of cashews," they would say, a tin cylinder that weighed nothing.

I pried the lid away slowly and looked down at the peanut butter, which had been gouged in a way that I did not dig brown butter for bread. "Shit," I said. Deep thrusts like quick jabs into the pasty meat of pulverized peanuts. Skippy. "Goddamnit." It made me ill. The police would not have noticed this. Clues on the molecular level. I knew now that I would have to clean out my entire larder, trash it, go shopping in a taxi, and restock. Wasted money. I did not even want to touch the unopened cans of peas and sliced pears, chili, corn. I imagined the dead man picking through the shelves, spinning cans around to read the labels, touching everything, coating my food supply with viruses.

Then another thought occurred to me. Detective Coleman had said the dead man had choked on a whole slice of bread. He didn't mention anything about peanut butter. But would he have mentioned that? The imprints of the man's fingertips were discovered in the mossy dough down his throat. I opened the peanut butter jar again and examined the gouges to see if perhaps he might have dug at the contents with those very fingers, a thought so revolting that I screwed the cap back on and almost threw the jar at the wastebasket next to the dishwasher. But the police might want to see it. I set it back in the cupboard. I was furious. Good God, a man's home is not only invaded but touched, probed, twiddled, tweaked. I would call Coleman in the morning and broach the subject. It would no doubt be a useless move, but it might help alleviate my revulsion. Let the majesty of the law remove it from my brain like a poultice.

That was that. I was going to bed. Take a shower, grab a book, read myself unto oblivion. Then I thought of the toilet corpse. How could I ever sit down on that thing again? How could I ever bathe or shower in the same room? I stood in the middle of the kitchen gazing at one of the four walls surrounding me and decided that the time had come to move out of this town. Leave Crestmoor for good, move on to another meaningless town, an idea that had been simmering on extremely low heat ever since my wife had left me. Get out of the death house. The boot in the ass that I needed.

Well, there was nothing I could do right now. Men in war took dumps in foxholes, it's all there in the history books. The indignity of combat is unparalleled. I would grab a can of Lysol and medicate my mind by spraying down the entire bathroom before using the facilities. A grand illusion to be sure, but one I needed. I would not be looking for a job tomorrow, I would be looking for a new place to live, an apartment, a motel, a haven to wait out the results of this terrible day, biding my time until the police confirmed that I was an innocent man and thus free to leave town.

I was peering under my sink looking for the Lysol when I heard a familiar sound outside: the rumble of a car on my driveway. When my wife and I used to have people over for dinner or a card game, they would be amazed at my ability to hear the subtle sounds of a car coming up the drive. But I was attuned to the aerial vibrations, the quiet rumble of an engine. Our guests remained oblivious to the arrival of new guests until the doorbell rang. I was like a magician to them, but you become sensitive to non-natural sounds out in the boondocks.

I stood up and heard the cessation of the engine. A police car? My magic did not extend to make and model. I was torn between annoyance and eagerness. Perhaps it was Officer Wilson returning with good news. I walked into the living room, shuffling soundlessly across the carpeting, a habit I had developed so visitors would not know if I was home. Tactic more than habit. The occasional door-to-door salesman did knock at times, people with religious tracts, or real estate agents making those difficult cold calls.

I parted the curtains an inch and peered toward the carport. Dark mass of an automobile on the driveway. I did not recognize it. The doorbell rang. Damn—my usual response to not knowing what I preferred to know immediately. I went to the front door and switched on the porch light. I wished I owned a peephole, but it was too late. My plan to leave Crestmoor rendered that idle wish moot.

I opened the door six inches and gazed out at the taxi driver. The light cast on him by the overhanging bulb, and the blackness behind him, made him seem a bit larger than in the stark light of day. He was wearing his cabbie cap, T-shirt, jeans, tennis shoes, had not changed clothes since last I'd seen him seated in the room at the police building. His head was cocked slightly as if he was waiting for the answer to a question not yet asked. I pulled the door all the way open and smiled. I instinctively reached with my left hand toward my billfold. He had not received a red cent for the no-show trip to the hospital or for the trip to my house. I had stiffed him twice. That came fast to my mind.

"Hello," I said brightly. "I bet I know why you're here."

"I bet you don't," he replied in the same dry tone of voice with which he had said, "Was that a mix-up?"

My left hand eased away from my billfold and hung itself on my left hip.

A somberness descended on the scene like an aegis cone. I raised my chin and peered at him.

"I have a couple of questions to ask you," he said. "Can I come in?"

I became instantly defensive. I did not want him in my house without knowing why.

"Does this have to do with the trips that you didn't get paid for?"

"No," he said.

I looked over at the car and recognized the taxi in the darkness, the rectangular unlit signage on the roof. But I could not quite make out the dark letters "Ace Taxicab Service."

"Are you on duty?" I said.

"Yeah," he said, reaching up and pinching the brim of his cap as if to tug it tighter around the crown of his skull. "I have to pull a couple hours on the night shift to make up for my losses today."

"Listen, I'll be happy to compensate you for all of that. My fault. I should have called about the hospital trip . . ."

He pulled the screen door open and said, "Can I come in? I want to ask you some questions."

I felt a flush of adrenaline. The man had touched my house without permission, virtually yanked the screen door. I heard a buzz, a voice, a click. I looked at his taxi and realized his two-way radio was on. The dispatcher was talking to other cabbies. This reduced my sense of apprehension. The driver was on duty, a working man scrambling for a buck. He was not here to cause trouble, he was trying to make up for losses. Married perhaps, children, frustrated maybe, battling blue-collar harpies. I had worked with men like him on loading docks, had endured their sad tales in bars.

121

"I was just going to bed," I said. "Can this possibly wait until tomorrow?"

"No, it can't," he said. He took a step toward me, filled the doorway. "I want to ask you some questions."

Christ.

"I just got off the phone to the police," I lied. It tumbled from my mouth. A false link to the law.

"I want to talk to you about something," he said.

A buzz, steady static, a click, a voice. I looked at his taxi again, then surrendered. He was on duty.

"Well, just for a minute," I said. "I had a bad day and—"

"Me too," he said, and barged in. "Barged" may be overstating it. I did give him permission. I decided to hang out by the door.

He walked into the living room and looked around, then walked to the hallway and looked at the bathroom. Of course I knew where all this was headed. I had been avoiding it physically and psychologically since the moment he had asked me if he could use the john—to go "number one," as Coleman had informed me.

He turned around and strode across the living room with his arms swinging slightly, like those of a gorilla. His shoulders rolled. He stopped in the middle of the room and looked at me. I felt as if I were now the visitor at the door. I could feel a slight breeze of night air. It cooled the sweat on my neck that I had not been aware of until then.

"I was talking to the cops today and they told me some stuff I don't understand," he said. His torso swayed slightly from left to right as if he was dodging Lilliputian arrows. He was trying to get to the point. "They said something about how you thought a man might be hiding inside your house when I came to pick you up."

My jaw parted to speak, but nothing came out. This was

it then. *The Confrontation*. The dissecting of my character. My immediate compulsion was to lie my ass off, but that was a child's ploy. Life had taught me that lies generally do not work.

"Well . . . as I explained to the police . . . when I got home today from the hospital, I found a loaf—"

A strange series of sounds came from his mouth: "Di, di, di, di," as he waved me off with one hand, palm splayed, erasing my words, "don't start giving me a lotta bullshit. You thought there was someone in your house when we went inside, right?"

I had a number of lines of approach that evolved quickly, but when I opened my mouth only a soft sigh came out. Why could I not simply say yes? A holdover from childhood? A belief in the sudden appearance of The Perfect Excuse? Why had I not tapped him on the shoulder at two in the afternoon and said, "Someone might be in my house"?

"What was that shit all about?" he said. "I want to know why you let me come in here when you knew there was a dead body in the bathroom."

Ah—a crack in the wall. An erroneous "fact." He was wrong about that. I took courage from his misunderstanding.

"I did not know there was a body in the house."

"Oh jis, jis, jis," he said, waving splayed hands. "I don't give a fuck what you knew. The cops said you let me come in when you thought there might be someone hiding in here, and then it turns out someone was *killed* in your bathroom."

This stopped me cold. His error meant nothing. I couldn't speak.

"You fucker," he said. There was the word. When men say "fuck" with its variations and permutations you know the gloves are off. "For all you knew I could have gotten killed. Right? Right? Right?"

Jesus but this was hard. Not his browbeating. I had endured browbeatings since I was a kid. But philosophers do talk about "peering into the abyss." You try to keep things secret, maintain appearances, practice courtesy, dreading the day the layers will be peeled away revealing deep down inside that you are not worth a shit.

I sighed and crossed over to the couch and sat down. I was tired enough now to go to sleep. I looked up at him. Again he was standing with his arms folded, all pecs and bulges and blue-collar outrage, the Colossus at Rhodes. I did not sense that he wanted to do me physical harm though. He was on duty. His taxi was whirring and clicking on the driveway. He wanted something more awful than violence. He wanted a straight answer.

"I didn't really know if someone was in my house . . ."

"Oh, knock off the bullshit," he said. "What kind of a person are you?"

I didn't answer. Did I know the answer? Of course not. I knew only what kind of a person I wasn't. And so did he.

He walked across the living room and looked into the kitchen. He crossed back over and passed by the bathroom and looked into the master bedroom. He was like a client looking to buy a house, checking out the square-footage, gauging the value of this cardboard castle. Except he strutted like he already owned the place. What exactly was he doing? I sensed he was walking off excess energy. He could not stand still.

"You did that, didn't you?" he said. "You let me come inside thinking someone was in here. You hid yourself behind me, didn't you?"

I nodded.

It was easy. The hard part was working up to the dreadful nod. It had taken approximately six hours. Why hadn't I just tapped him on the shoulder instead of letting him go in there? Everybody present knew the answer. I would like to quibble though. It was not simply because I had no character. That's the obvious answer of the nickel-psyche variety. I did not warn him of a potential intruder for two reasons: I was afraid he wouldn't go into the house at all, and I was too embarrassed to let him know I was paranoid. Why would I reveal a thing like that when the odds were fifty-fifty that I might be wrong? Take a gamble. Live on the edge. Protect all that goddamn dignity I've been hoarding for years.

"You're a coward," he said.

No, I wanted to say. It goes much deeper than that.

"Sorry sonofabitch to let me walk into a trap," he said.

I wanted him to go away. His taxi buzzed, clicked, whirred, a sound like cicadas in the treetops.

"I'll give you money," I said.

"What?"

"And then I'm going to ask you to leave."

"Oh, you'd like me to leave, wouldn't you," he snapped. "I didn't know what the fuck was going on until those cops told me the whole story. I couldn't believe what I was hearing. You let me walk into a *trap*."

He was covering old ground now. Talking off excess energy. It was as if he was trying to talk reality out of existence. He couldn't believe what I had done, and what might have happened to him. Toilet corpse.

I remained silent and looked up at him, let his geyser flow, the steam of dockworkers wrestling with absurdity, simple hardworking men too ignorant to deal with the subtleties of idiocy. Lunchbox men who drank beer, watched football, and took proper care of their wives and children and friends.

"Don't look to me to be a fucking witness for you in court," he said.

I nodded.

"I hope they hang your ass."

"For what?" I said with a frown.

"For being an asshole."

Verdict rendered. Fair enough. I eased myself up off the couch and reached for my billfold. I opened it, and a death moth fluttered up into my face.

He laughed with derision. "You must not open that fucker very often," he said. "You do like those like free rides, don'tcha."

I removed five twenties and held them out to him. "Here's one hundred dollars. Please take it. I want you to leave."

He snatched it with a fist. "You want me to leave, huh? Now you're being honest, huh?" More sarcasm. I remained mute.

He stuffed the money into his T-shirt pocket and headed for the door. He stopped, turned, and looked at me from shoes to forehead. "I told the dispatcher down at Ace not to take any more calls at this address. If you need a taxi, call your friendly neighborhood cop."

He pushed the screen door open and walked out. I watched it close slowly, the hydraulic pump sighing. I shut the door and glanced at my watch. 8:45. I shuffled toward the bathroom. I did not care about the corpse anymore. I was going to go "number two" and then hit the sack. But when I got into the bathroom and turned on the light, I could not bring myself to sit down without a hit of Lysol. Not even depression can make a dent in basic fear. But what did I fear? Corpse germs on my bare ass? I went back to the kitchen, picked up the can of Lysol, and headed toward the bathroom. The telephone rang.

I stopped dead on the living room carpet. Now who. Now who. Now who. Not a question. A plea for mercy. I did not know anybody in this town who would call me at this time of night. Except the police. And the Ace Taxicab Service. And the hospital. Maybe Morton had died. He wasn't married. Perhaps he had given them my number, a proxy next-of-kin in case of an emergency. I deferred to the fact that I did know a lot of people in this town who might call me at this time of night. I had to answer the phone. It kept ringing. Sometimes I let my phone ring until the caller gave up. But it rang and rang and rang.

"Hello?"

"Peter!"

Oh God.

My ex.

"Yes?"

"What is going on there?"

"We're divorced, Laura. I told your lawyer I don't want—"

"The Crestmoor Police Department called me and said you were brought in for questioning about a what . . . a dead body in the house?"

I inhaled deeply, sighed. It made a wind noise in the phone. She heard it.

"Well?"

"There was an intruder in the house today while I was out looking for a job. Apparently, he took a slice of my bread and accidentally choked on it."

"Accidentally choked? Nobody chokes on purpose. When are you going to start talking like a normal person?"

"He died trying to vomit into the toilet," I said.

Was that normal enough for her?

"Oh Christ," she said. "I suppose you left the back door unlocked again."

This was a sore point between us. I had done that twice during our marriage and she had made a special point of

127

never forgetting it.

"A man died in the house today and I'm going to bed now," I said.

"The police called and asked me questions," she said. "I thought you had strangled someone to death."

"It was a transient," I said. "A hobo or something. They're still investigating."

"I don't like this, Peter. I don't like the police calling my sister's house and asking questions."

On this point we were in perfect agreement.

"I'm not in charge of the police department," I said. "You'll have to take that up with them. I suggest you talk it over with your lawyer. Send me the bill. Goodbye."

"Don't you dare hang up on me."

"You know as much about this situation as I do. I have nothing more to tell you."

"Are you still working?"

"Yes."

"Where?"

"At the factory."

"With that drunk maintenance man?"

"Yes . . ."

"You sound like you got sacked."

I remained silent, thus confirming her accusation. I am forced to concede that something enters my voice whenever I get sacked. I had lost numerous jobs when we were married, and a certain timbre entered my voice each time I tried to be evasive in Laura's presence—a sort of toned-down false bravado as if to say, "Huh? No, fine, great—everything's okay at this end," like the reply of a junkie trying to convince his parole officer that he's off the skag.

"You got sacked again, didn't you?" she said. She was like the taxi driver. This was a day of interrogations.

"Is there anything else?" I said. "If not, this conversation is over."

"Sacked and broke," she said. "You're going to end up in jail for vagrancy."

Click.

That was me. I had never hung up on Laura before. Throughout the divorce proceedings I had tried to comport myself with a modicum of civility, but what the fuck. And anyway, she was probably right. I would end up in a prison cell with the car thief. Maybe he could teach me how to steal ATM machines. They say penitentiaries are colleges for criminals. I could use a degree that was actually worth something.

I took the phone off the hook then. The odds of her calling back were slim but, as I say, I had never disconnected the line out of sheer rudeness. She was the type of person to whom the last word was life's blood. I was that way in high school. I could never let an argument go until I had browbeaten my friends into conceding I was right. I regret that. The odds of my having been right about anything between the ages of fourteen and seventeen were worse than beating the house in roulette, but it was the heart-pounding sensation of being right, the breathtaking certainty of possessing all the facts, that ultimately alienated my friends. I see it now as a form of juvenile bullying. But I do not think they took me very seriously. They were more concerned with fast cars and hot chicks than examining my opinions from every angle and concluding that I was brilliant. It was important for me back then to have people think my argumentation was brilliant, since I was a flop at everything from basketball to trig.

A shrill sound came from the telephone, a signal that the receiver was off the hook. It stopped after a while. The phone company computer was programmed to give up. Artificial intelligence at its best.

I went to the kitchen and checked the back door to make certain it was locked. Give Laura credit where credit was due. I thought I had locked the door that morning, but there was a parallel construct at work here—going to the store to buy a quart of milk and coming home with fifty dollars' worth of groceries and no milk. Certainty is a precarious illusion.

I carried the Lysol into the bathroom and looked around at all the porcelain and chrome fixtures, the pink tiles on the walls. Like a room in a hospital. Smooth slick surfaces easy to wash and wipe. I sprayed the toilet first, the ring seat, then lifted it and did the rest, wondering vaguely about the presence of a ghost new to the afterlife. I had read *The Tibetan Book of the Dead* in college, that safe haven where undergraduates toy with mortality like a shuttlecock. A nurse once told me that patients frequently related out-of-body experience stories, baffled middle-aged heart patients who floated above surgeons mining the chest cavity and stitching aortic muscles. Temporary ghosts yanked back down to the operating table for a short trip to consciousness and suffering. The nurses grew accustomed to those odd stories. They could only listen and comfort. Nurses know more than priests will ever know. The question on my mind was whether the intruder's spirit was watching me disinfect the throne room.

I gave everything a quick once-over before shutting off the spray can of illusions. It was mostly the ring seat that bothered me. I let it dry for five minutes, let the death germs curl and die, then shut the door and put it out of my mind for the next few minutes. The scrubbing of urinals had ceased to bother me in the army after a few days of getting down in there with that plastic brush and really going after those hard-to-get-at stains, sprinkling the porcelain with industrial-strength Ajax powder. Funny how timid twenty-year-olds can be when it comes to washing commodes, the work their mothers do regularly at home. Young troops would rather be jacking bullets into rifles and blasting imaginary enemies.

I took my shower, dried my hair, and carried my clothing into the master bedroom, where I dumped it on the floor. A ritual I enjoyed now that my wife was no longer there to snarl about the hamper. I have often wondered if life with a man, a new husband, comes as a shock to women who grew up without brothers, the slobs of the earth.

I walked barefoot on the soft carpet as I set about closing up the house prior to retiring. Check all the locks, the doors and windows, turn off the lights, put the beast to sleep, maybe for the last time. I wanted out of there and the sooner the better. That would not be much of a chore. Before I got married I was a bedouin, often changing apartments in college, or moving to other towns, and in the army I was stationed only two or three months in one place before transferring to another, even if it was only to another barracks on the same army base. I developed a slight affinity for moving on, eschewing roots, but it was not a fixation, itchy feet to head on down the road as in so many country-western songs—the drifter who can't be tamed by no high-toned woman. But there was a little bit of that in me, which had emerged when I made it clear to my ex that this was not a house I wanted to own.

I checked the spare bedroom, the bathroom, and the kitchen. I was passing through the living room when I heard it again, the close approach of an automobile, the muted aerial vibrations that heralded arrivals at parties and which nobody heard but me. Damnit—another visitor in my driveway. At this point the only lightbulb on in the house was in the master bedroom. The ambient light would leak out into the night, this I knew. I would not be able to fully darken my house to signal unwanted visitors that it was too late for a friendly call.

I sidled up next to the picture-window and parted the curtain a crack. The taxi had returned, and this time the logo on the roof was fully lit, "Ace Taxicab Service" black letters stark against the bright yellow rectangle, although the company was not a part of the Yellow Cab empire. A universal, recognizable color. I wondered if Yellow Cab had trademark rights to that color. The thought passed through the part of my mind that perpetually refuses to focus on things at hand. But I had grown used to it. It did not impede my general ability to focus. Other things too numerous to mention took care of that department.

The taxi engine shut down, the roof logo went dark. Cursing, I hurried into the bedroom and yanked my pants and shirt back on, slipped my naked feet into my shoes, and shuffled into the living room to peek past the curtain again. "Fuck," I whispered. What did the bastard want from me now? More money? Did he leave something behind? I peered at the dark shape of the vehicle, waiting for the driver to emerge, when suddenly the doorbell rang. I had missed his emergence. He was already at the door.

I switched on the living room and porch lights, took a deep breath, and fixed my expression. We were square. We had nothing to say to each other. He was simply a rude stranger ringing my doorbell too late at night. Perhaps I would send him away with a threat to call Ace and report his obnoxious behavior.

I opened the door and looked at him through the screen. I had the urge to reach down and snap shut the lock on the flimsy aluminum barrier between us, but I held off.

"Ace Taxi," the man said.

It was a different driver. He was holding a clipboard.

"I didn't call for a taxi," I said.

He raised the clipboard to his face, pinched the brim of his cap, and frowned. "Is this four-eighteen Crestmoor Drive?"

"No, it's not," I said. "This is Crestmoor Road."

"Here's the address." He lowered the clipboard and turned it so I could read it. I glanced at a sheet of paper clipped to the board. While my eyes were distracted he yanked the screen door open and bulldozed his way into my living room, bumping into me. He swiped at my legs with a foot and caught my ankle, preventing me from stepping back. I fell to the floor. He flung the clipboard away, shut the door behind him, and looked down at me. He removed his cap and flung that too, revealing a head of hair instantly familiar. I had seen that black coif inside my stolen car.

Every muscle, bone, and fiber of my being was infused with adrenaline. Assault is something adults do not experience, it is a playground thing of children badgered by bullies. I was rising like a kite driven upward by a wind when the gun came out, drawn from behind him and pointed with the swift motion of experience. He had drawn that thing before.

"Stay on the floor, fucker."

I went back down slowly, the black hole of the muzzle like the flash of a camera bulb making me blink. The adrenaline peaked, plateaued, held. I sat motionless, gazing at the pistol, while his head swiveled back and forth taking in the living room.

"You live here alone?"

I nodded.

"Speak speak speak."

"Yes," I said.

"Nobody else here, right?"

"Yes."

"Ooookay." He stepped back and did the damnedest thing. He twirled the gun with an actor's élan, gripped the butt, and pointed the muzzle at the ceiling. "Get on the couch."

cushion, and placed my hands on my thighs.

He pointed the gun at me and said, "Stay put, lonely-boy."

Keeping the gun aimed at me, he edged over to the kitchen and looked in, then crossed the living room and looked down the hallway toward the bathroom. The barrel remained fixed on my face as if connected by a steel rod. The sensation was this: a boy stretches a rubber band around his thumb to the cocked middle finger. Every boy has done this. You point the fake gun at a friend's face, making him twist his head, blink, snarl. You have rubber-band fights. The projectile stings the face. Child's play, infuriating. The difference here resided solely in the result. There was lead in that thing.

"So they took genius-boy away, huh?"

"What?"

"What? What? The police. They took genius-boy away, right?"

"The police removed a dead body from my bathroom," I said.

He nodded. "What a fucking idiot." He glanced into the master bedroom, then came back and stood in front of me. He looked at the telephone. "What's with the phone? Why isn't it hung up? Is somebody on the line?"

"No, the line is dead."

He moved around to the end of the couch and picked up the receiver, held it to his ear, and said in a dull tone, "Hullo hullo hullo." He waited a moment, then set the receiver back down on the table.

"Good. Let's keep it that way."

He stepped around in front of me.

"All right, what did they say?"

"Who?"

In owl falsetto he mimicked me. "Hoo hoo hoo? Who

do you think?" He spoke rapidly. The jitters of a break-in artist, I assumed. I suspected his adrenaline level was high. A man barges into a house, points a gun, there is a window of personal chaos like storming a beach, scouting the layout, drawing a perimeter, setting up guard posts.

"The police?" I said.

"Who else has been in here today?" he said. "Who do you think I'm talking about? Are you playing mind-games with me? Don't try to out-think me, chump. I never lose at mind-games. I'm the king of the mind-games."

This was my first hint. The man was not normal. It's true that breaking into a house was not normal, but a part of me assumed I was dealing with a commonplace burglar, a normal sociopath, but then I had never spoken with a sociopath before. I had never pulled hard time, and in spite of what some people might think, the army did a fair job of weeding out insane recruits. The only people I had ever met who spoke in terms of mind-games were undergraduate students.

"What do you want to know?" I said.

"Everything." He looked around the room. "Now you stay put. No matter what I do or where I go in this house, you stay put. A bullet leaves this gun at a velocity of eight hundred feet per second, so unless you can run faster than that, you would be well advised to obey me."

He crossed to the far corner of the living room, where two chairs had been placed side by side for the guests that used to come but stopped coming after my divorce. Not big furniture, foam-padded, relatively light. He grabbed one by the back and dragged it across the room so he could sit down and face me.

"This will make it easier on both of us," he said. "Now we can talk man-to-man and eye-to-eye."

I nodded.

"He nods," the man said. "He nods in agreement with me. I think that's a mind-game. I think you're playing a mind-game slash body-game."

My eyes were on the gun. His right elbow rested on the arm of the chair, the barrel of his weapon pointed toward the bathroom. He crossed one leg over a knee. "Let's get this straight," he said. "I cannot be buffaloed. I want you to tell me everything, and I know that you know what I mean by everything."

I started talking. "The police came here this afternoon and examined a dead body in my bathroom." I was snatching at images as they came to me. There was no continuity. I did not know what he meant by "everything" but I would say everything that came to me. "The man apparently—"

"No, no, wait, back up, back up. I mean about the car. Where's your stolen car?"

"The police have it."

"Tell me about it. What's going on with your car?"

"They found my car and took it to the police station."

"What do you mean *they* found your car? *You* found your car."

A fresh stream of adrenaline like ice shot through my system. He had seen it. He already knew what he was asking. I pretended I did not know this. I felt myself retreating into the haven of ignorance. I would tell him everything that had happened without interpretation of what had happened. This I would give to him: the appearance of incomprehension, the inability to understand my experience.

"I found my car parked on a street where it was abandoned."

"I saw you," he said. "You didn't even know I saw you, did you?"

"No."

"I drove right past your sorry ass and you didn't even

know I saw you."

I shook my head no.

"Speak speak speak, I speak English, don't give me that body-language shit. I'm recording everything right here, baby, it's going right here." He tapped his ear with a finger. "I don't record images, I'm not a goddamn camera, I record *sounds*."

"I didn't know you saw me," I said.

"Damn right you didn't know. You're a stupid motherfucker. I saw you trying to start your car. You don't know jack shit about cars, do you?"

"No."

"Fuckinay right you don't."

He got up suddenly and went toward the bathroom. His back was to me but he wiggled the gun in my direction. A reminder. Eight hundred feet per second. He disappeared around the corner but I stayed on the couch. I understood the velocity of bullets. In the army you touched a trigger and a target one hundred meters away shuddered.

The light from the bathroom came on and cast its yellow angles on the hallway wall, cast the shape of his body in shadow. Manshape. We fired bullets at manshapes on the rifle range. Cops fired at them on TV, in the movies. Head-and-shoulder shots.

He came back into the living room shaking his head and smiling wanly. "Dumb fucker. Jesus." He waved the muzzle at the bathroom, using it as a pointer. "So what was the verdict?"

I took a guess. "The coroner said he choked to death on a piece of bread."

The man looked down and gave up a series of soft belly chuckles and quietly said, "Goddamn stupid bastard."

He abruptly looked at me. "What's your name?"

"Pete."

"Pete? Like in peat moss?"

I nodded. He did not remark on my body language.

"Pete and peat. Those are homonyms."

"Yes, they are."

"You know what a homonym is?"

"Yes."

"How do you know that?"

"I learned it in school."

"Fuck school. Let's get back to the point. What's the verdict on the car?"

The man must have thought I was a mind reader. The attitude of a narcissist, I supposed, someone who believes that everybody around him knows exactly what he is talking about at all times and hangs on his every word. I decided that one possible hope of my survival resided in trying to stay one step ahead of him. A man who had brought up the subject of mind-games moved in directions that I was familiar with.

"The police examined my car. A headlight was broken. After they arrested me and took me to police headquarters they called a tow truck to take the car to the impound lot."

"And . . . ?"

"They examined it for . . . I don't know . . . clues. I'm not very familiar with police work."

He frowned and began slapping the barrel of the pistol sidewise against the cup of his left palm. A thoughtful tap. A carpenter might do such a thing with a pair of pliers, a folding ruler. "Dumb bastard walked right in front of my car."

I took note of the word "my" but let it pass. When you steal something, it becomes yours. The history of imperialism.

"Why did they arrest you?" he said. The barrel stopped slapping his flesh. He held it up as if the pistol itself was waiting to hear my answer.

This stung me. I should not have mentioned the arrest. I had to stay sharp. Don't reveal anything that this man does not need to know while at the same time revealing that which might be defined as "everything."

"I saw my car parked on the street so I got into it. A moment later a policeman showed up and arrested me. He thought I was driving it when the accident happened."

The intruder's eyes sparkled. "They thought *you* were driving the fucking car when the pedestrian got hit?"

Note that he did not say, "I hit the pedestrian." The car did the hitting. A narcissist never does anything wrong. Personal pronouns disappear. The passive voice intrudes. My evaluation of this man as a "narcissist" of course is not to be equated with the evaluation of a psychotherapist. I know little of the technical complexities of psychology, other than the fact that half the people I ever met were insane.

"It was coincidental," I said. "I got into the car, and a moment later the policeman arrived and approached the car under the assumption that I was the driver. He suspected me of hit-and-run, of leaving the scene of an accident." Should I include the drunk-driving charge? No—although the man seemed pleased by new information. He was responding as if I had told a brand of dirty joke that makes people chuckle rather than guffaw. I thought it best to maintain an element of humor if possible. There was a precedent for this. I had seen it in the movies: "I let you live because you made me laugh, Charley."

"So the cops think you're to blame for the accident?" he said.

"Yes. I have to make a court appearance."

He chuckled a little more, then looked at me without a hint of humor. "Did the guy die?"

"No. He was knocked unconscious. They took him to . . .

a hospital."

He nodded. "Dumb fucking bastard," he mumbled—to himself of course, consulting himself, talking things over with himself. But who doesn't do this? Everyone talks to their own mind, answers their own questions, makes judgments, draws conclusions, though usually during mundane chores, shopping for groceries, should I buy peas or corn? People in grocery stores move their lips.

"Why do you refer to him as a dumb bastard?" I said.

"Because he stepped right in front of me. He was waving like he wanted a ride. I don't pick up hitchhikers, especially after I steal a car. Unless it's a woman. I'll pick up a woman hitchhiker in a stolen car. That's the only exception to my rule. You gotta be ready to make exceptions to rules, see? You gotta be prepared for contingencies, see?"

He was lecturing me on how to become a successful person. I nodded to let him know I was filing away his brilliant advice.

"So the guy is still alive, huh?" he said.

"As far as I know."

Without moving his head, he glanced thoughtfully down at his gun. I had the sudden urge to tell him that the victim had *definitely* identified me as the driver. I felt a responsibility for saving two lives now, my own and Morton's. He might go after Morton. But the likelihood of either rescue appeared slim. This man seemed a killer. I had the impression that he was acquainted with the man who had died in my bathroom.

He began wiggling his fingers as if beckoning a dog. "Come on come on, what else?"

I spoke as if we were simpatico. Maybe we were. He wanted to know everything. I complied.

"The police took me to headquarters and interrogated me and made me write a witness statement."

"What did you say about me?"

This seemed a leap in logic. There was a fragmented quality to his line of inquiry. He was making assumptions about me as if scanning a map, a big picture that existed solely in his mind.

"I tried to convince them that I was not driving the car," I said. "I told them I was walking home when I saw my car go by."

"Me. What did you say about me?"

"I told them that a man with dark hair was driving my car. I was so surprised to see my car go by that I didn't get a good look at the driver. It happened too fast."

Again the chuckle of a bawdy joke. "You didn't see shit. But I saw you good. I was looking at you when I drove by. I was doing this." He sat erect and rotated the pupils of his eyes to the right, hard askance, the peer of a spy, a nefarious villain, a slick private-eye. "I saw everything. I saw you standing there like a dumb bastard."

I nodded.

"Did you notice that I wasn't speeding?" he said.

"I did notice that you were not driving very fast."

"You see, that's where guys make a mistake. When you hot-wire a car you should never drive fast. It's a dead giveaway. That's how guys get caught. They think because they're driving a stolen car they have to speed. Shit. They blow right past a cop hiding behind a billboard and the chase is on. It's fucking unbelievable how stupid some people are. They got no goddamn sense. It makes me sick to be around stupid people."

He fixed me with a hard gaze. "Did they believe you?"

Believe which part? We had spoken of many things. I had to interpret his private language, estimate his direction of thought, leapfrog his logic. "I did my best to convince them that I was not driving the car. But I was found sitting in the car, so they assumed I had hit the pedestrian."

His pupils rotated, scanning my face as I spoke, forehead to cheek to jaw to eyes to moving lips. What was the purpose of this questioning? I assumed he would shoot me. Paranoia was replaced with fair assumption. I was waiting for it to happen.

"So the cops think you might be the driver, huh?" he said.

"I don't know that I convinced them otherwise. You know how the police are. They have to—"

"Oh yeah, baby, I know how the police are. Why the hell did you follow me?"

"It was an automatic response. I saw my car going by so I chased it."

"See, this proves you have an inferior intellect. There was no way you could catch the car. Your brain is defective. You don't have the faculty to reason things out properly."

"I know," I said. "I started running after the car before I thought about it."

"See, the thing is, when people do things automatically, they're relying on nature to take care of them. You have to develop your mind, see. You can't let the animal nature make your decisions for you. You have to conquer it if you expect to survive. You have to be able to think fast and make smart decisions. Do you see?"

It was another lecture. Where did this man come from? I glanced at his clothing. No hint there. A taxi driver. Suddenly I sat perfectly motionless. A visceral bell of memory was rung by the faint familiarity of the taxi cap. It had not really fit this man's head well. It seemed a trifle small. A dread sprouted in my chest.

"So you couldn't give the police a good description of me?" he said.

Try as I might to do otherwise, I could now speak only in a monotone. My emotions had been stilled. "I told them that a

142

man with dark hair drove past in my car. That's all I was able to tell them."

He nodded thoughtfully, gazed into the middle distance.

"How about genius-boy?" he said.

"I'm sorry, I don't understand what you mean."

"The genius who choked on the bread."

My shoulders rose of their own volition. "The police didn't tell me much about him."

"Did they identify him?"

"I don't know."

He pursed his lips and thought this over. "Do they think you killed him?"

"They questioned me about it. They were suspicious of me because I had already been brought in for hit-and-run. A policeman drove me home from the hospital. When I got home I called the taxi company because I needed to go shopping. The taxi driver came to my house and asked if he could use my bathroom and I said yes. He went in and found the body, then he ran out."

"Why were you at the hospital?"

My mind was not staying sharp. I gave up on that feeble ploy. In five minutes I might be dead. I might be wherever souls go. I might be haunting my rented house for all eternity. I would encounter the spirit of the toilet corpse, who might make things clear to me as he wandered on the astral plane.

"I went to visit the man that I was accused of hitting with my car."

"Yeah? No kidding? That was real nice of you."

His glib manner annoyed me, altered my feelings, sharpened them. I felt less bereft, more focused. "I wanted to see how he was doing and to tell him that I was not the one who hit him."

"I get it. You wanted to cover your ass, right?"

143

"I wanted to console him."

"You wanted to find out if he could identify you as the driver, right? I didn't give you enough credit. Smart move. If he kicked the bucket, you wanted to make damn sure he told the police you weren't at the wheel, right?"

He was infuriating me, not only because he was making assumptions about my motives but also because there was truth in what he said. Morton had thought it was me who hit him. I had wanted to make certain he did not tell the police an untruth, a factual error, a deathbed statement that could put me in jail.

"So what was the upshot?" he said.

"Of what?"

"The visit the visit, what do you think we're talking about? Listen, bozo, I'm trying to get a fix on the layout here and you're playing mind-games with me. Knock that shit off and tell me what I want to know."

My dread evolved into simple fear. This man could not be reasoned with. A manic child was more rational. I felt all hope ebbing. Would he shoot me in the head or the heart? Like that, all things of the earth lost their significance. I was going to die tonight.

"The police have no idea who you are," I said. "I told them that the man must have broken into my house and opened a loaf of bread and ate a slice and choked on it. That's all they know, as far as I know."

"Nobody knows nothing. Tell me about it," he said. "The whole human race is clueless. It was easy to get into your house. We walked in the back door. You left it unlocked."

The fact that I would be dead in a few minutes did nothing to lessen the sense of anguish I felt knowing that my ex was right—the last flicker of my life would be devoted to embarrassment. Even at the portico of death the dread of humiliation remained inside me. If this man were caught, Laura would get the facts from the police. "The dumb bastard left the door unlocked." Was that my wife talking or the man who killed me?

"We were watching you from the woods the whole time. We saw you trying to start your car. You gave up easy. You didn't even pop the hood."

I was tired of hearing about my shortcomings as an auto mechanic. Hood popping, battery wiggling, what is all that to me? Machines defeat us. I gave up popping hoods in my twenties. You stand before the maw of iron and wires and pretend to be looking for something that is hidden under the surface, a flaw that can't be seen, a fuel pump that has given up the ghost, an alternator that will not perform, a spark plug cracked, melted, ruined, why bother? Car nerds like Morton can do it, but the ordinary guy? He's only kidding himself. But still, my vicious critic did have a point. Is it too much to ask an ordinary chump to wiggle a battery cable or eyeball the wires to see if one is loose? Yes. I might as well drop my paycheck into a slot machine and hope for a million-dollar jackpot. Machines mow us down.

"Where are your fucking socks?"

"What?"

He pointed at my feet, his arm rising and dipping like the drill of an oil derrick. It was exaggerated, sarcastic body language. I looked down at my shoes and saw an inch of bare skin.

"I'm not wearing any."

His arm stopped. The expression faded from his face. It reminded me of Detective Coleman's lifeless expression at certain points during my interrogation. "I can see that, motherfucker. I didn't ask if you were wearing any socks. I asked you where they were."

"In my bedroom."

A hideous grin shaped his lips. He raised his eyebrows and began shaking his head slowly. "*And . . . ?*"

"They're on the floor."

He closed his eyes. "All right, let's try this again. Why are you not wearing socks? Are you a hippie or something?"

"No. I was getting ready for bed and I had already taken off my socks. I heard your car pull up in the driveway so I put my shoes on to answer the door."

"See? Was that so hard? I ask you a question and I get a lot of yackety-bang. I see a man not wearing socks and I wonder what the fuck his problem is. People wear socks unless they're hippies. You don't look like a hippie to me. You look like Johnny Middle-Class. You look like the man in the gray flannel suit. You look like you never did anything interesting. I'll bet you never did anything interesting in your entire life, did you?"

"No."

"I knew it. I can't be buffaloed. I see a man and I know right away what kind of a person he is, how fucking meaningless his life is. Your life is meaningless, isn't it?"

I nodded.

"He nods. Have you ever been married?"

"I'm divorced."

"I knew it. You look divorced. See, this is another aspect of my mental superiority over everyone. I can look at a man and tell right away whether he's married or divorced or whatever. You see, I've always been more perceptive than other people. But I don't let on, see. When people find out that you're smarter than them, they put up walls, you know what I mean?"

"Yes."

"You gotta play it cool if you want to take advantage of

people. How come you got divorced?"

As of this moment my hatred of the man would never be surpassed. I did not like him talking so glibly of my relationship with Laura. I thanked God that Laura was in Albany. Had we not gotten divorced, this man might still have come to our door on this very night. Forget the random forks in the road that lead us to the present moment. Laura might have made me wiggle the cables on my battery before starting out on foot for Apex, but that did not mean this monster would not have intruded on our lives. I saw Laura's face clearly in my mind. I saw her face changing expression when she had gotten the news of her father's death four years earlier. The collapsing of the flesh around her mouth, followed by tears, her entire face becoming wet and ruddy. My heart went out to her. She loved her father.

"You're not a taxi driver, are you?" I said. This I would give to Laura, the woman I had fought with so many times before we separated. The thing sitting on the chair four feet away from me would not get past this last wall.

"Welcome to the real world, bozo," he said.

"Where did you get that taxicab on the driveway?" I said.

A sly look came onto his face, the look of a child found out. "I borrowed it," he said with a single breathy chuckle.

That's when I knew for certain. I did not know the details, but I knew. I looked at the pistol held loosely in his hand. He gave it no more respect than a squirt gun, bobbling it as he spoke, the finger touching and slipping away from the trigger. I did not know if it was on safety. I had never handled a revolver in the army, only the Colt semi-automatic. I supposed the safety was set up to be quickly pushed by the thumb, a slide mechanism, but my furtive glances provided no information. I had to assume the safety was off. Is this where the phrase "rule of thumb" comes from?

"Where's the taxi driver?" I said.

He cocked his head to one side and said, "Out there."

"In the taxi?"

"Naw. He's out there. Don't worry about him. You and me got business. Do you own a shovel?"

"What?"

"Don't start playing mind-games with me. When a man says 'what?' he's buying time. I asked if you have a shovel. You know good and goddamn well what a shovel is."

The answer was yes but I said nothing. I was torn between the knowledge that I was going to die and the uselessness of trying to prolong my life. Why do we try to prolong life even at its worst? It's because we're used to it. It's all we know.

"This isn't much of a house," he said. "Attic? Basement?"

"I don't understand what you're saying."

"Of course you don't. That's because you're intellectually inferior to me. You have a hard time following what I say because you have a smaller brain than me. You're like a dog, or a cat. Did you ever try to train a cat? You might as well try to train a toothpick. People say cats are smarter than dogs because you can't train them. That's the stupidest thing I ever heard. You wouldn't say that about people. You wouldn't say the smartest people are the ones who can't learn. Cats are stupid."

He stopped talking and looked at me as if expecting a response to a question.

"I never thought about that before," I said.

"Of course you didn't. Nobody thinks about the things I think about. People live out their boring lives doing what they're told, then they die. I've met people that if you told them to die they would do it if they could. They would flex their die muscle. People are stupid." He looked at the bathroom. "Like genius-boy. He choked on a piece of bread. I laughed

148

my ass off. See, the thing is, he thought he was smarter than me. He thought he could put a slice of bread in his mouth and swallow it whole. See, he was trying to impress me. He wanted to show me I was wrong when I told him to chew it twenty times. That's the rule I live by. Chew food twenty times. You should have seen the way his eyes bugged out when he found out *he* was wrong. Jeez. Some people have to learn the hard way. That was the last thing he ever learned."

I pictured the scene. The choking man. The laughing man. Now it was my turn to die. "Why didn't you give him the Heimlich Maneuver?" I said.

He snorted. "He would have stuck that slice of bread in his mouth even if I wasn't there. That's how I played the game. I wasn't even there as far as he was concerned. See, I wanted to teach him a lesson. I wanted to teach him that you can't go through life expecting others to save your ass. You got to be smart and look out for your own ass. It's the survival of the fittest, you know? The dumb people die early. But I don't believe in a master plan. It's more like water running downhill. Gravity is just there, you know? The dumb people go down. The smart people don't. That's why I'm alive and he's dead. The guy was a fucking genius. I could see it in his eyes while he was choking. His eyes were big and round like he was saying, 'Oh, I get it, Benny. You were right and I was wrong.' That's what I saw in his eyes. The shock of truth. He realized I was never wrong. He realized how stupid he was. Then he ran into the bathroom."

Benny.

"So do you got a shovel in the basement or the attic or some place?" he said. "You don't have a garage. That's where people store crap. This isn't much of a house. How come you didn't build a garage? Someone could steal your car." He grinned.

149

"I rent this house. It has a crawlspace in the attic and in the basement. I don't keep anything in either place."

"I once knew a guy who grew pot in his attic. He had lamps and shit. He had to crawl around to water his pot plants. It worked pretty good. The cops never did catch on."

I produced a slight series of nods. I felt I had to respond in some way to everything he said. I sensed that he was the sort who needed to know that his words were being comprehended, that I might set him off if I did not make it clear that I was listening and understanding.

"So do you own a shovel?" he said. He kept coming back to that with a simple sort of politeness as if the answer were so important that he did not want to risk havoc until he found out where the shovel was.

"It's in the storage shed," I said.

"Where's that?"

"Out in the carport."

"Ain't nothing out there."

"It's built up against the wall of the house. It's not very big."

"All right," he said, leaning forward, standing up, rolling his shoulders and craning his neck like a dockworker at the end of a relaxing break, ten minutes of lounging outside a warehouse and having a smoke with his pals. "Let's get going. We got work to do."

"What do you mean?"

"No questions. Into the kitchen. Let's go." He picked up the clipboard where it had landed on the floor, picked up the driver's cap and slapped it onto his scalp.

My mind raced ahead of me into the kitchen, where three cutting-knives were stored in the block of wood that I had purchased for Laura one Christmas. Handy invention. I bought it out of desperation. I find it impossible to shop for people. I find it intolerable that Americans are required to spend money through the coercion of tradition. Valentine's Day. Mother's Day. Birthdays. Thanksgiving. It's all bottom-line and profits. Sentiment is weighed and measured like gold dust. What were the chances of my grabbing a knife and sticking this man? None, of course. A trigger moves a fraction of an inch.

I walked ahead of him into the kitchen. As we entered I automatically reached to my right and switched on the light. I did not even think about the fact that he might object to my sudden move. The light came on. He did not seem to mind.

"I want you to make me a sandwich," he said.

By now I knew not to ask him to repeat himself, a human instinct for clarification of ludicrous statements that I consciously had to control. I could expect anything to come out of his mouth.

"What kind?" I said.

"Peanut butter."

I went to the breadbox, removed the plastic bag, opened the cupboard, performed the moves of sandwich making.

"Got any Peter Pan?" he said.

I paused—a momentary stumble—then moved on. "Skippy," I said. "I have no Peter Pan."

"I like Peter Pan. Skippy tastes too much like peanuts. Funny, huh? Peanut butter should taste like peanuts but I like Peter Pan."

I nodded. "I have only Skippy."

"That'll do."

"I have to get a knife," I said, touching the silverware drawer.

"Go ahead," he said, wiggling the gun at me.

I slid the drawer open and looked down at all the bread knives, the forks with their hard tines, the useless spoons, the

151

smaller cutting-knives with their serrated teeth, the spatula and the apple-peeler, the kitchen clutter that was of no use to me. I picked up a butter knife and opened the peanut butter jar and looked at the gouges that he had obviously made earlier in the day. I fixed the sandwich.

"You buy good macaroni," he said.

I nodded.

"Thanks," he said as I handed him the sandwich. "I ain't et in hours."

This made me wonder where he had been during the hours after he ran away from my car. I wanted to ask him. Go to the grave with final knowledge. But what was the point? As I said, all things of the earth had lost their significance, especially words. But then a thought occurred to me. "Did you come into my house this afternoon?" I said.

He nodded. "I been in and out of here all day. I been using this joint as my hideout. I bet I could live here for a month without you knowing it. You're stupid."

I began scratching at my cheek in order to quell my rage. Month my ass. He had left the bread out on the counter where I found it. "No—*you're* stupid," I wanted to say, but he had the gun.

He ate the sandwich standing next to the doorway, watching me and shoveling it in, chewing. "Glass of water," he mumbled with his mouth full.

I filled a glass at the sink and handed it to him, but he waved the muzzle indicating I should set it on the nearby counter.

I closed the sack of bread and put it away, screwed the lid onto the peanut butter jar, and placed the food-soiled knife into the sink without bothering to wipe it clean.

After he finished eating he drank all the water.

"Paper towel," he said.

I tore off a sheet and handed it to him. He wiped his lips, then slowly and methodically wiped his fingerprints off the glass. He smiled at me while he was doing this. He set it on the counter with a click and tossed the towel into the wastebasket.

"Good shit," he said. "All right, let's go. Out the back door. Show me the toolshed."

I opened the door and stepped into the night. The sky was cloudless, the moon full. The white varnish of lunar paint illuminated the edges of everything, the leaves of the high branches in the woods beyond the property line, the sidewalk that led straight to a concrete incinerator built before the burning of trash was outlawed. I led Benny around to the carport and onto the concrete slab. The ambient light beneath the flat roof revealed an oil stain centered on the concrete. I have never owned a car that did not manufacture an oil stain on a garage floor. I stopped and pointed at the toolshed, a five-foot square wooden box eight inches thick, built flat against the wall at eye level. It had no padlock. I had removed that after years of pretending someone might steal something from it. A pain in the ass to unlock whenever my ex wanted the bushes trimmed.

"Open it."

I opened the box. It was dark, difficult to see the tools.

"Got a flashlight?"

I reached down and lifted a yellow plastic flashlight from one corner.

"Does it work?"

"Yes," I said as I snapped it on. I kept the beam out of his face. I was one step ahead. Do not do anything by accident. This will prolong my life. All things of the earth ceased to have meaning except precision moves.

"Goddamn," he said. "You keep fresh batteries in the

sucker, huh?"

"Always," I said. A fixation that I had embraced when I was a young man newly away from home. My father never kept fresh batteries in his flashlights. Simple things like batteries, electrician's tape, paperclips, staples, Elmer's glue, had to be bought if we children needed them for projects. Even screws and nails. We lived on the ludicrous edge of need, never prepared for anything.

"Most people let their batteries go dead," he said.

Yes—in some ways I was simpatico with this monster. He held out his left hand and I gave him the flashlight. He whipped the beam around inside the box.

"Shovel," he said.

I reached up and took it from its perch. Each tool had its own hanging nail. I glanced at the hedge shears. Foot-long blades. The cutting edges were a bit rusted. After Laura went away I stopped worrying about the symmetry of our bushes.

"All right, into the cab," he said.

I was holding the shovel with both hands. The gun was pointed at my belly. I was two feet away from him, and his finger was a fraction of an inch away from the hammer-release. The idea of a nexus, a moment, a window of opportunity passed through my mind, flitted, and faded. Speed was everything and he had the edge. But I did not want to get into the cab. That my death was imminent altered the shape of the cosmos, the saddle that Einstein speaks of, it became two dimensions with no thickness at all, was made only of words. Now, or ten minutes from now, or an hour, it was all the same moment. This man intended to kill me. I would pass through Einstein's word-portrait into something else.

"Why?" I said.

"We got work to do." He backed away and whacked the air sideways with the pistol, urging me toward the taxi. My fists gripped the wooden handle of the shovel, I could feel the flesh growing white at the knuckles. It felt good. It felt like I was hanging on to life. I turned and walked toward the taxi. I heard the double doors of the toolshed close. Covering his tracks, no doubt. I thought of running, but that had become a part of my being ever since he had drawn the pistol. Along with that was the wariness, the sensitivity to any opportunity to get out of the situation. There were flaws in this man's claims of mental superiority. He had it in him to make a mistake. He had already run a man down by accident. He had left the bread out where I could see it. My mind became a spinning radar dish, seeking a fragile moment when he would be distracted—a spinning, useless radar dish.

"Toss the shovel in the backseat and get in the driver's seat," he said.

I opened the rear door expecting the corpse of the driver to spill out. Everything was on my radar. But the backseat was empty. I set the shovel on the seat and looked at Benny, who was pointing at the driver's door. I opened the door and climbed in and felt for the key—radar business: duck down, start the car, drive forward onto the back lawn. Plans were born and died faster than the life and death of a star.

He climbed into the backseat and sat on the far right side. I heard the shovel clatter to the floorboard. He leaned forward and pointed the muzzle at the side of my head. Then he reached across the seat and held out the ignition key.

"Okay now, I want you to back out onto the road and head toward the woods."

I started the car, backed out, and aimed the hood toward the mass of moonfrosted trees. The path of the road led between them. I had never walked through the forest on the right side of the road, only the section behind my house. The entire forest covered an area perhaps half a mile in diameter. It had always been in the back of my mind that the forest would be clear-cut one day to make room for real estate developers.

"Where are we going?" I said.

"Don't worry about that. I'll let you know. Did you ever drive a cab before?"

"No."

"We're going to take the scenic route. I bet this is the first time a customer ever asked a cabbie to take the scenic route." He chuckled.

I nodded in the darkness. The presence of the gun felt like water in my right ear. I guided the vehicle along the asphalt road between the trees. We traveled only a half-minute or so before he said, "Slow down. It's right along here somewhere."

I slowed. I looked in the rearview mirror. There was no traffic behind us, no traffic in front of us.

"Hit the brights for a moment," he said.

I looked at the dashboard, the lit dials, the knobs, and said, "I don't know how to do that."

"Pull the fucking *turn*-signal with your left hand," he snarled with the childish scorn of someone who knows something.

The brights came on. We cruised for a few seconds, then he said, "Dim it and slow down."

I did both.

"Turn left here."

I slowed and saw a left turnoff into the woods, a dirt road set between close trees. A lovers' lane perhaps, or something the county forestry department had fashioned. Or both.

"Yeah, this is it," he said. "Just follow it."

It was bumpy with dried rutted mud, fallen branches crunching beneath the wheels. But I could see that a vehicle had been here recently. Fresh white cracks in the branches on the road ahead of us, broken branches off to the sides. Did the road go all the way through the forest and out onto a field? Was there a place to turn around? Did it matter?

I saw something small and white hanging from a bush.

"Stop here and shut off the engine," he said.

I parked.

"See that?" he said. "That's a handkerchief I hung there so I would know."

The narcissist had spoken. He was compelled to explain his every accomplishment like a tour guide explaining the practices of aborigines in a museum exhibit: the sharpening of flint arrowheads, the grinding of maize. Note the sophistication of these primitive peoples who had yet to learn the secrets of smelting iron, copper, tin.

"Okay, Pete, how much do I owe you?" He shined the light at the dashboard. "Oops, you forgot to turn on the meter."

I glanced at his face beyond the gunsight. He was grinning with the expectation of the second-rate stand-up comic who laughs at his own jokes.

I didn't give him what he wanted. I didn't laugh. I assumed he would wait until I was outside the cab before he fired the gun, dragged my body into the underbrush, and drove away.

"All ashore," he said. "Hubba-hubba."

Wrestle with the gun, I told myself. Last ditch. But he sat back and waited for me to open the door. I got out. The wall of the woods was dark. I knew the terrain well enough to know that if I ran I would stumble over a root. Eight hundred feet per second. A fool's ploy. Everything was linked to velocity. A man could barely stroll these woods in daylight without risking a sprained ankle.

Benny climbed out holding the flashlight and the shovel. He left the driver's cap in the backseat. He aimed the beam into the forest. The light lost its effectiveness ten feet into the trees. Leaves and branches fragmented the light, a mirror image of my mind. The shovel, the woods, I sensed where this was leading and wondered if he intended to belt me on the back of the neck with the blade to forgo the need for a gunshot. But who would hear it out here anyway? We were a mile from town, there was no traffic. We were alone in the universe.

"Go where the light is," he said, holding the beam steady and allowing me to begin picking my way farther along the two-track. I heard him stumble and say "fuck" a few times, but he did not have the advantage of the light at his feet. He was using it as a guide and a machete through the dark tangles.

We had traveled perhaps fifty feet when he said, "Whoa." I stopped as he came up behind me and shined the flashlight around. "There's your buddy," he said, and flicked the beam to the right, where I saw the taxi driver lying at the base of a tree a few feet into the bushes. His wrists were bound behind his back and a strip of what appeared to be duct tape was wrapped around his head. The driver's back was to us, he was lying on his side, but I assumed he was gagged. I saw the body for only an instant, then Benny directed me to keep moving farther down the road. Soon we were in a small clearing. The road appeared to end here, although there was room between the trees for vehicles to travel farther. But the roadbed beyond this location was overgrown with weeds. It looked as if no vehicles had come this far in a long time.

"How tall are you?" he said, but before I could answer he sidled up next to me and looked at the top of my head. He was a few inches taller than me.

"Okay, good," he said without waiting for my answer. "Get over here in the middle of the clearing and lay out flat on the ground."

"This isn't necessary," I said. It came out fast. I wasn't even aware of what I was saying. My vocal chords had taken over, my mind felt soft and hazy, I could smell the shrubbery all around, the leaves, the pale nostril flavor of dried branches, the dust of the earth. "The police think you're in the next county. I have no intention of identifying you, ever."

"Stretch out there, Pete," he said, using the circle of light like a whisk-broom. "Right there in the middle." He meant a space that he himself might have cleared after he bound the taxi driver and propped the body beneath the tree.

"What's the point of this?" I said. "Take the taxi and drive across the state line." Like all Americans, I had been inculcated with the belief in the sanctity of state lines. Home free. The law can't touch you if you cross a state line. Cops are honest, they would not violate the sovereignty of Kentucky, New York, Arkansas, Oregon. They hit the brakes and leap out of their police cars and grab their Smokey hats and slap them to the asphalt in rage as Bonnie and Clyde and Machine Gun Kelly roar laughing into the sunset.

He glanced at me as if unaware that I had been speaking.

"Get down there. I ain't got all night."

I sat down with my knees raised and my heels pressed against the ground.

"All the way, stretch out flat," he said.

I did what he told me, wondering what the statistics were on people who knew how they were going to die versus people who were caught unawares by accidents, strokes, collisions, robberies, stray bullets, there are so many ways to die. Then there was suicide. It occurred to me that by complying I was committing a form of suicide. What was I doing? Through observation, analysis, logic, I had concluded that my time was up, yet here I lay as if I had no choice at all, none, a conclusion based solely on the presence of the gun.

Benny picked up the shovel with his right hand. He poked

at the earth near my feet. He drew a line perpendicular to my shoes. I raised my head and watched in the trembling light. He scratched at the earth like an artist making a sketch. He proceeded to draw a rectangle around my body, leaving a space of perhaps six inches on all sides. As the shovel scraped past my ears I thought, My God, is this how the mind of a sociopath works? Is this how crazy people approach problems, figuring things like an upholsterer taking the measure of an unfamiliar piece of furniture? Did something as simple as the digging of a hole baffle him to the extent that he thought he needed a sketch? Can any human being be that simpleminded?

The approach was practical though, this registered on me as he finished up. His practicality could not be faulted, insofar as he was the man with the shovel and gun, and I was the man laid out on the ground, a helpless audience to his childish ideas.

"All right, up and at 'em," he said.

I got up off the ground and looked down at the rectangle crudely engraved on the dry earth. He held the shovel out to me.

"Okeee," he said. "I want you to dig a hole in the ground about, say, I don't know, two feet deep. Maybe three. We'll see." He raised his eyebrows. "Stay between the lines."

So I was not going to die in one minute, or ten. Maybe not even an hour. It takes a long time to dig holes. I jammed the tip of the blade into the earth, which was surprisingly soft. But this was earth in a forest, not out on the sunbaked plains. It gave easy. I pressed the edge of the spade with my foot and heard the metallic sifting as it sank. My urge was to fling the dirt into his face. Maybe he had taken this into account. He already had positioned himself so that he was ten feet behind me and off to one side where he could watch my progress.

160

He spoke as I dug. He said things like this: "I once read in a book that before Columbus discovered America a squirrel could climb a tree in South Carolina and walk all the way to the Mississippi River without touching the ground." I wanted to bait him. Did he think South Carolina existed before Columbus set foot on an island whose inhabitants he promptly misnamed? It was possible. I wanted to discuss his claims of intellectual superiority and find out if he equated it with factual accuracy, or was he talking in more abstract terms, the self-satisfied terrain of hubris, the proud fraud of the IQ. Maybe he had once completed a crossword puzzle and was exhilarated by his achievement. I pictured him doing this in a prison cell, and then walking about the yard in San Quentin showing off the puzzle and smiling with half-lidded eyes as he passed it around for approval. My imagination was taking me places I would rather not go. It was getting revenge on this man through silent sarcasm. I wanted to fling dirt at him, then swing the shovel like a baseball bat while he slapped dust from his eyes, I wanted to hear the ring of a skull struck by metal, wanted to bat the gun from his hand. I began to go over the events of the night wondering at what point I might have given myself an edge and prevented this from taking place. Why had I not reached down and locked the screen door when he first arrived? Why had I not wiggled the battery cables at dawn? I had no illusions. I knew what I was doing. I was digging my own grave.

I heard a noise behind me. I glanced around and saw Benny easing himself to the ground and leaning back against a tree. The posture of a supervisor. A seated sergeant watching privates digging foxholes, filling sandbags, raking gravel. Men who could not make it on the outside, that's how we privates dealt with the fury of being supervised by men with beer bellies. Fury is a private's right. I had contemplated

161

reenlisting with the glory of each promotion, but dissuaded myself. The average soldier receives three promotions before he snatches his discharge out of an officer's hand and runs to the nearest bar. Private E-2, PFC, Specialist Fourth-Class, these were the typical promotions. Some men made buck sergeant, but most of the men I knew never rose above the rank of the corporal class.

Thoughts like these passed through my mind like a slow river as I bent to my dreadful labor. My body was not used to this, the awkward half-bent posture of a shoveling man. It was exhausting. I grew overheated. The sweat on my back cooled as it was absorbed into the fabric of my shirt. Benny said nothing when I stopped to take a breather. He seemed to understand the nuances of hard labor. The dirt piled around the hole like the fringes of a beard. I stayed between the lines, the idiotic precision of an imagined perfectionist.

The shoveling grew easier the deeper I got, the earth softer but heavier with latent moisture. I did not speed up the digging as the dirt came out easier, nor did I slow the digging as one might be tempted to do in a situation where the end result was unpalatable. I'm talking foot-dragging. I was well acquainted with that aspect of my personality. I picked a plausible pace, was watched as a man on an assembly line was watched by an efficiency expert with a stopwatch in one hand and a bottom-line to be met for his own overseer. Before I knew it, I was sinking into the mire of recapitulation. This would be my final resting place. What was I leaving behind? What had I accomplished in my life? It was over now. There was no future. I could take an accounting. I had accomplished nothing. The past had never been prologue. I was born into an epilogue. The final page was about to be turned on one of those blank books you buy in the novelty section of a store, along with cartoon calendars and ballpoint pens with plastic daisies sticking from the tops.

When the entire length of the hole was two feet deep, I stopped. I was like a lazy scholar hoping the teacher would forgo the assignment of homework. I did not want to make it three feet deep. I turned and looked at Benny and saw his head cocked back against the tree, his mouth wide open, his eyes shut. My God, he was asleep. The moment froze, a tableau, a photograph: the flashlight rested loosely in his left hand and the gun loosely in his right hand, his finger nowhere near the trigger. The boredom of watching another man work must have sedated him, the lateness of the hour, he had been busy all day, on the lam, fortified only by peanut butter and macaroni.

I stumbled rushing from the hole, tripped on the edge, made sounds, and his eyes flew open. My movement toward him was like a zoom-lens angling on the gun as he raised it. *Blam!* No better word for it. The bullet passed my left shoulder like a hornet. "Back off!" he shouted. The passing of the bullet took my momentum with it. I stood stiff as a waxwork.

He hauled himself up off the ground with his flashlight fist braced against the tree, the pistol pointed right at me. "The fuck's the matter with you!" he shrieked. "You didn't think you were smart enough to dry-gulch me, did you?" This was bravado, I could tell. He seemed rattled in spite of his words. "I wasn't asleep, you dumb bastard. I just closed my eyes to see what you would do and you fell for it. Nobody can outsmart me. Now get back to work!"

But he knew what he had done. He had fallen asleep on the job. The narcissist caught unawares. He was furious with himself, and furious with me for witnessing his imperfection.

"I missed you on purpose," he said as I turned back and stepped down into the hole. "I could have blown you to hell but I shot past you. You thought I missed, didn't you?"

I nodded as I prepared to stab the earth again.

"Yeah, that's what you thought, you dumb bastard. Look at me, you idiot. Look at me!"

I had my back to him. Somehow I felt that a bullet in the back would not hurt quite as much as a bullet in the chest. Doubtless there was nothing to that theory, but it was a necessary illusion. Facing a man with a gun is intolerable.

I turned all the way around and stood with the shovel jammed into the earth. He was pointing the pistol at my heart. "I'm good with this," he said, rocking the muzzle up and down. "I can drive a nail into a board fifty feet away with a bullet from this thing. I never miss. That was a warning shot. If you try anything again, you'll get it."

I waited for him to finish.

That's when I heard the mournful sound.

We both heard it.

We turned our heads, his to the right and mine to the left, looking down the road. A crunching, slithering sound came from the bushes.

"The fuck?"

Benny pointed the flashlight along the road. A wildcat creeping through the woods? This occurred to me, who had never seen a squirrel in this place.

The bushes shook. Benny caught and held the leaves with the circle of light. A writhing, squirming figure edged itself onto the road like a massive snake. The taxi driver was wriggling from the spot where he had lain.

"Shit!"

Benny took off running down the road. The flashlight beam jerked like an angry cane devoid of mass whacking the cabbie. Benny's arms were pumping. His back was to me. My body knew the moment had come before my mind could put it together. I was after him with the shovel raised, speed firing from my thighs like sparks, fear drawing me toward him like a magnet, physics exploding on this dark road, speed light magnet *blam*, my shovel caught him on the back of the head and down he went. The flashlight sprang from his hand and spun in the air, bounced onto the ground, lit his crumpled form, lit the snake twenty feet away, blinded me, and rolled to a stop aimed at Benny's right ear.

I raised the shovel intending to kill this man, break his head like a cantaloupe, but even in that black moment the moral imperative flooded my mind: murder. To put it in more mundane terms: never kick a man while he is down. A district attorney might take that view in the well-lit confines of a courtroom. What has the law got to do with reality? A rich man can get away with murder, but a poor man?

She. It.

I hammered the flat of the blade onto the hand holding the gun and heard a hideous crunch. Benny's body writhed a moment and lay still. I squatted and picked up the pistol and heaved it away. I grabbed the flashlight and ran to the cab driver. He was lying motionless on the road. Had his crawl from the bushes been his last death struggle? Had the shot awakened him, drawn his departing spirit back to his body? I set the shovel down and moved toward him, preparing myself mentally and emotionally to do the things I did not want to do, the things you have to do. Touch the jugular. Feel the flesh cooled by death.

The man was lying on his right side, his back to me. I squatted to see if there was bleeding in the hair. He was breathing, his torso expanding and contracting. "It's okay now," I said softly. Had any of the policemen told me his name? I could not remember. I wanted to say his name, to call him back from the tunnel of dying, let him know that help had arrived. His hands were tied behind him in childish shoelace loops. I began working at the rope. Where did Benny get a rope? Where did he get duct tape? I jiggled and unloosened the rope. When it came off, his left arm rose slightly from the binding point. It must have been half-dead, the circulation cut off, the muscles asleep. He lay without moving. I quickly unknotted the rope at his ankles. Benny the genius had not done so thorough a job on the ankles. I pulled the rope around the feet and flung it away. I rolled him onto his back and looked at the duct tape strapped across his mouth. It was slightly lifted from his lips. This had allowed him to make that ungodly bobcat moan. I had to tear at it, pressing my fingers into his cheek to get a grip. The tape tore easily. I peeled it away from his beard and he was on me in an instant.

"Bastard!" he shrieked. "Bastard!"

He exploded full-strength and mauled me as I squatted awkwardly balanced, his fists pummeling my face, flinging me backwards, kicking me as I tried to speak, to explain, to clarify. The flashlight flew from my hand, the bulb blinking out. I curled onto my side in the fetal position, each point of my body that was bruised by his blows throbbing like an island of pain in the sea of my flesh. I faded in and out of consciousness.

The things I ought to have done, I did not do. I lay listening to the diminution of the driver's footsteps until they became silent. The half of my mind that cared enough to assess my situation—the radar-dish half—turned its attention toward Benny, but I heard nothing in that direction. I lay like a pebble dropped into a still pond while my troubles disappeared in all directions, concentric waves expanding into the trees. I thought of the grave. Didn't Benny the genius realize that the police would inevitably find the grave and link it with the only fugitive apprehended within a radius of one hundred miles of Crestmoor? But he did not strike me as a man who had a firm grasp of consequences. He struck me as a man who lived in the present—the absolute present-tense of NOW— and to whom plans were a surefire thing. The future was a given. He would succeed at whatever half-baked scheme drifted through his brain. No, his motive for burying corpses in the hole had no connection with rational analysis, of this I was certain.

Thoughts like these passed through my mind as I lay on the ground. My mind was the only thing in motion, so to speak. I was in pain. I felt resigned. I could have stayed on the ground until starvation set in, followed by death, rot, bones, squirrel-chew, and discovery by a band of Boy Scouts bent on mastering woodland lore. But my idle surrender to fate was interrupted by the sound of the taxi starting up. My God. The driver had found his vehicle. I had forgotten about it. I had not taken the key from the ignition and apparently Benny hadn't either, but then my mind had not been on the key when I clambered out of the taxi, it was focused on the business to come. What mattered now was that I was lying in the middle of the road and a man who had assaulted me was at the wheel of a one-ton vehicle.

I levered myself to my hands and knees and crawled into the bushes, but this proved unnecessary because I heard the sound of the taxi receding. He was exiting the forest. I rolled over like a log to a sitting position. I hoisted myself erect, grabbing hold of a horizontal branch from a sapling, the only aid I had received, it seemed, in weeks. Up, human. My mind was like that. Pan was on my side. I was a mongrel in need, a creature of nature. But this is, and always will be, true. Our machines infect us with hubris. My thoughts ran that way, thanking the tree, the gods of the woods, for the extended branch.

I came erect and peered around in the darkness trying to

get my bearings in relation to the road. The fading sound of the taxi was off to my left. I walked forward from the bushes through which I had just crawled. The road was only a few steps away, but in the darkness I might as well have been in the Yukon. I looked up and saw a star path through the trees, the space where the road had been carved, there were no branches overhead.

I squinted at the ground where the scuffle had taken place. The yellow flashlight had been flung ten feet away. I walked over and picked it up, worked the switch with my thumb, and the fucker came back on. Miracle. When I was a child there were no miracles, only trips to the store to purchase whatever piddling tool I needed to perform my child projects, Scotch tape, paperclips, batteries.

I scoured the ground with the beam and found the shovel, picked it up, and walked slowly back toward the body of Benny, thinking that I ought to do what my conscience had forbidden me to do in the throes of self-preservation. I had never chased and/or beaten a man in my life. It had been a minor miracle that I had not cut loose the guy wires of civilized restraint and pounded his body into butter. Believe me, I had felt the urge inside me when I swung the shovel against his skull, and it had shocked me, held me back from taking another hammer at his defenseless head. But now I was thinking in cold-blooded terms.

Give him a solid chop with the edge of the blade and save the taxpayers the cost of a trial, execution, burial in a pauper's grave, or the more economically feasible procedure of cremation. The pummeling I had taken from the cab driver had instilled this appalling attitude in me. The entire day, in fact, had contributed to the effect.

Benny was lying face-down on the ground. Genius-boy had taken his last dive. Out cold. The sight of him enraged me. This self-proclaimed mental giant lying like a useless sack of shit exacerbated the insanity inside me. I stuffed the flashlight into my right pocket, the vertical beam caressing the side of my face. I tucked the shovel under my armpit and bent down and grabbed Benny by the feet and began dragging him toward the hole. His weight was a moot point. I calculated two hundred pounds but he might have been buoyed by the skateboard of my fury. Mentally defective, was I? His taunt gave me strength. I walked backwards until I came to the hole, then maneuvered his body into it. I fully expected him to rise to consciousness, groan, struggle, come up fighting, but I would have clubbed him again. This was my state of mind at that moment. The only rational thought was "tit for tat," if that can be viewed as rational. When he came to, I wanted him to find himself hoisted on his own petard. I had been told that "petard" came from the French and meant "to fart," as opposed to being raised on a pike of some sort, which was my original misconception. Whenever I hear that phrase I envision medieval drunks seated in taverns farting their lives away.

As I yanked him into the hole, I twisted his body so that he would be facing the stars when his eyes fluttered open to a world he had made. He fit perfectly. He was taller than me but the parameters he had drawn with the tip of the shovel would have contained any average American male.

I stabbed at the little hills of loose earth I had scooped from the ground and began shoveling it onto his body. I wanted him dressed appropriately when he came to and realized that the tables had been turned. I worked with a fresh fever. "Wake up!" I shouted. I did not recognize my voice. I might have been Grendel howling across the moors, my shorn arm in the hands of an angry Beowulf. At one point I accidentally poked him with the tip of the shovel, trying to lay down a pile

169

of dirt in the space between his left arm and ribs. He twitched. I had made contact. I stood back from the hole with the shovel in my fists, and the lights of an automobile swung into the woods and came roaring down the road in my direction. I froze in the headlights. I figured it was the return of the taxi driver. Who else knew I was here? The police, that's who. The taxi driver had made the call on his two-way radio after he had driven away. This I learned later. As soon as the flashing red lights came on, as soon as the cruiser stopped and two uniformed policemen leaped out and pointed pistols at me, as soon as they told me to drop the shovel, I returned to reality like a spirit yanked from the dark tunnel of death, a departing ghost sucked back into a body lying prone on an operating table.

I assumed the position but not on purpose. I followed the handle of the shovel in a race to the ground. I was unconscious before I landed beside the grave where Benny was covered from neck to shoes with a layer of freshly tilled earth.

Four

By the time I came to consciousness, the entire woods was lit like a fairyland. Spinning red lights flashed against the trees. Headlights illuminated the ground. Cops were everywhere. Two medics were leaning over me. Voices buzzed. They did not speak English. They simply spoke. I could not make out the words. My cognitive powers had been depleted by the sum total of everything that had occurred since the moment my car had failed to start.

"How is he?"

That I did comprehend. It was a cop voice. Hard. It brought my cognitive powers together as a team. I started to function, beginning with my hearing and traveling down to my feet.

"He has bruises but there doesn't appear to be any serious wounds."

My shirt had been opened by a medic, my pulse taken. I was a Xerox of Morton on Hawthorne, minus the blood. I wanted them to place me on a stretcher, drive me away from this hell, and place me in a white, antiseptic room at County Heaven where Angels of Mercy would hover about me with gossamer wings, where prescription drugs would be stacked like cannonballs at my bedside.

"He appears to have fainted."

171

A confirmation of what the cops, with their drawn pistols, no doubt had surmised.

"Sir, are you able to stand up?"

I was gazing at the star path. I decided not to play possum. After all, how many years could I get away with such a ploy? Not enough.

"Yes," I whispered. I made to sit up on my own, but they helped me. Men in white, men with badges, I was surrounded by authority figures. Too late of course. Where were my protectors when Benny was engaging in his terrifying mind-games? I glanced at the grave as I arose, but Benny was not there. I looked farther down the road and saw an ambulance backing away, lights flashing, and I knew he was in custody. This helped calm the seas churning within me. Grendel slipped into his cave, threw his one good arm around his mother, and wept. It was all up to that fierce bitch now to settle the score. I'm talking the police, of course, blind justice, the majesty of the thing we buy with our taxes. Benny would have his day in court, and his life in prison.

My right wrist was clutched and carefully but firmly brought around to the small of my back. Then the other wrist, the snap of handcuffs clicking like bones manipulated by a chiropractor.

"That's him," a voice said, and I recognized it. I squinted through this fairyland of lights and saw the taxi driver standing in the background near his cab, which was parked behind the second police car in line.

"What's your name?" a cop said.

"His name is Pete Larkey!" the driver shouted. "That's the guy!"

"Sir, could you please go stand by your vehicle?" another cop said.

The driver walked backwards and sat against the fender of

his taxi. Folded his arms. Glared at me. I looked away.

"What is your name, sir?"

"Peter Larkey."

"Sir, are you injured in any way?" the cop said.

I started to say no. Injured meant broken bones to me, blood, missing teeth, but then I realized I was in fact injured, injured in so many ways. "Yes," I said. "That taxi driver beat me up."

"Fuck you!" he shouted.

A cop walked over to the driver and began speaking quietly to him.

Another cop shined his flashlight in my face and made a thorough examination of my surface appearances. God only knew what he was seeing. Had I bled? Was I badly bruised? I was filthy, this I knew. Sweat-stained, leaf-strewn, frosted with dust. An innocent man at the absolute rock bottom of life.

"I want that taxi driver arrested and charged with beating the shit out of me," I said.

I knew then that I could not trust my voice. The bicameral mind had become unlinked, the snake brain unleashed, I would begin howling like Grendel.

"Up yours!" a dim voice hollered. Another cop led the driver around to the rear of the taxi, where he could fume without interfering with police procedure.

"Come with me, sir," a cop said.

I nodded. I could not trust my voice but the power to keep my mouth shut was still in me. He guided me to a car, opened the door, helped me inside. When the vacuum pressure squeezed my body, the sounds of the world were muted. The entire two-track was blocked by police cars. I didn't know how many. White lights everywhere, red lights painting the moonfrosted treetops crimson. How much thought went into the dramatics of a police bust? Had psychologists been consulted to determine the maximum intimidation effected by lights and sirens and badges and paramilitary uniforms? The tin star was obsolete. Power demanded pizzazz. My mind curled around these thoughts like latent smoke from a dying campfire. I had been handcuffed and seated inside a rolling jail. What sort of twisted ironies were these? What were the motives of the gods? What sin had I committed? I will tell you: the sin of innocence—the one sin the gods will not forgive.

I fainted again. When I came to consciousness, my body was covered with a fine sheen of sweat as that accompanying a broken fever. I was no longer Grendel. I was just Pete Larkey, unemployed loser, staring into the face of Detective Coleman.

"How do you feel, Mr. Larkey?"

"Tired," I croaked.

The rear door of the vehicle was open. Coleman was leaning in and looking at me.

"I'm obligated to inform you, Mr. Larkey, that you are being held on suspicion of assault, kidnapping, and attempted murder."

But of course. A logical outcome for a man too stupid to wiggle his cables.

He advised me of my rights. Advised. Such a word. It had the quality of an afterthought—Oh, by the way, Mr. Larkey, anything you say can get you The Chair.

"I did not do any of those things, Detective Coleman. I myself was assaulted this evening by a man who broke into my house and held me at gunpoint."

"Who assaulted you?"

"A crazy man whose first name might be Benny. I don't know that for sure. They took him away in an ambulance. He forced me to dig that grave in the road. I hit him on the head

174

with a shovel." I paused a moment, then said, "I did assault him, but only in self-defense."

He pondered this for a moment, then said, "I'll be right back, Mr. Larkey."

He closed the door. I closed my eyes. What purpose would it serve to keep my eyes open? When had open eyes ever worked to my advantage? I sat in the vacuum silence until the door opened again. A policeman helped me out. Detective Coleman was standing next to him. He told the policeman to remove my cuffs, then asked me to take a seat in his unmarked car. He escorted me down the road past two more police cruisers. The road was no longer packed with vehicles. The taxicab was gone. The two-track was empty all the way to the asphalt road, Crestmoor Road, which bisected the woods. A single cruiser with red lights spinning was parked at the entrance to this evil Eden that stretched to the backyard of my house.

Coleman opened the shotgun door and I climbed in. He walked around the front of the car and took his place behind the steering wheel.

At this point, a policeman came up to the car with a thermos and handed it through the driver's window.

"Would you care for some coffee?" Coleman said.

I nodded. He filled the thermos cap with coffee and handed it to me.

"You said you were forced at gunpoint to dig that grave," Detective Coleman said. "Tell me again who forced you to perform that action."

My soliloquy was succinct. I spoke of everything that had happened to me since the moment Officer Wilson dropped me off at my house. I took careful pains to describe in detail the simian posture and attitude of the cab driver when he arrived for an explanation as to why I had not warned him that there might be someone inside my house, a detail that was true and of which I was ashamed and which I admitted without hesitation. There is no modesty in a war zone, a flood, a natural disaster. Rip up those long johns and bind the wounds. I made it clear beyond the shadow of a doubt that I had feared the taxi driver. I described his exit, and the subsequent phone call from my ex-wife. Check the phone records, Sherlock. You will see that I am an innocent man. Ma Bell will back me up. Long distance from Albany. Case closed.

I watched Coleman's face as I covered the events that I knew he would be most curious about. Exactly what happened after the taxi driver left my house? The next time I saw the driver he was bound and gagged. Check the duct tape for fingerprints. Yes, mine will be there, along with those of a man who no doubt has an extensive file at the FBI. He will be identified. Unless he was wearing gloves when he muzzled beard-boy—his claims of mental superiority were not to be dismissed so glibly.

Coleman did not interrupt my narrative. I sensed that he was hanging on my every word, waiting for the stumble, the lapse of consistency, the confused time element, anything that might indicate I was making up what might sound like horseshit to a man who needed to determine whether I was the sort of person who could assault, kidnap, murder and/or bury alive a human being. Why I might do such a thing was a question I would leave up to Coleman to answer, and believe me, I would find his answer extremely interesting.

But I was able to see things from his angle. I understood cops. I watched TV. Already I had been investigated for hit-and-run, a corpse had been found in my bathroom, and a cab driver had reported that I had knocked him unconscious, etc. So I understood Detective Coleman's position. I would lay out the facts without a stumble, without the telling pause, the stutter-stop that renders suspicious a narrative being made up on the spot by a lying motherfucker desperate to save his guilty ass from a well-crafted, taut, and one-time-only noose. I would say what must be said. I was an innocent man.

"I want you to give me a complete physical description of this man who held a gun on you," Coleman said. A strange request. All he had to do was follow the ambulance to the hospital and strip-search the bastard.

I started with the top of Benny's head and worked my way down to his shoes, which I had gotten a good look at as I dragged him to the hole. When I finished the description I handed the empty thermos cap back to Coleman. He screwed it on tight, then asked me if I was up to accompanying him to the grave.

I nodded.

As I climbed out of the car I pondered the possibility of a lawsuit against the taxi driver, and even the cab company. The man had no right to assault me, even if he did believe I had bushwhacked him and bound him for burial. This wasn't the Wild West, where two-gun justice prevailed and circumstantial evidence was the rule of law. I did feel a bit ambivalent about putting the cab driver in that sort of jeopardy though, facing a criminal lawsuit with possible imprisonment. I suspected he watched as much television as I did. Maybe he had grown up in an environment where violence was the norm, where it wouldn't occur to a man not to viciously attack someone who had bushwhacked him and attempted to bury him alive. Mountain people. Desert scum. On the other hand, I liked the idea of suing the taxi company. Go for the deep pockets, as the TV lawyers say.

"Did you search my house?" I said.

"No, Mr. Larkey, we have not done that yet."

Yet.

The single most frightening word in the English language.

Coleman had a large flashlight, the sort that holds a dozen batteries, big lens, dazzling beam. I was not cuffed but there were plenty of uniformed men around. I looked for Officer Wilson but did not see him. He was a day-shift cop. I supposed he was fast asleep in bed right then, or else watching TV. Hearth and home.

Coleman asked me to show him the spot where the taxi driver had been lying bound and muzzled with duct tape. We walked toward the scene of the dig. It made me ill to walk in that direction. Held at gunpoint. Slave labor. Oh God how I looked forward to the moment when Benny would make his perp walk into the police station. I envisioned cops restraining me behind a barrier as I shook my balled fists, spat, and hurled Druidic curses in his direction. The orgasm of vindication.

"I drove the taxi along this section of road," I said, pointing left and right as we walked deeper into the forest. "I don't remember exactly where I was forced at gunpoint to park the cab, but it was right along in here."

He shined the light at the ground. I was hoping to see incriminating tire tracks, but the earth was dry, and anyway they would have been scattered by the cop cars that had come for me. No matter. I was certain the cabbie would be more than willing to mark the exact location where he had made his escape from the homicidal Samaritan whom he had dispatched with his fists.

"The place where the driver was tied up is farther along," I told Coleman. I felt like a GI returning to the scene of a battle forty years later. The grim nostalgia of a near miss. Did Audi Murphy remember with vivid clarity the actions of his war, his battles, his disasters and heroics? How did he feel shooting at actor Nazis and watching remembered buddies die in combat? How did he feel about getting paid to relive the hardest years of his life?

A strip of yellow tape was now strung across the road between two red safety cones, though slack enough that we had only to step over it. We walked another dozen yards, and I saw little yellow flags planted in the ground indicating potential pieces of evidence, one of which was a wad of duct tape that I had flung during the mission of mercy that had led to my severe beating. I should have left the sonofabitch tied up and just gone for the police. What had made me tamper with evidence? Altruism? According to economists there is no such thing on the entire planet. Everybody is out for himself. Let the cops handle it, Charley, I have to go home and start planning my career on a loading dock.

"This is where the driver was lying," I said.

"Could you describe the precise position of the man as he lay on the ground?" Coleman said. "Be careful not to step on any of those flags."

I approached the spot and stood with my feet close together. The ground had been stirred up where I had been assaulted. "His head was here, his feet were there," etc. I painted the picture. I pointed out the place where I had fallen backwards and he had hit and kicked me, and the place where I had crawled to safety in the bushes. The sapling which had helped me up from the ground stood mute witness.

Coleman and I walked another twenty feet and that's where I stopped and pointed at the ground.

"Right here," I said. "I hit him on the back of the head with the shovel and he went down. I grabbed his gun and threw it."

"Which direction?" Coleman said.

I pointed off into the woods, the trees, the thick underbrush.

"So we ought to be able to find the gun in there," he said.

I nodded.

He turned to two uniformed cops who had followed us. He approached one of them and spoke quietly, then came back to me.

"From this point you say you dragged the man to the hole?" he said.

I nodded. I indicated swatches of disturbed leaves and slightly scarred earth that marked the path of my two-hundred-pound Olympic tug.

We followed it until we came to the scene of the main event. A cop was snapping pictures. Portable studio spots had been set up around the scene and were running off a battery. I concluded that these props had been brought in during my second period of unconsciousness. No need to wiggle those cables. The setting was eerie, a Hollywood soundstage with appropriate stark shadows. The centerpiece was the two-foot-deep grave.

"Be careful where you step," Coleman said as we approached.

Little yellow flags were everywhere. I took a quick scan and noted that all the footprints seemed to be mine. No doubt the police had taken note of that too. The place where Benny sat had no loose dirt because I had taken special precautions not to fling the dirt in his direction, the sort of planning I am best at, the sort that eradicates any possibility that my word can be backed up by evidence.

"The man was sitting against that tree," I said, pointing at it, running my finger up and down as if to punctuate the veracity of my witness statement.

This too must have been what it was like for returning GIs trying to piece together scenes of their old battles. Vague recollections that took place in a maelstrom of action. The memory plays tricks. The stone wall, the bunker, the hillock changes size. Some things have the clarity of sharp photographs, and others are blurred. Is this placid sepia picture-postcard image the spot where I battled for my life against the dreaded Hun?

Coleman took a long, studied look at the entire scene, just as he had taken a long, studied look at the landscape surrounding my house that afternoon. He stepped to the grave and looked at the little hills of dirt that bordered three sides of the hole. He squatted and peered at the ground, tracing the border with his flashlight.

"Are these the marks you mentioned?" he said, slowly drawing a rectangle with the light. Here and there were the still-extant lines that had been drawn by Benny with the tip of the shovel. I had kept within the lines as per instruction.

"Yes!" I said with undue enthusiasm. "He drew those lines himself!" Benny's manic perfectionism would be his undoing. He had left behind evidence of his involvement. What more did the police need? A warm flood of exoneration roiled inside me.

Coleman stood up but said nothing. I was disappointed by his response. I expected him to match me yahoo for yahoo — "Turn Peter Larkey loose and call the DA!"

"How long did it take you to dig this hole?" Coleman said.

I gazed at my handiwork. "I don't know. It may have been forty-five minutes. Possibly an hour. I lost track of time. I wasn't thinking about time, although I will admit I was thinking about how long I had left to live."

He nodded as if he understood this contradictory train of thought. Was he buying my story?

"Why did you dig the hole only two feet deep?"

"That's what he ordered me to do."

"Yes, I understand. But I have a problem with that. If the man intended to bury you and the taxi driver, it doesn't seem to me that two feet would be deep enough."

I stared at him for a moment, then looked at the hole.

He continued: "It seems to me that there would be room enough for only one body in that hole."

He was not buying it. I read between his lines. The hole was deep enough for only one victim of a brutal homicide. I spoke quickly, perhaps too quickly. "He did say that I might need to dig it three feet deep but he wasn't sure. He said . . . he said to me, 'We'll see.'"

Even I wasn't buying it. I had left that detail out of my oral statement. It now had the quality of a story not so much being made up on the spot as being *revised* on the spot, the sort of detail a cornered man might add to give verisimilitude to his bullshit.

"At any time did he actually tell you that he intended to kill you and place your body in this hole?"

"No. He . . . he . . . he never came right out and told me anything. He forced me to do things at gunpoint, like make him a peanut butter sandwich. But he never told me what he wanted me to do until it came time to do it. He was a strange fellow. He kept bragging about his mental superiority. He told me that my brain was defective."

Coleman cocked his head ever-so-slightly sideways. This was another detail that I had left out. My narrative had been linear. Pure action. No speculation as to motive. Jack Webb states it on *Dragnet*: "Just the facts, ma'am, just the facts." But until this moment at the graveside I had no reason to inform Detective Coleman that my assailant had made disparaging presumptions about my intellect. Perhaps my defective mind had unconsciously left out those details on purpose.

"Why did he say that about you?" Coleman said.

"When I told him that I ran after my car this morning, he basically said I was stupid to have run after the car since it would have been impossible for me to catch it. He said I didn't have the faculty to reason things out properly."

"But you ultimately did catch it."

I paused a moment, then said, "That's true."

"Did you mention that to him?"

"No." I looked at the grave, then looked at Coleman. "I didn't think of that. But even if I did I wouldn't have said it. I didn't want to say anything that might have annoyed him. He seemed like the kind of person who would get mad if you made him look foolish."

Unlike the ingratiating nods that I had been flinging at Benny all night like soothing faerie dust, Coleman did not nod at my commentary. He took another long look around at the scene of the crime, then told me to come with him.

We walked to the yellow police-tape where the two men who had shadowed us were waiting silently like extremely well-trained guard dogs.

"Excuse me just a moment," Coleman said. "I need to talk with these men."

I flung some faerie dust, then turned and looked at the starkly lit scene, which up until then had possessed the artificial quality of a Hollywood set. Cops were poking around in the bushes here and there, painting the trees with flashlight beams, bending to peer at things on the ground like hardy dwarves in a Disney fantasy digging for diamonds. But now it changed. I saw the hole for what it was. My body might never have been found. My last resting place. God only knew what Benny had in mind for the taxi driver. Perhaps he would have eyeballed the excavation and then told me to dig down another two feet. The lit set became nothing more than a grisly crime scene, minus the corpses. My dislike of the taxi driver began to fade. Of *course* he had attacked me with the ferocity of a junkyard dog. Was I not a "Benny" character in the eyes of the cabbie? Our bones would have commingled in the damp earth until the arrival of the Boy Scouts. Perhaps a spring rain would have uncovered a tibia or femur. Some poor twelve-year-old decked out in merit badges might have called his scoutmaster over to examine the remains of what he thought was a fallen deer. The upshot was hideous to contemplate. Imagine a grown man in charge of twenty idealistic boys inadvertently extracting a grinning skull from the earth.

My skull.

"All right, Mr. Larkey, I would like you to accompany me to your house now."

As Coleman's car emerged from the orifice of the woods, I thought of praying. I could not get a fix on Coleman's attitude. Was he buying my story? I felt that my future was in his hands, and I preferred that it be in the hands of God rather than *the gods*. The gods were playful. The God of the West did not toy with lives. He was Merciful and Just, and Peter Larkey was an innocent man.

But I did not pray. It was in me though. A silent beseeching. My innocence so far could not be established beyond the shadow of a doubt. It was like a receding horizon. Each question I answered seemed to move me toward or away from the ideal destination. But I was judging things from Coleman's point of view. Did I sound like a lying motherfucker or was I showing all the signs of an innocent man overwhelmed by events commonplace to a homicide detective?

My every move, utterance, nuance, eyeball flicker, and baffled stutter was being weighed and measured by a man who was familiar with set patterns. Perhaps he already had drawn his conclusion about my guilt or innocence in the way that a chess master can see the endgame long before his lesser opponent has made his fifth move. What happens in the mind of a chess master who perceives that he will lose when his opponent slides his rook to the one single fatal square? Does the master play it out for the enjoyment of jousting, even though he knows he is going to lose? Or does he bank on the possibility of a critical error that might later be executed by his opponent? Does he tease himself with minor suspense? Or does he attempt to rattle his opponent by reaching into his handy bag of mind-games? How many chess masters softly snort with derision at key moments?

Two cop cars were parked in front of my house. The emergency lights on their roofs were lit but not revolving. No blood-red disks scything the far moors, just idle cops awaiting further instructions. The Fourth Amendment was intact. They were waiting for me to invite them in, and I was more than willing to accommodate them.

Again I was escorted to the front door of my cracker box by lawmen. What did they make of this endless waltz? Who was this man who up until nine thirty this morning had lived his life on the edge of town in a state of anonymity? Recently divorced. A loner. A recluse intimately connected with bodies scattered across the landscape of the pleasant township of Crestmoor.

"Walk me through it," Coleman said as we stepped into the living room. He was carrying his industrial-strength flashlight. The living room lights were still on. It was all as Benny and I had left it. "Show me everything the man did and tell me everything the man said from the moment he rang the doorbell until you got into the taxi."

I began with my surreptitious peering out the window at the sound of a vehicle rolling onto my driveway. I felt as if I was rehearsing a scene already performed, blocking out the action of a play that had closed after opening night.

Here is where I sat on the couch. Here is the chair that he dragged across the room. He said this, he said that, he treated the gun as if it had no bullets, he bobbled it, waved it around haphazardly. It occurred to me that Benny had never served in the military. There is something about getting bitch-slapped by sergeants that gives you a lifelong respect for triggers.

"After he forced me at gunpoint into the kitchen, he told me to make him a sandwich." I opened the cupboard and pointed at the jar of Skippy. "He preferred Peter Pan but I didn't have any."

I reached for the jar as if reaching for a book that Coleman might like to peruse, but he told me not to touch it. I felt foolish. I felt as if all the cop shows I had ever watched on TV added up to nothing. You do not tamper with evidence, manhandle potential court exhibits, smear fingerprints.

I pointed at the glass Benny had drunk from. "He did use that, but he wiped his fingerprints off after he drank the water."

Coleman told one of the officers to place the glass into a plastic bag. The cop pulled a bag from his back pocket and opened the mouth wide, slipped it over the glass without touching it with his fingers.

I told Coleman about the peanut butter jar, the macaroni tub, anything that might have Benny's fingerprints. Step-by-step we were moving toward a horizon over which stood the land of innocence. I felt hopeful as I led them outside to the moonfrosted landscape. I took them around to the carport, where I pointed at the double doors of the toolshed.

"He closed them himself before we got into the taxi," I said. "There may be fingerprints on the knobs." The knobs were made of plastic, the underrated, sturdy, low-rent cousin to glass.

"Is there a padlock for these doors?" Coleman said, pointing at the iron clasp that once had barred the door from imaginary intruders.

"There used to be but I stopped locking it awhile back," I said, feeling guilty. I was confessing to a lapse of security, like a soldier who never bothered to padlock his footlocker due to laziness, slovenliness—a total fucking dud.

The policeman who had placed the glass into the bag took out another bag and used it as a glove to reach beneath the wood of one door and pull it open. It came easy. Coleman swept the inside of the box with the flashlight beam.

"The shovel was hanging there," I said, pointing to a space that was emptier than any space I had ever seen in my life. I now wished I had performed a routine in the past that I had seen other men do, which was to paint an outline of each tool against the backboard of the box, but that had seemed the sort of thing a father might do, a gentle reminder to children that *this* is where the goddamn shovel, saw, or hammer belongs. Not my father, though, and not me. I was upholding the family tradition of never doing things in a practical manner.

Coleman shined the flashlight around the carport.

"Describe for me exactly what happened after the shovel was removed from the toolbox."

I went over it again. Both hands on the shovel, gripping life. I went beyond the facts to the truth, which I was learning were not the same thing. I told him that I had the urge to hit the intruder with the tool but that I held off due to the distance between his finger and the hammer-release. Shovel into the backseat. Me into the driver's seat. Back the taxi all the way down the driveway, swing the car around, and aim it toward the woods.

Coleman shined the light down the driveway as if watching its ghost ease onto the road. He turned and looked at me.

187

"I hate to put you through this again, Mr. Larkey, but I'm going to have to take you to headquarters and get a written statement."

I hung my head. "Yes. I know. It has to be done," I said this to the garage floor. I spoke to the oil stain. My ex had asked me a dozen times to clean it up and I promised I would. I never got around to it. What would it have mattered anyway? My Ford leaked oil the way grass grew. The way bushes got shaggy. The way I lost jobs. The way the sun set and the moon rose. I craved stasis in my life.

Coleman asked me to come back into the house. I followed him inside. The uniformed man followed me. After we entered the living room Coleman turned to me and smiled. "Mr. Larkey, before we go to headquarters I am going to have this officer frisk you. This is just a security precaution."

"I understand," I said.

"First off I would like you to empty your pockets."

I complied. I had nothing in my pockets except a comb and a billfold.

"Would you mind opening your billfold and showing me the contents?" he said.

I opened it and pulled out twelve dollars. I pulled out my driver's license and credit cards. I have three. Two of them don't work anymore. I pulled out the various scraps of paper I have accumulated over the years, phone numbers of people I have not called since I was single, back when I would phone buddies to meet me at bars, even the names of women I may or may not have had the nerve to call. It's hard to get dates when you're broke. I once called a woman and asked if she would join me for a beer at a neighborhood tavern. She told me she was all beered-out for that week. I got her message. Loud and clear. Most messages from women are loud and clear.

The cop gave me a brief but efficient frisk. I assumed he was looking for a pistol. That's probably true of all frisks.

"Thank you, Mr. Larkey," Coleman said.

I reassembled the pitiful remains of my life and stuffed them back where they had come from. Coleman asked for my house key. The police would be making a thorough search of the place, just as they would be making a thorough search of the woods for the pistol that was in neither of my pockets.

On the way to the police station I gazed out the front window of Coleman's car but didn't say anything. I wondered how seriously he had taken my assertion that I had waived my right to remain silent. I regretted that. I wanted to remain silent for the rest of my life. I had been running on unprecedented adrenaline levels for hours it seemed, and I was coming down hard.

"I'm tired," I said. "Is there some place in your building where I might be able to lie down for a bit?"

He glanced at me with a somber look. "I'm afraid you are going to spend the night in jail," he said.

Why did I ask such a question? Of course they had a place where people like me could lie down and grab a few winks. People suspected of assault, kidnapping, and attempted murder have bunks supplied by taxpayer largesse.

"You will be allowed to contact a lawyer," he said.

Lawyer? Who—Bud Seifert, the shyster who managed to give away everything I owned to my ex? Why would I want to talk to that incompetent little prick?

"I do not need a lawyer," I said. "I am an innocent man."

He remained silent for a bit, then said, "In my experience, innocent men are those most in need of lawyers."

189

I looked at his profile in the lights as we entered the township of Crestmoor proper. Was that a police joke or just levelheaded advice? But I knew what he meant. No use squalling to the police that I was being held unjustly. In this nation, policemen, judges, juries, and executioners work out of a different department than lawyers.

"I know," I said. "I just want to lie down. I'm tired."

"Perfectly understandable," he said.

A police cruiser was escorting us back to the station but there were no red lights or sirens. I glanced at my watch. It was 11:30 p.m. This day was almost over in a literal sense. But it would never be over. I had experienced enough days that never ended to recognize the signs.

When we arrived at the station, I was escorted to the same room where I had made my second written statement of the day. All this writing. I felt as if I were back in college. Liberal arts majors do more writing than most majors. It's voluntary, of course. The dissection of the complete works of Western literature. Thousands of meaningless sentences to win that sparkling A+ on the final GPA. I sat for an hour or so in a small room putting it all down on paper. I spent part of that hour with my eyes closed, trying to remember the exact wording of the conversations I had engaged in with both the taxi driver and Benny the mental giant, the genius who had turned his back on me at the wrong moment. It was difficult. The memories were filtered through the humiliation of admitting to the driver that I had allowed him access to my house that afternoon under patently false pretenses, and filtered through the fear of death during my back-and-forth with the gun-wielding Brainiac. I used quotation marks in the places where I clearly remembered the dialogue: "I'm the king of the mind-games." That sort of thing.

After I finished writing the statement, a uniformed

policeman took it away. I had another wait while Coleman evaluated my paper. During the interim I was offered free coffee and donuts, but I turned them down. I did not want my brain battling caffeine when the door to the iron-bar motel slammed shut.

I did not see Detective Coleman again until the following morning. I spent the night in a jail cell, although it did not look like Andy Taylor's jail, no bars, no Otis Campbell wandering in drunk at two in the morning, no Deputy Fife snorting and stomping around the office because he finally had someone to guard. The door had a window embedded with wire mesh. The room was modern, yellow-painted, and devoid of furniture other than a bunk bed. I was alone in the room. It passed through my mind that the homeless could be quartered in such small spartan places if the taxpayers could be convinced to treat hobos decently, but my mind often wanders through the Elysian fields of altruism when I am at the mercy of hard times. The light went out while I was undressing. I crawled beneath the covers of the lower bunk, and the last thought I had before I faded was that this was like going to sleep on an army bunk. My incarceration was like the army in ways too numerous to mention.

If I dreamed that night, I wasn't aware of it. I had no recollection of the mystifying machinations of the subconscious when I began to drift awake around 6 a.m. It appeared that I hadn't moved throughout my sleep. When I shifted my limbs to roll over I could feel the ache of having remained in the same position all night, could feel the bruises from the kicks and pummelings I had undergone at the hands of the taxi driver. The memory of the events of the previous night generated a desire to slide back into sleep. Almost forty years old and snoozing in a slammer. I was too fed up to be amused by the downward spirals that had so often amused me in the past. I kept my eyes closed for a while but knew my batteries had been recharged. I would have to get up. I was hungry. I had to go to the bathroom. I had to start the first day of the rest of my miserable life.

A guard was sitting on a chair outside the cell. He showed me to a restroom. Then he escorted me to Coleman's office. On his desk was a tightly wrapped and still warm sack from the local McDonald's. Egg McMuffins and coffee. Coleman told me he had gone home and slept and was back in the office an hour before I woke up.

"So how are you feeling this morning, Mr. Larkey?"

"Better," I said.

"Good. Good. Why don't you dive into this?" he said, shoving the paper bag across the desk toward me.

He waited until I got started on the food, then said, "I have some interesting news for you. We have identified the body of the man who was found dead in your bathroom." He spoke as I was chewing, perhaps as a policeman oblivious to the unpalatable link between corpses and sausage, but I was famished. I listened raptly as he went on.

"We obtained his ID through his fingerprints. His name was Oscar Easley. No address. Unemployed. Last known residence, Joliet Correctional Center." Coleman was reading this from a sheet of paper, which he slapped down on the desk. He smiled. "Your basic drifter."

I felt mildly vindicated. I had speculated all along that the man who had been found in my bathroom was some sort of hobo. Perhaps he had hooked up with Benny along the road. But there was no sense of elation at having learned the stats. A nobody from nowhere had choked to death on a slice of bread in my house. I had heard the details first-hand from the man who had refused to give the poor sap the Heimlich Maneuver.

Then Coleman frowned. "Mr. Larkey, we have a number of small problems."

I did not frown. I was used to this sort of prologue.

"We took a written statement from the taxi driver concerning the events that he was directly involved in. He has accused you of hitting him on the back of his head and knocking him out after he left your house."

This did not come as too much of a shock to me. I was already certain that he thought I was the man who had rendered him unconscious and tied him up and transported him to the woods. I had been certain of it since the moment he had beaten the shit out of me.

"I've gone over his statement a number of times and have compared it with the things you told me, and I will tell you that for the most part your stories substantiate each other. He described the encounter that took place at approximately eight thirty last night, and"—at this point he held his right hand in a horizontal position with the fingers splayed, then rocked the hand like an NBA pro skillfully dribbling a basketball low to the court in the universal body language for comme ci, comme ça—"the stories meshed. However, according to his statement, after he left the house, you followed him outside and hit him on the back of the head with a blunt instrument."

"Not true," I said quietly.

"We have the medical report. It would appear that he took a violent blow to the back of his skull."

I shrugged. "I can't substantiate that. All I can say is that I did not do it."

Coleman looked down at my statement, leafed through a couple pages, then looked up at me. "It says here that you spoke to your wife on the phone at approximately eight forty-five."

"That's correct. She called me. I'm sure the phone company would have the record of the call."

"Oh it does, Mr. Larkey. We checked. We spoke to your wife last night."

I closed my eyes and nodded. And here all along I had thought our divorce was final. I would never get away from that woman. She must have been thrilled by the call.

"She has corroborated your conversation."

"Good," I said. "Am I going to be released?"

"I'm afraid not, Mr. Larkey. There are still some problems with your story."

"I didn't know there was any problem with the truth. I have told you the truth. What problems are you talking about?"

"It's just this, Mr. Larkey. The man whom you call Benny is in County General. He has made an accusation against you."

I stopped chewing.

I would have asked what accusation but Coleman was one step ahead of me. He was probably experienced with the speechless shock of innocent men.

"He told us his name is Benjamin Gruner. He said he came to your house last night to ask directions. He said he was lost. He said he turned away from you for a moment, at which point you beat him into unconsciousness with a blunt instrument."

The McMuffin dropped from my right hand. It did not matter, though, because my appetite disappeared before the food hit the floor.

"That's not true," I said. "Why would I do a thing like that?"

I instantly regretted my words. They had the quality of answering a question with a question, the sort of thing guilty men do to buy time.

But my question might as well have been rhetorical. The detective did not respond to it. He sat at his desk and watched my face.

I looked down at the spoiled remains of my breakfast, then looked up at Coleman. "The man is a congenital liar."

Coleman picked up a cup of coffee and took a sip, set it down, raised his chin and gazed at me.

"Mr. Larkey, my people have been searching the forest all night and we have not been able to find the gun that you claim you threw into the woods."

Claim? The connotation of that word did not elude me. Doubt was being cast on my statement. My poor, pitiful, truthful statement.

"Well, they will have to just keep looking because I threw it in there and the gun could not possibly have run away."

"Oh, we will keep looking, Mr. Larkey. If it's in there we will find it."

"It's in there goddamnit," I said. "I threw it, so I know it's there."

"Why didn't you keep it?" he said.

"What?"

"You say you took the gun out of Mr. Gruner's hand. It would seem to me that once you had possession of the gun you had control of the situation. Why did you not keep it? Why did you throw it away?"

I was flabbergasted. Why does any man do anything he does when his world is spiraling out of control? I had come to within a hair's breadth of being killed and buried.

"Because I wanted it out of there," I said. "I didn't think it through. It was intuitive. Get rid of the goddamn thing, that's all I was thinking."

I lowered my eyes to the desktop and saw a series of images like a rapid montage from a motion picture, guns being kicked away, dropped off bridges, flung out of car windows, get the gun out of the picture and the playing field tilts at a different angle, depending on who is holding the next weapon in line. In my case, a shovel.

"Mr. Gruner denied having stolen your car yesterday."

He let that hang in the air.

I sat back on the chair and smiled. "Of course he denied it. He's a liar." I almost said, Why in the fuck would he admit that? I was learning a new way of communicating that I had not learned on television. I was learning that you almost say things to the police, and then don't.

"And as far as the hit-and-run accident," he continued, "we do not have any evidence that anybody but yourself was driving that car yesterday morning."

Here is what I wanted to say: Your inability to establish my innocence does not confirm my guilt. But here is what I said: "Did you check for his fingerprints on the steering wheel?"

"We checked. We didn't find his fingerprints."

Of course not. He wiped them off before he jumped out of my car and ran away. Brainiac attends to the details.

"He must have wiped them off," I said.

"Possibly." Coleman leaned forward and looked down at a sheet of paper. "Mr. Larkey, we took a statement from Mr. Morton yesterday, and he told us that he saw you driving the car that hit him. He said it was your car and that he saw you behind the steering wheel."

"Did he tell you that he had been drinking at the Lemon Tree Lounge prior to the accident?"

"Yes, he did."

"Did he tell you why he walked in front of my car?"

The detective paused at this moment and looked at me with an expression that I can only describe as "speculative."

"Why do you say that, Mr. Larkey?"

"Because that's what the man who held me at gunpoint said. He said Morton walked in front of my car."

"Did Mr. Gruner refer to your friend as 'Morton'?"

"No . . . he never said Morton's name."

Coleman nodded. "Mr. Morton told us that after you left the Lemon Tree Lounge he had a last drink, then headed home on foot. As he was approaching his house he noticed your car coming down Hawthorne Drive. He said he flagged you down because he wanted to find out if you had purchased a new battery or whether you had adjusted the cables on your old battery to get your car running."

"I wasn't driving the car."

"He told us that you slowed to a halt. He said he stepped into the street to walk around to the driver's side door, but as soon as he got in front of your car you ran him down."

This was news to me, insofar as Benny had not described it that way. Flagged down — then Benny stepped on the gas and ran over Morton. Not surprising. Morton was walking where Little Lord Fauntleroy wanted to drive. Or perhaps Morton was just another witness to dispose of. Another surprise contingency.

"You have my written statement," I said. "I saw my car stopped momentarily on Hawthorne Drive."

"Yes sir, you did write that in your statement."

"Everything I wrote down was true."

"Mr. Morton told us that he recognized you at the wheel."

"He had been drinking. He thought he saw me. When the car went past me, I myself barely saw the man at the wheel."

Coleman nodded. "When Officer Wilson saw your car parked at the curb on Hawthorne Drive, you were sitting at the wheel with the engine running and your eyes closed."

"That's all in my statement. I did not lie about that." I stared at Coleman, but then it occurred to me that my last

197

statement could easily be misinterpreted by the sorts of people whose job it is to interpret spoken English. "I did not lie about *anything*," I added, as if I had meant to pause for dramatic effect.

I continued: "Benny told me that he and this man Oscar entered my back door after I left the house to walk to Apex Auto Parts. He told me he laughed when Oscar started choking on the bread."

Coleman was attentive, but his eyes were not hardened with doubt. He was listening to me repeat that which I had already said, had written, had lived.

"He told me he wanted to teach the guy a lesson. He called him genius-boy. I guess they weren't close friends." I hadn't written that on my statement. It was an inference. But I said it now. "The man is some kind of sociopath."

I was looking at the desktop when I said this. I was looking at the paperwork on Oscar Easley. His epitaph. I looked up at Coleman. I could not fathom what he thought of all the things I had been saying. If the taxi driver's statement was true, if I had bushwhacked him and dug a grave to bury him, then I myself qualified as a sociopath. I lived alone at the edge of the woods. I had no friends. I was a loner. An outcast. Divorced. Broke. Then a bastard cabbie walks into my house and intimidates me into giving him money. Perhaps I had cracked, flipped out, went over the edge. Even a man without a mentally-defective brain might be driven to an act of violence if pushed hard enough by the injustices of life. The cab driver may have been at the wrong house at the right time to give my loose screw the final twist. I had to assume the detective was considering things along this line. That's what I paid taxes for.

Suddenly I said, "Did the cab driver have my one hundred dollars on him?"

An ill feeling came over me. My one hundred dollars must have been in Benny's pocket when he barged into my house. Ten thousand bad pennies come back. I tried to think. Would the fact that I myself did not have one hundred dollars on me speak to my innocence? The taxi driver must have mentioned the money. Maybe he thought I had clubbed him to get the money back. I recalled my frisk at my house. Then I knew. The one hundred dollars, that's what the "security procedure" had been about. I felt duped, as well as mildly embarrassed. Coleman had played a trick on me. I had gotten my tax-money's worth.

"Benny must have taken it off the cab driver."

"Possibly," Coleman said. "But his possessions were searched at the hospital. He had no money on him."

"Why did you search him?" I said.

"Because of your accusation," Coleman replied. "He too is under suspicion."

I felt like a fool. The lying Brainiac was not home free in spite of his lies. We were both in the same boat. This gave me a glimmer of hope, as does all fool's gold. But I could not help feeling that Benny had an edge. How could a deranged man like Benny hide from the police? How could he leap from my car and run away without being seen by anybody in Crestmoor? I will tell you how. He was a college-trained criminal. Guys like him learn their lessons well. Joliet. Sing Sing. Parole is graduation day. "Remember not to speed after you hot-wire a car!" the teacher chirps as the graduate struts toward the gate.

"Mr. Larkey, I am going to ask that you accompany me back to the woods."

Dread sprouted unbeckoned. I did not ever want to set foot in that forest primeval again.

"What for?" I said.

"It's the matter of the pistol," he replied. "We need your help finding it."

He watched my face as he said this. Would I blanch at the prospect of being asked to find something that did not exist? Would my eyes betray me? Would I crack, flip out, and admit that there never was such a weapon, and that everything my two accusers said was true? I was The Shovel Man.

"Okay," I said.

Interpret *that*, Sherlock. I will admit it. The doubt that was being flung about me like a net was getting on my nerves. I had held no antipathy for Detective Coleman from the moment I had met him. I liked him. I liked his professionalism. I liked the sense that he could see past any bullshit flung toward him due to his years of experience on the force. But his persistent chipping at the truth was getting me down. I wanted him to believe *me* and not the liars of the earth like Benny, or men who did not know the whole truth, like the taxi driver whose take on reality was based on, influenced by, and limited to his terrible experiences. He was a metaphor for the entire human race.

Accompanied by a police cruiser, we drove back to the scene of the crime. It was seven thirty in the morning and the sun was up. Midsummer. Had this been winter it would have been dark outside. Cold. There was something wrong about visiting the scene of a crime on such a beautiful day. Not a cloud in the sky. This visitation needed darkness, ground fog, the hooting of owls. But as I said, I had never seen a living animal in the woods. Of course, prior to this week I had been in the woods only twice since I had lived in Crestmoor, once with my ex and once by myself. The animals had probably been hiding, lurking, waiting for me to go away, not unlike most of the friends I had lost throughout my lifetime.

We turned onto the dirt two-track that led into the forest. During my encounter with Benny there was darkness all around, but now in the daylight I could see through the trees, could see blue sky past not only the branches but the trunks. It seemed a young forest, insofar as there were no thick-trunked trees of the type that might be felled by lumberjacks. I had no idea what sorts of trees they were. I know nothing of nature. I am made of brick, asphalt, plasterboard, television, paper cups, cheese wrapped in plastic. I am an American.

"We'll walk in from here," Coleman said, driving just far enough into the woods to allow the cruiser to pull in and park behind us, our escort, chaperone, bodyguard, armed and ready to cut me down the moment I made a futile dash to freedom through the saplings. It made me feel strange to be followed by benevolent men with guns, as though I were neither innocent nor guilty, but was another of those entities who inhabit the world of The Third Thing. Maybe "Limbo" is the word I am thinking of.

The forest was silent. I could see all the way to the site of the grave in the daylight, though it was a good fifty yards. The lovers' lane was straight. Why had it been carved through these trees? Had the county done it? Who would care if a blight took down this useless tract of wild growth? But maybe tree disease was like hoof-and-mouth disease. One bad patch of bark and the entire continent collapses like a circus tent.

"We made a determination that the taxicab was parked right here," Coleman said, pointing at a yellow flag off to the side of the road. He did not say how they came to that determination. Footprints, a statement by the cabbie, Holmesian deduction, but I did not ask. I would keep my mouth shut, pay homage to Jack Webb, and try to stick to the only facts I knew. That method seemed to have served the cabbie well.

We continued on our way. I looked off to my left in the direction of my house. I could not see the house. The distance was so great that the skinny saplings closed the gaps, filled in the blanks, hid the sky in that direction. I could have walked the distance within ten minutes. If the ground was not so littered with brush and tangled roots I could have run it in three. It occurred to me that it was a good thing I had not attempted to make a run for it on the previous night, drawn toward my house like a moth to a useless flame. Bullet in the back. Benny insulting my intelligence as I lay dying. "Eight hundred feet per second, chump." I wondered how he knew the velocity of the bullet. Read it in a book? Made it up? Could he actually have served in the military? As a washout or a dishonorable discharge, I supposed. Or maybe they had taught him velocity in crime college.

"This is where the cab driver was tied up," Coleman said. Little yellow flags stood all around. I wondered when the flags would be taken down. After my sentencing?

"What I would like you to do now, Mr. Larkey, is show me exactly what happened last night."

A reenactment, that's what he wanted. I looked around at all the flags that were like masking tape on the floor of a theater stage indicating where the actors should stop and stand, talk, and move on to the next bit of tape. I made a wide circle so that I would be "coming at Benny from behind," so to speak.

"We were both running," I began. "I was behind him. He was running toward the cab driver. I came at him and raised the shovel over my head and hit him like this." I swung the imaginary shovel, gave Benny enough time to hit the ground face-down, then I raised the shovel again and slammed the flat edge of the blade onto his hand.

I stopped.

"His hand," I said. "Was his hand broken? Did they find any damage in the hospital? It made a terrible sound when I hit his hand. I was sure the bones were broken."

Coleman raised his chin and peered at me. "Why don't you continue with the demonstration," he said. His voice was level, giving away nothing.

I tried to remember. Did I toss the shovel at that point? The GI returns to his old battlegrounds and can remember nothing with clarity. The most significant moment of his entire existence is a fog of sound and horror.

"I squatted down like this," I said. I reached toward one of the flags. What did that yellow pennant indicate? "I picked up the gun and . . ."

I threw it.

He watched the arc of my hand, then looked off into the woods. He looked back at me.

"You are right-handed, correct?" Coleman said.

"Yessir."

"The man fell face-forward to the ground?"

"Yes."

"So you grabbed the gun with your right hand, and then threw it."

"Yes."

"Was it possible that you might have turned about and faced another direction before you threw it?"

"No. I just grabbed it and threw it."

"Give me a better sense of what you did. Demonstrate it again for me."

I reached for the invisible gun, lifted it, and chucked it into the trees.

"So you were squatting when you tossed it," he said.

"Yes."

"Which means you probably did not throw it as far as you could have thrown it if you were standing."

I shrugged and nodded.

"Is it possible that you stood up before you threw it?"

"No. As soon as I got my hands on it I threw it. I wanted to get that thing away from Benny as fast as possible. I squatted down and grabbed it from his hand and threw it."

"Was he still holding onto it?"

"It was under his hand. I smashed his hand pretty good with the shovel."

I abruptly stopped talking, hoping he would pick up the cue and give me a little feedback on the hospital scene. But he didn't. He turned his back to me and looked off into the woods.

I glanced to my right, where the uniformed officer was standing by at a distance of fifteen feet. Watching. Listening. Observing. I could not help but feel that this was the most interesting case that this young officer had ever taken part in. It certainly was for me.

Coleman turned back. "We have searched every square inch of ground in that direction and we cannot find a pistol," he said. Something had changed in the tenor of his voice. It evoked two concepts: either I was lying, or his men were incompetent searchers. He did not say this though. His eyes said it. That was my take. I sensed that he was no longer on my side. I sensed that I was now a bona fide suspect in more than one assault, kidnapping, and attempted murder. I had been caught burying a man alive, which did not speak well for my cause.

"I don't know what to tell you," I said. "I'm not the guilty party here. Benny held me at gunpoint and made me dig that hole."

I pointed down the road.

"We're done here," Coleman said.

I was driven back to headquarters in the rear of the police cruiser. Coleman did not accompany us. I gave this some thought as I was escorted into the police station, and I came to the conclusion that Coleman had probably gone to the hospital. To check on Benny's hand? Or to release him on his own recognizance and set him free to roam the world searching for more victims to intimidate and insult and rob and bury alive? The general consensus of society seemed to be that this was all the government was good for. This was an unfair take though. The police knew no more about what had really happened than did the taxi driver. History is bunk. That is another consensus. I could not help but feel that the worst thing in the world was to know the truth. Philosophers down throughout the centuries had been searching for The Truth, and the question at the forefront of my mind as I was led back into my jail cell went as follows: Just what exactly did the philosophers intend to do with all that trash?

Five

I sat down on the bunk and for the first time since all this had begun I felt uneasy. By this I mean I had experienced fear in the presence of Benny and even the cab driver, though to different degrees, but I was beginning to comprehend the situation in a new light. Until now I had been taking refuge in the concept of innocence, as if it were a magic word that bestowed protection. But now I wasn't so certain that this was not simply the delusion of a naive mind. How many men had been incarcerated for years only to be proven innocent, usually through the evidence of DNA? It's in the papers with disturbing frequency. Released after fifteen, twenty years, a life sentence for murder, rape, burglary, commuted by a governor, the smiling man walking free after his life has been ruined by twisted justice, sleeping lawyers, biased juries, or simple incompetence. I felt very uneasy. My faith in the majesty of the law was showing cracks, like those in the wall of a dam signed-off on by experts. Suppose this brainiac con man Benny was able to convince everyone that I was the guilty party. I had been found shoveling dirt onto his face. He was unconscious. My God, the mileage a man like himself could get out of *that* scenario.

I lay down on my cot because it was too much for my tired shoulders to bear. Benny talking to reporters, weeping even, the insidious incorporation of crocodile tears, "I am homeless, I came to Crestmoor looking for work, and this . . . this Larkey fellow hit me on the head when I came to his house to ask directions. I have a wife and child in Tucumcari. I wanted to send money home. I heard there was work in the box factory. My brother-in-law passed through Crestmoor last year and told me what a friendly town this was, but Pete Larkey almost killed me and tried to bury my body, even though I was still breathing." Flashbulbs burst in his face. Front-page photo. My cadaverous mug inserted at the bottom right-hand corner, the phiz of the monster who attempted to murder in cold blood an ordinary Joe just trying to put food on his family's table.

My God.

He had it in him. I had never met a person in my life to whom the social mores meant less.

I knew I would have to contact Bud Seifert and place my fate in his hands as I had done during the divorce negotiations. This did not bode well. It tired me to think about it. I drifted toward sleep. It was obvious that my life was over. It would be my word against Benny's, plus the police by now had mountains of evidence that I had been ranging across Crestmoor the previous day running people down with cars, hammering them with shovels, duct-taping them, and burying them alive.

I lost consciousness while leafing through my files to find the sin that had heaped this punishment on my shoulders. Was there something more vile than mere innocence about which the gods were furious? Benny would have laughed at my search. "You? Vile? You've never done anything bad in your life, you wimp." But then maybe that was my true sin: existence without purpose.

It was all too much.

I slept for hours. The wheels of justice ground as slowly as ever. Dickens speaks on this subject in the most tedious book I ever read in my life: _Bleak House._ It was required reading in an English class, along with a half-dozen other books by authors such as Wilkie Collins and Mary Shelley. It took me the entire semester to get through that single volume, the only book I ever truly thought of as a _tome_. I read the other novels when I wasn't trudging through Dickens's padded serialization. He must have been paid by the word. I wished to God I had been. I was probably the only student in the class who finished the thing.

"Larkey! Wake up!"

Now it was _Larkey_ and not the affable _Mister Larkey_. I no longer felt that I was in the good graces of Detective Coleman or the other policemen who had gazed upon me with polite curiosity as the evidence mounted up. Doubtless they had all judged me and found me guilty in their own minds. But this was the voice of the jailer, a different turnkey than the one who had locked me up earlier, a man who had not met me and thus had no reason to think I was anything other than a despicable serial killer placed under his charge.

I opened my eyes and looked over at the doorway where he was standing. Keys in one hand, open door braced in the other.

"You got a visitor, Larkey. Make yourself presentable."

My clothes were in disarray. I had not undressed but apparently I had kicked off my shoes at some point during my slumber, a half-awake thing that I had done before in my life. You wake up with overheated feet, work the shoes off with your toes, and forget you ever did it. I once had a bizarre skin rash on my hands that forced me to sleep with rubber gloves coated with lotion. I would wake up and find the gloves flung halfway across the bedroom, my sheets and pillowcase saturated with a medicinal stink.

I sat up and put my shoes back on, stood and tucked in my shirt, tugged at my clothes, made myself presentable. I imagined I would be following orders similar to this when I was finally sentenced to The Big House. I hoped it was San Quentin. I had not been to California in a long time.

"Who is my visitor?" I said as I exited the room and entered the hallway.

"Just follow me," the cop said. I took a close look at the insignia on his sleeve. Deputy Sheriff. He was bulked up, in his mid-twenties, probably took himself more seriously than his job, which he apparently took very seriously. He was not going to brook any affability from a prisoner.

We walked down the hallway in the opposite direction of Coleman's office. It gave me a sense that I was being disassociated from hope. I began to wonder who in this burg would visit me. Morton? Had he recovered and left the hospital to take a last good look at me before giving a sworn affidavit to the DA that would send me up the river for life? Or maybe it was one of the garage mechanics to whom I had spoken after Morton's encounter with the underside of my car. Who did I know in this town? It didn't matter. My visitor was from Albany. I nearly went into cardiac arrest when I saw Leonard P. Dexter standing in what I quickly realized was a visitor's room. You've seen them in the movies. Is there anything in life that has not been portrayed in the movies, including things that don't exist, werewolves, vampires, fire-breathing dragons? I froze as soon as I stepped through the doorway and saw him standing there wearing a business suit and holding a briefcase. My brother-in-law who had attended my wedding years ago. He now looked even younger, fit, healthy with wealth. He was a CPA, and by the cut of his clothing he appeared to be more successful than I ever would be.

"Peter," he said with the peculiar non-inflection of a man naming things in a museum exhibit. "Bituminous. Paleolithic. Deciduous. Reptilian."

"Hello, Leonard," I said.

I glanced around the room to see if any fire-breathing dragons had accompanied him from Albany, but I did not see her anywhere. Did I sigh with relief? No. I doubted I would ever sigh with relief again as long as I lived.

The deputy directed us to a table. We sat on opposite sides. There was a solid board like a faux ping-pong net that separated us. You've seen them in the movies. I knew not to reach across the board to shake hands. I had seen a plethora of visitor's rooms in the movies as well as on TV. No touching. No exchange of gifts. There was no wire-embedded wall of glass with a telephone to speak through, but maybe only because the Crestmoor City Council did not feel the cost would be justified by the number of homicidal maniacs that graced their township annually.

"Laura asked me to fly down to see you," Leonard began, setting his briefcase in front of him on the table. He glanced at the deputy as he did so. One false move and bullets would fly.

"Why?" I said.

He smiled. He had the air of an insurance salesman, a realtor, a Kiwanis member, razor-cut, clean-shaven, smelling of Old Spice, a buttoned-down exec to whom a trip to a police station was as foreign as a trip to Transylvania.

"To make bail."

"Pardon me?"

"The police called us in the middle of the night and told us that you are suspected of attempted murder."

"I'll bet that was a thrilling call."

He shrugged. "Things have been pretty dull in Albany lately. These phone calls from the Crestmoor police have livened things up."

"Did she come with you?"

"No. I told her I would make the trip alone."

"If she's so goddamned concerned about me why didn't she come herself?"

"Are you certain you want the answer to that?"

"No. But what's this about bail?"

"She doesn't believe for one second that you are guilty of anything. She asked me to write the check." He paused and took a deep breath. "Look, brother, she doesn't hate you. I might as well tell you this. She feels sorry for you. She knows you don't have any money and could not possibly cover the bond. I agreed with her. I always liked you, Pete, but I know the kind of guy you are. Whatever the hell's been going on here, you're no killer. We'll get you a lawyer."

The blood was rushing to my cheeks. I felt naked, exposed. I knew what Leonard and the whole family had always thought of the loser that Laura had hooked up with. A woman will hook up with anything under the right circumstances. I could tell you horror stories about the women who married the slobs I knew in college. What happens to a woman's mind when she falls in love? Is love an affliction like alcoholism or more like a swat on the head with a shovel?

"Not that idiot Seifert."

This amused him. "I don't think your divorce lawyer is the man for the job. I've already spoken to my own lawyer. He's going to recommend someone in this part of the world."

Someone expensive I hoped, since Laura apparently was willing to pay for my bail bond, court costs, and cremation.

I looked down at the tabletop. I felt morose, wistful,

embarrassed. I had always liked Leonard, even if he was a wealthy and successful relative. Is there anything more annoying in the world than a brother-in-law whose life runs like a well-oiled machine designed to print money? Yes. A brother-in-law like me. The few times that I had met with Leonard in the past he always sported a slight smile as if he was entertained by the curiosity his wife's sister had chosen to whither thou goest. Doubtless he had known second-raters like myself in college. It was unlikely he viewed me as an insane serial killer any more than did Laura. I tried to see myself through his eyes, and saw a Hard-Luck Charley who did not possess enough money to make bail in a ludicrous set of charges that would supply plenty of laughs at the next Albany soirée.

"They think I did it," I said in a well-chosen morose tone of voice. I looked him in the eye and waited for him to say the immortal words, "*Did* you do it?" but he was having none of that.

"Laura asked me to tell you that when things here are cleared up you will be more than welcome to come stay in Albany until you . . . ," and here his voice faltered uncharacteristically. I interpreted his hesitation as compassion. "Until you get your act together."

"Those are her words," I said, letting him off the hook.

He nodded, then leaned forward and said, "Listen, brother, I agree with Laura. You're finished in this town. It doesn't matter what really happened here, your landlord is probably going to kick you out. You're welcome to stay with us until things settle down."

Goddamn my battery cables. The last person on earth I wanted to be indebted to was my ex. Plus, I knew that her sister didn't like me. Laura was the first person in the Collins family ever to get a divorce. Her sister Bernice placed a lot of weight on uninterrupted lineage. She once paid fifteen hundred dollars to a genealogist to trace the Collins family across the Atlantic. She was a born psycho.

"I appreciate your offer, Leonard."

That was my way of saying yes. I did like Leonard, always had. He struck me as one of the few men I ever knew who understood women.

Leonard covered the bond. He drove me away from the courthouse in a rental car. The newness of the vehicle, the odor, lifted my spirits, which indicated to me how simpleminded I was. I would not be going back to my house. Leonard had taken two rooms at a Motel 6 on the edge of town. I would be staying there overnight on his nickel. My house was in temporary police lockdown. The motel was within walking distance of the Lemon Tree, another place I had no desire to go to again. I would have liked to burn down my house and walk away from it, but it was a rental. There was nothing inside that cardboard box that I wanted. Starting life over again is easy when you have nothing. Except I did need the legal papers that define us as human beings, the documents you stuff into boxes and can never find when the problems of life sniff you out and demand verification. Birth certificate, army discharge, things of that nature. I have never possessed a passport, have never left the continental United States, but the idea appealed to me now. Go live in Mexico. Go to Vancouver. Get away from the U.S. with all its strange violence, its webs, its weirdos.

It was almost noon when I got settled in my room. There had been a long wait at the courthouse for the judge to set my bail, for Leonard to cut the check. I wondered if Benny had to undergo a similar process in absentia. I supposed that if he died my goose was finally cooked. My word against a dead man whom I had tried to bury preemptively. It turned out that Leonard was already acquainted with my defense lawyer, a man named Eviston. They had met on social occasions that are participated in by people completely unlike me. Leonard was a CPA who moved in high altitude circles. "He's a good man," Leonard said to me on the drive to the motel. This was supposed to cheer me up. Leonard's faith in my innocence was touching. It was not his faith, though, but the faith of Detective Coleman that I desired. I had not spoken with him since my reenactment out at The Site.

What did he make of all this? Had his years of experience taught him to recognize the signs of innocence? I tried to reassure myself, to bolster my own spirits, to take heart in the fact that every word I had said to him was true. But what good was The Truth when you were caught standing by an open grave shoveling dirt onto a man's body?

Maybe I would have to plea-bargain down to a lesser offense and spend the rest of my life trying to explain to a prison shrink that my actions fell under the aegis of temporary insanity. I would not deny it. I had been out of my mind when I dragged that asshole to the pit and began slopping dirt onto his unconscious carcass. I wanted him to wake up and see just what happens when a raving narcissist bites off more than he can chew.

This made me think of Oscar. Choked to death on a slice of bread, and Benny would not deign to give him the Heimlich. I would gladly speak for the prosecution at his trial, if he went to trial. The charge? Being an asshole. I would mimic the words of the taxi driver, who apparently had it in for me for reasons that were not unfathomable. I had sent him into the bathroom knowing full well he might not come out alive.

My shrink would have a field day dissecting that aspect of my personality. He would probably pocket a big chunk of change from the State to find out what the taxi driver already knew: I too was a jerk.

"Laura said she would accept a long-distance phone call from you if you wanted to talk to her," Leonard said after I got settled. I nodded and told him I would probably call her later in the evening, but for now I just wanted to lie down in the quietude of the motel and get some sleep.

"I'll be next door if you need me. We'll go to the store later and pick up a few things for you," meaning toothbrush, change of clothes, etc. And, of course, dinner. I was completely at the benevolent mercy of my wealthy brother-in-law, to whom this trip doubtless had the quality of a delightful jaunt. I pictured him calling his associates at his office in Albany that morning: "I have to fly down to Crestmoor and bail my brother-in-law out of jail. The cops nabbed him for attempted murder." "Who—Pete Larkey?" "Yep, they finally caught up with him." "It's always the quiet ones." "Golf Saturday?" "You bet, pal." They ring off. Leonard smiles to himself as he packs his suitcase while his wife scowls in the background, and his sister-in-law sits at the kitchen table mortified over a cooling cup of coffee and wondering why she didn't marry Philip Canby, that pre-med student who now owns a chain of foot clinics in Baltimore.

I sat down on the bed and toed my shoes off and let the bottoms of my feet sink into the wall-to-wall carpeting. I removed my watch and deliberately did not look at the time. Why bother? What had Time ever done for me? I unbuttoned and removed my shirt, then dragged my comb and billfold out of my back pocket. I set the comb on the nightstand next to the bed and opened my wallet to look at the twelve dollars I had been carrying with me since I had given the taxi driver the bulk of my ready cash.

I pulled the bills out to spread them, count them again, a five and seven ones, and a death moth fell from the fan of paper. It did not flutter into my face. It dropped like a fingernail-clipping onto my lap and lay there motionless. It was the tiniest thing, one wing enfolded against its body, and the other spread as if it had died in death throes trying to wriggle out of its leather coffin. How could such a tiny thing possess the spark of life? What is life anyway? A molecule? An electron? A particle? A wave? Einstein and his obsession with matter in motion. He was asking stupid questions. Here is the real question: How small can something be and still be alive? Did Oscar Easley lose more life than this moth had lost at the moment of his death? I reached down and touched the insect with the little finger of my right hand, tried to coax it to move, but it was dead. I nudged it, attempted to transmit the vital force like God touching Adam in the Sistine ceiling, but it spun to the floor, its final resting place the carpet of a Motel 6 on the outskirts of a town nobody ever heard of.

I lay down on the cool bedspread and closed my eyes.

When I awoke it was still light outside. I got up and peeked past the curtains, something I had always done upon awakening as if expecting the worst, and was never disappointed. The rental car was gone. Leonard was probably out having a drink with the man who was being paid to defend me against the calumny that would ship me to The Big House.

I could not let myself think that way. I had to remain loyal to my belief in truth and majesty. I let the curtain drop and walked over to the night table. I picked up my watch and looked at the dial: three thirty. That made me feel good. It was a good time of day. It was summer, there was not a cloud in the sky, and it was three thirty. It should always be three thirty. I allowed myself to think this way. I supposed that men in prison had similar thoughts on disparate subjects that gave them comfort. I had occasionally wondered why it was that men sentenced to The Chair, or even to prison for life, did not just kill themselves preemptively. There was nothing to look forward to, except the illusions of appeal, pardon, commutation, parole. Cling to life. It's all we know.

I was hungry. That's what life is. The search for food. Everything has revolved around that since the dawn of man. Find food. Find money to buy food. Surround yourself with gold and trade it for food. Prolong life to prolong the hunt to prolong life, etc. I sat down on the bed and put my shoes back on, my shirt, and stood in front of the mirror above the dresser and tried to make myself look presentable. I would not wait for Leonard to get back from his jolly afternoon snort with the lawyer. Maybe they had gone to the Lemon Tree. I did not want to know. I would never go there again. Rudy Flanagan would never say, "What'll it be, Pete?" to me again as long as I lived. I would see to that even if the State didn't.

I made sure I had my key, then I stepped outside the room and shut the door. I had never stayed at the Motel 6 but I knew it was only a few blocks from a McDonald's. Sleep, eat, drink, all the businesses cluster for the buck. I walked along the road wondering how many people in passing cars already knew me for what I was, the asshole who tried to bury a man alive. What were the papers saying? I didn't dare look at the morning edition, even though I kept passing newspaper boxes. My name would be in there, my address, the sordid details, the trial-by-media. Would the girl behind the counter at the Golden Arches gasp and refuse me service? I was entering a new world, fame tainted with vile rumor. How did innocent convicts deal with this, much less guilty convicts?

But nobody took notice of me in the McDonald's. I had been afraid I would have to eat on my walk back to the motel, but there were only a few people at the tables. I sat by a window and had my Last Meal, as I thought of it. Big Mac. Fries. Coke. It reminded me of my youth. College. High school. Grade school. In my father's youth, a hamburger was fifteen cents and a bag of fries was ten cents. It was a different world back then.

When I left the McDonald's I looked in the direction of my house, which was over the horizon. I calculated fourteen blocks from where I now stood. Traffic was light on the boulevard that linked up with Crestmoor Road farther south. For now, I was a free man, but how long would that last? Innocence and freedom were like oil and water in the universe I currently inhabited. It made me sick to look in that direction. How could I have done such a thing—drag a man into a ditch and cover him with dirt? What was inside of me that I had never examined before? The business of allowing the taxi driver to enter the bathroom even though I believed there might be an intruder seemed an extension of an unclean spirit that inhabited me, a thing capable of inexplicable violence, which was manifested by my appalling actions.

Or were they really so appalling? Was I merely human? Would any ordinary man have reacted the way I did? I was now thinking the way a lawyer might talk in court. But this is what lawyers do, extrapolate and manufacture innocence-by-association. Anybody would have done such a thing, and my client asserts that he did not go to the woods with malevolence on his mind or in his heart. Mister Benjamin Gruner is a liar, and the taxi driver is another one of his victims.

I stood with the sunlight warming my face. Had the police

found the gun yet? How could the gun have disappeared? I had full faith in the ability of the police to find anything. Every square inch of the woods would be searched in a situation this bizarre. I had picked up the gun and flung it, but I was not Superman, the Hulk, a steroid geek capable of tossing three pounds of steel five miles through the air. Goddamnit! Why was everything working against me? Lost evidence, lost fingerprints, the proof that I was the victim here, the innocent, the falsely accused, what kind of lousy fucking luck was dragging me toward the rocky shoals of three-to-five in Sing Sing?

I started walking south then. I did not want to go back to The Site, did not want to enter my house where poor Oscar had died under the laughing scrutiny of Benny the jerk genius asshole who would not help him dislodge that slice of suffocating bread, but within ten minutes I was back on Crestmoor Road moving toward Hawthorne Drive. I looked back at the parking lot of the Lemon Tree Lounge but did not see Leonard's rental. He and his drinking pal had probably chosen a classier joint to idly discuss my case before getting down to the serious business of comparing and contrasting liquid-center golf balls versus cork.

I crossed Hawthorne Drive and looked off to my right where the previous morning I had seen my car pause momentarily before moving on with Benny at the wheel and Morton on the road. I felt bleak. I wanted to leap back through Time and race to warn Morton. Look out! My car is after you again! I had not been at the wheel either time that my Ford had injured him. The thing seemed possessed.

I peered in the direction of my house. The road was empty. Even if someone had stopped to offer me a lift I would not have accepted a ride. This was the essence of all my troubles: interacting with people. I would have to watch out for that in the future. If I moved down to Mexico I would not be able to speak the language and thus would be left alone, the hermit Americano who lives out near the beach. He pays us for groceries once a week in U.S. currency and never leaves his hut. We think he is a sad man. The children peek at him from behind the trees, but we admonish them to leave him alone with his troubles. We hear strange noises coming from his hut at night but we cannot tell if it is weeping or laughter. *Vaya con Dios, pobre hombre.*

I neared my house and looked at it with revulsion. As far as I was concerned I no longer lived there. I did not want to enter that pit of turmoil and death. I kept my eyes askance as I passed the driveway and continued along the bisecting asphalt road that ran through the forest. I could see in the distance the place where Benny had forced me to turn left at gunpoint and enter the lovers' lane. As I said, the trees were skinny but not sparse. I could see into the woods, but what the trunks lacked in width they made up for in profusion. I could not see to the far side of the forest, which led into what I supposed were farm fields. I had never had cause to drive in that direction. Truth be told, I had never had cause to drive in any direction at all, not in Connecticut, Mill Valley, or Phoenix. I was a directionless man, tossed on the random currents of life, pulled toward meaningless destinations. Until today. Today I was going into the woods and do what the police had failed to do. Find that fucking gun. How could they have missed it? I imagined scores of men trudging through the woods with heads bowed, eyes scouring the ground. You see men like that on the news, searching for whomever must be found after relatives have reported them missing. You see them in the movies where the searchers are always successful, usually with deplorable results.

I came to the dirt two-track and turned left toward The

Site, my eyes already scanning the ground, even though realistically I could not have tossed the gun this far. But what did reality ever have to do with my life? Reality was an illusion—I approached my destiny as if the world was being created with every step I took. The past was not prologue. There was no precedence. I was in virgin territory. If I thought for one moment that the police had turned every single leaf and stone in this forest I would have given up before I left the McDonald's. Total denial was my only hope.

I came to the place of The Scuffle. Little yellow flags were still planted in the ground on wire stems. They were like hieroglyphs telling a story that could be interpreted only by men schooled in flags. But I could read it. I had written it in the dirt myself, and the taxi driver had added the punctuation marks. Here was the flag where I had landed on my ass, here is where he kicked and pummeled me, here is where a wad of duct tape had found its final resting place. The gun would not be here. Why had I not brought it with me instead of flinging it away like an orange peel? Benny was out cold, and if he had recovered and come at me I could have shot him, or else flung the gun aside and relied on my rage to take on a man suffering from a serious concussion. The taxi driver could have aided me . . . or else aided Benny. Probably the latter. The driver might have held me down while Benny plugged me, then thanked the driver for saving his life. The possibilities were endless. But why speculate? Deal with the illusory reality of NOW. I walked past The Scuffle and approached the scene of The Shovel Blow To The Head. I saw fewer possibilities here. If I had not hit Benny, he might have plugged the driver and then me, and then run for it. He would have been in the next county, the next state, before anyone found our bodies. The corpses eventually would have been found, probably this very afternoon. The taxi company would have put out the call to the police, and they would have driven into the woods like good search dogs. The bloody bodies of myself and the driver, and the two-foot grave, would have baffled them unto eternity. Benny would have made his escape. But all the evidence was now directed against me. I was suspect Numero Uno. Benny probably wept when he told his tale of getting assaulted at my front door. He would hold to that story. Inveterate liars are good at it. He would have shown up in court as a witness for the prosecution, wearing a new suit, a fresh haircut, with a long finger extended in the direction of the man who had shoveled dirt onto his carcass: me. The Accused. "I came to town to find a job, Your Honor, and he mauled me."

The prosecutor no doubt would mention the fact that a dead body had been found in my house earlier in the day, and that I had intentionally run a man down in my Ford and left him to die on the asphalt.

My defense lawyer rises to object, but it's already on the record: Mr. Peter Larkey is a debased sociopath who gets his kicks making people suffer.

I looked farther along the road in the direction of The Grave. I might as well call it that. Denial has never actually benefited me. I measured the distance with my eyes. I had chased him at least fifteen yards before I hit him. I had no memory of reference, of relativity, I had simply taken off running. I had to put a stop to the linear progression of the terrible inevitability.

I turned so that I was "facing" Benny's back and recalled the moment of the overhead swing. Benny fell. I altered my target and hammered his hand.

I squatted near a yellow flag and made as if to pick up the gun. My memory of that moment was inexact. I grabbed it and tossed it, flung it in an arc into the woods. I looked in the direction I imagined I had thrown it. I had no memory of the force of ejection. The gun left my hand and a sensation of safety, of less danger, had come over me. Benny was unconscious and defenseless, which allowed me to leap up and run to the driver.

I looked into the woods. I could see sky between the trunks. The gun was in there somewhere. The police could not possibly have missed it. This was logic. My logic. Another tool in my arsenal of useless weapons. Anything can happen in the heat of a chaotic moment. Ask a man who has returned to an old battlefield. Everything has changed. The stone wall he hid behind as the Germans approached turns out to be a random collection of medium-sized rocks, but in his memory it was a massive shield built by Titans.

I raised my eyes to the treetops.

As I said, I had never seen an animal in this place. The fact that I had never seen or heard birds during my two trips into the woods a long time ago could be accounted for by the fact that they would have gone silent at the approach of a human being. A logical conclusion. Squirrels hide. Deer freeze. Man— the center of the universe, as Albert Einstein so hubristically put it—stands there thinking he is alone while timid, savage eyes measure his every move. In what I imagined to be the direct line of my throw, I saw what appeared to be a bird's nest. It was twenty feet off the ground near the crotch of two branches, a Y where the bird who had built it had gathered enough twigs to fashion an avian condo. It hung like Spanish moss, although perhaps no more than a foot down the side of the trunk. Maybe storm drip had pulled the mud and twigs earthward. What did I know of nature, of the way things worked in the wild, the way creatures dealt with frustration? Why do beavers chop down trees with their teeth and build shelters? How could an animal have the innate intelligence to build a house? What did Albert Einstein know of beavers? But then experts are theorists who answer their own questions to their own satisfaction and then award themselves medals.

I made my way into the woods perhaps ten feet and looked up the tree. It had a thick trunk with low, skinny branches that I could reach if I made the effort, leaped, pulled myself up like a boy who thinks that climbing trees is a feat that will help him achieve the goals of adulthood. I'm talking about myself here, when every accomplishment seemed like an unheralded omen: you will grow up to be successful.

I leaped. I was thirty-eight years old and on the cusp of physical uselessness, but I caught hold of a lower branch and scrambled with my feet before common sense could tell me no.

A chin-up, another grab, and I was on the sylvan ladder. From there it was just a matter of slow and gentle steps, testing the strength of branches, a thing learned in boyhood, a part of the foolish idea that doing something complicated and meaningless was a portent of great things. I embraced the trunk with my left arm as I snatched at branches that helped me to climb higher. In my youth I had found that pine trees in city parks were best for this. Branches all the hell over the place, rendering less significant the achievement of climbing to the top of a fir and gazing out over the rooftops of the city.

But I was larger now, heavier, thus unfamiliar with sway. My weight set the upper trunk in motion. This began to seem a bad idea. What if the trunk snapped and fell? How old was this tree? But I was only five feet below the bird's nest, so I continued on. If the gun had lodged in the nest through the fantastic unlikelihood of my artless panic toss, I would find out. I told myself it was not too late to turn back. But I needed to reach in and feel those pounds of cold steel lying in hiding like a laughing child. As I made the final push I moved slower

224

and held tighter, the tree swaying, a breeze seeming to pick up at this altitude, until I came face-to-face with the bottom edge of the nest, the strung waterfall of twigs mud-baked tight against the trunk.

I reached up and poked my hand into the nest, and realized I might be bitten by a bird, a squirrel, a snake for crying out loud, even spiders, lizards, but all I felt was a hole. Emptiness. Twig walls. No eggs, no life, just an abandoned nest.

"What are you doing up there?"

I made an awkward move to shift my chin so I could look down. Benny was standing on the road grinning up at me. "What kind of an idiot are you, Larkey?"

It was like seeing Lucifer. In my childhood I had dreams of haunted houses that scared me awake, but they did not compare to the sight of that demon below me with a grin on his face and murder in his heart. I could smell his heart from twenty feet.

"Get down here, asshole," he said. There was a lilt of laughter in his voice, bully laughter, preamble to gleeful violence.

I did not speak. I embraced the trunk with both arms and looked in the direction of Crestmoor but did not have a clear view of the town or the road that ran past my house.

"Nobody's coming to help you, Larkey, so get your ass out of that tree and I mean right now."

I looked to the top of the trunk, which narrowed to a spray of small branches, useless. There was no up, there was only down. Nonetheless, my altitude gave me a false sense of security, which I badly needed.

"Don't insult my intelligence, peat moss," he said, lowering his head and shaking it with disgust. "You know I'm going to get you down out of that tree, and when I do you'll be sorry you made me do it the hard way."

225

He was right. I knew I could not stay here forever. When I was a child my grandmother used to recite a rhyme: "Timothy Ticklefeather L.L.D. lived in the top of a very tall tree, he gathered the rain in his godpoppa's cup and nibbled on the nuts that the squirrels brought up." The citizens came from town to talk the man down but in the end Timothy climbed higher until he disappeared. As a child I wondered why anybody would give a damn that a long-bearded doctor of letters refused to come down from a tree. But I never wondered why he went up there in the first place. I understood it intuitively.

Benny knelt on the road as if in genuflection. He reached to the back of his belt—then whipped his fist around with a fluid motion and gripped both hands as one would to aim a pistol with especial accuracy. "Get your fucking ass out of that tree or I'll shoot," he said. His left hand was bandaged.

Here it was then. I could feel the decision-making process dwindling. Take a bullet at the top of the tree, or climb down and take it on the ground. If the bullet didn't kill me, maybe the fall would. The choices were limited to two: death here or death there. I raised my face to the blue sky, then looked directly at the tree trunk. I leaned my forehead against the bark and closed my eyes. I tightened my embrace. I would take the bullet and the fall. My last living act would be to refuse coercion. I would thumb my nose at my entire past.

"Let's go, Larkey. Down. On the ground. Right now."

I wondered if my ex would learn the facts surrounding my death. Would she be understandably amused? Of all the ways a man might die, only her ex-husband Pete could engineer a scenario like this. It warmed my heart in an odd way to know that my last thought would be of her. We had once been in love. All fear left me then. As my friend Morton said in the cloying darkness of the Lemon Tree Lounge: "Was I born for a purpose, or for no reason at all?" It now occurred to me that this might be the answer: we are born for a purpose, but we die without ever learning the purpose because it's none of our business.

"If you don't climb down I'll shoot you down," Benny said. "It's gonna hurt, Larkey. But don't worry, that'll just be the pain coming to say goodbye."

I readied myself for the shot. Perhaps I would literally, technically, medically die halfway to the ground, my ghost floating out of my descending body. My death would be a poem.

"You're a moron, Larkey."

I tried not to squint my already closed eyes, but some things are impossible. The survival instinct cannot be abrogated by logic. A bullet travels eight hundred feet per second. Only something as ignorant as a human body would try to shield itself with a squint.

I felt the tree vibrate. I opened my eyes and looked down. Benny had leaped to the first branch and was pulling himself up. He was climbing the tree. "Hit me with a goddamn shovel you sonofabitch I'll break your fucking neck!" he grunted as he levered his bulk onto the lowest branch that would give him firm footing.

Where was his gun?

Why didn't he shoot me?

My last image of him was pointing that thing at me—but what thing? Had I really seen a gun? As the hulk squirmed below me I thought back a few seconds and pictured what I had seen, and in that instant realized he had been bluffing. A quick whip of the hand, an emulation of aiming, but it was only his fingers pointed at me. I did not see a muzzle, I saw only what he wanted me to think I saw. Everything about his posture had said "gun," but he was bluffing. It had the quality of a verbal threat, playground bullying, intimidation—but it was simply the malevolent body language of a raised fist. I became furious that he had planted terror in my mind with his mock stance.

I began my descent.

He had already made ten feet, but the slob was not used to climbing. God only knew, but he might have spent the last ten years lying slack on a bunk in San Quentin. His breathing was heavy. His face was red with effort and rage and desperation. His bandaged hand was giving him trouble. I surprised him with my sudden concession to gravity. I felt like a child as the branches slowed me, bent to drop me lower, I was Batman in gymnastic free fall. He froze and watched as my body approached, then tried to duck as I stomped the top of his head.

He fell.

A ten-foot drop with branches impeding his descent accompanied by desperate cries of "agh" and "shit" and landed with a thud.

I reversed direction and climbed back to my perch beneath the nest. Benny staggered to his feet, came at the tree, gripped it like a throat and began throttling it, but the trunk was too thick to do more than make the leaves tremble in unison with the breeze.

"Nice try," I said. I knew this would infuriate him, but so what? My destiny was a given. I would live or die. There would be no citizens coming from town. Benny had left the hospital, this was all I knew.

He looked up at me with the somber, expressionless fury of a man who has no response to the worst of all possible put-downs: nice try. I'm talking emasculation. Man is the center of a universe that will not budge.

"I brought gasoline with me, Larkey. I'll burn this fucker

to the ground."

I looked along the road but saw no vehicle in which he might have hauled a gallon of gas. I had heard no sound of a car approaching. He had walked here, I was sure of it.

I leaned a bit farther out from the tree, gathered a wad of phlegm, and spat. It spread like an umbrella as it fell. He could see the spittle coming toward him, his eyes as wide as a child's. He turned, ducked, ran back to the road swatting at his head as if battling bees. I was wrong. "Nice try" was not the worst insult. Spitting held that title, was as old as the human race, older than the spoken word.

He looked at the backs of his hands as if to check whether I had hit my target, then looked up at me.

"I don't know what you think you're doing, Larkey," he said. "You're only making it worse. See that hole?" He pointed at the grave. "When I get you down out of that tree I'm going to finish the job I started last night. I'm intellectually superior to you, so you can't win. You're like a little kid, Larkey. Only little kids spit. Why don't you come down and fight me like a man?"

"Beg me," I said.

"What?"

"Beg me and I'll come down."

This made his face red. He did not have a comeback. I had given him an order, do this and I'll do that.

"Do I threaten your ego?" I said. I was taking my cues from him. I remembered our conversation from the night before. He was a word man. "Does your neck hurt from looking up at me?" I said. Observe, remark, and annoy, that was his method. Where are your socks, are you a hippie? Distract and rattle. Easy to do when you're pointing a gun at someone—or sitting in a tree. I leaned out and spat again.

"I'm going to kill you, Larkey," he said. It was the grumble of a bear circling prey crouched inside a fortress, a cluster of rocks, a beaver lodge.

"When?" I said. "I'm waiting, Benny. When are you going to kill me? You're too slow. I bet you were a slow learner in school." Saying these things made me feel as if a strong wind was blowing through my mind. I was baiting him. Did I have a death wish or simply a wish to hurry the inevitable? I was in a position I had never been in before: total helplessness. Most of my helplessness in the past had involved exits that I had deliberately ignored.

I looked up at the nest again, the thing that had lured me to this precarious perch. I reached up and took hold of the lower half of the nest and tore it gently away like the bottom half of an ice-cream cone, hoping the gleaming blue steel of a .38 would reveal itself, but nothing dropped from the hole, not even a sparrow skull. It was empty. My theory had been proven entirely wrong, but this was nothing new. It was a confirmation of all the theories on the subject of hope that I had ever entertained. Then a small rock hit my hand. I looked down and saw Benny chucking another rock at me. His bandaged palm was cluttered with rocks that he had gathered while I was testing my theory on hope.

"You'll come down bleeding!" he shrieked.

"Only girls throw rocks!" I shouted.

I could not help but feel that the banality of my remark would make him go ballistic. For one thing, girls do not throw rocks. Boys throw rocks. They think rock-throwing will help them achieve great goals—perhaps in the major leagues. Girls braid dandelion stems and collect seashells. I expected him to stop throwing the rocks and extrapolate upon my banality, mock me, but he was beyond sarcasm. I had penetrated his soft heel. If he had possessed an axe, I would have been down in no time.

The rocks proved too much for him. He dropped them and began rubbing his shoulder. "What the fuck are you doing up there anyway, you intellectual midget?"

Now we were back to that.

He looked around in all directions, then looked at me. "I know where you live," he said. "You'll come down sometime. You can't get away from me. You'll never get away from me. The cops will never catch me. You'll go to sleep every night for the rest of your life scared shitless!"

With that he turned and began trotting toward the center of the forest. He passed the grave and disappeared from view, became a dwindling noise in the underbrush. How I wished I had found the gun in the nest. At this juncture I would have finished the job I had started last night and allowed a goddamn jury to parse the concept of "intent."

I clung to the trunk, with my forehead against the bark and my eyes closed. I assumed Benny was hiding in wait. If I climbed to the ground, he would break from the bushes like a charging bull and finish me off with a rage greater than mine because he had only tricked me into thinking he had a gun, whereas I had branded him with words. The power of language is immeasurable. The men who wrote the Bible understood this. Language is the true magic of the world. Lives are altered by nouns and verbs. Wars begin in the moist depths of vocal chords.

"What are you doing up there?"

I looked down and saw Officer Wilson standing on the road.

His police cruiser was parked thirty yards away. I had not heard it, but maybe Benny had. Maybe Benny was no different from myself, attuned to the approach of police vehicles in the way that I was attuned to the approach of guests when my ex and I held parties. This was not an unreasonable assumption.

A man who lived like Benny would have his radar out at all times, harkening to the sounds of potential capture. Not unlike myself at all.

I began working my way down through the branches. "Unholster your weapon!" I shouted. "Benny is here!" I scrambled without élan, no longer feeling like a comic-book character at ease scaling heights. "Pull your gun!" I shouted. "Benny tried to kill me!"

I caught quick glances at Wilson as I came down. He did as he was told, though not necessarily because of my warnings. He backed away as he drew his weapon. Thank God for that anyway. I didn't care why he did it, just as long as he had it ready when Benny exploded from the bushes in a self-destructive leap of revenge.

I dropped the last five feet and squatted like a monkey. Wilson held the barrel skyward, professional wariness masking his face. My head swiveled back and forth in true simian fashion. I was poised and ready. The two of us could take Benny. He would die today if I had anything to say about it.

"Are you all right, Mr. Larkey?" Wilson said.

"He went down the road," I said, rising and pointing deeper into the woods.

"Who did?"

"Benny. The guy that . . . that . . . tried to *bury* me last night."

He turned and looked beyond the grave where the road succumbed to the jungle.

"You saw him here?" Wilson said.

"Yes! He . . . he . . . he tried to climb the tree. He wanted to *get* me!"

The sheer force of my news ought to have spurred him to action, but he merely stood looking along the road, then back at me, then along the road. I knew now that he doubted

232

my word. He had found me up a tree, hugging the trunk, obviously a nut whose word held no weight.

"You saw him?" Wilson said.

"Yes! He tried to climb up and drag me down. He threw rocks at me."

I looked at the base of the tree, searched for the rocks he had dropped, but saw nothing except another in a long line of odd stories devoid of evidence.

"How long ago did you see him?"

"A minute ago! He must have heard you coming. He gave up and ran down the road."

"Come with me," Wilson said.

He led me back to his vehicle. I was in for it again. The bracelets, the compression chamber, the ride north. Did County General have a psychiatric ward?

"You have to go after him! He threatened to kill me!"

"Get in," Wilson said, opening the shotgun door.

I slid in and sat staring through the windshield. Wilson took forever to walk around the front of the car and climb into the driver's seat. When he got settled he said, "Benjamin Gruner escaped from the hospital a little over an hour ago. We've been searching for him."

"How did he escape?"

Wilson looked at me. I read his eyes. The facts in the case were none of my business. The investigation was ongoing. He plucked his microphone from the dashboard and spoke to the dispatcher. There was jargon, code words, numbers, but I caught the English part. "Last seen in Weaver's Wood."

What did he say?

He hung up the microphone and looked at me. "Did he chase you up the tree?"

I was caught off guard. I had never known the name of the forest behind my house. In the heat of all this I was sidetracked by a curious historical fact.

"No," I replied. "I was already up there."

A cop-squint creased his face. "What were you doing up in the tree?"

Oh God. How long must I go on revealing my idiocy? Why did people ask me questions I did not want them to ask? Why was it that every question I was confronted with in life filled me with shame and embarrassment? I took a deep breath and let it out slowly, as slowly as every truth that ever came out of my mouth.

"I was looking for the gun," I said.

"What gun?" he said. His voice had an edge. Cops do not treat guns lightly.

"The gun Benny held on me last night when he made me dig the grave."

Wilson looked ahead to the spot where the piled earth surrounding the grave had dried to the color of the road. "We know where the gun is," he said.

"You do?"

Why did I say that? You say things like that to guests at parties. You do not make policemen repeat themselves.

"Yes, we found the gun," he said.

I closed my eyes. My hand involuntarily slapped my face and held. Absolution.

"Did you think the gun was up in the tree?" he said.

It would never end. I lowered my hand and nodded. Now he would know that I had no faith in the police department. Who did I think I was, Holmes outwitting Lestrade?

"I don't get it," he said. "What made you think it was in the tree?"

"I thought I might have accidentally tossed it up into a bird's nest at the top of that tree. I thought maybe . . . you know . . . your men overlooked it."

He leaned forward and peered in the direction of the place where I had perched. "We brought search dogs in this morning but they didn't gather at the base of the tree."

"You did?"

"If that gun was up there, they would have barked."

"Are dogs really that good?"

"You would not believe how good bloodhounds are," he said. "They can find anything anywhere if it's been touched by a man. They could smell a snot-rag on the moon."

A single chuckle erupted from my belly.

"The driver had it," he said.

"What?"

"The taxi driver had the gun in his possession."

The radio barked. Wilson picked up the mike and spoke, but I did not hear what he said. I heard only what he had just finished saying. The taxi driver had the gun.

He hung up the mike. "Hold on a sec. We're backing out of here."

He started the engine, threw it into gear, turned his torso and slapped an arm across the seatback, and guided the cruiser in reverse at a high rate of speed toward Crestmoor Road. I thrilled at the weird sense of flying backwards. I was a participant in the crucial action of legal reckless driving. He braked. He flipped on his overhead lights, the red flash painting the sunstruck trunks. "Reinforcements coming," he said. "We'll stay right here."

I sat frozen, my shock at the news he had given me suspended as I listened for the sounds of sirens, but I did not hear any. The reinforcements were approaching with silence and cunning. Surround the woods. The lasso effect. Tighten the noose! I could already smell the perp walk.

"We found it during a search of his taxicab."

"What?"

235

"The gun."

He misunderstood my question. He had interrupted my thoughts, my fantasy, my pleasure. I was, in fact, asking him to repeat his statement. But I did not correct him.

"He confessed to taking it," Wilson said. "Detective Coleman was talking to the driver in his office when the call came through from the hospital. Apparently, Benjamin Gruner took advantage of a lapse of security." Wilson seemed reluctant to make this statement. It did not reflect well on the majesty of the law in Crestmoor. "He made a trip to the john and didn't come back. There was an adjoining room. It had a door of its own to the john, but it was supposed to be locked. A nurse allowed him to go in there alone. He should have been accompanied by a deputy."

"Maybe he jimmied the lock," I said.

He glanced at me but made no comment. I could not keep my mouth shut. But I had done this before, the amateur who pretends to see things a professional has overlooked because he is inured to the obvious. My pretensions are legion.

"Could you do me a favor, Officer Wilson?" I said.

"Glad to, Mr. Larkey."

"Could you not tell anyone why I was up in that tree?"

He looked out through the windshield, raised his chin, rubbed his Adam's apple with his palm and said, "Based on what you told me, Mr. Larkey, I can only conclude that you took refuge in the tree while being pursued by a dangerous man. That's where I found you anyway. I'll leave the detailed explanations up to you. I'm certain Detective Coleman will want to hear your side of the story."

I felt ashamed for having made the request. It was something that would be asked by a teenaged boy appalled at the prospect of cheerleaders glimpsing his reality. But I had surrendered to it. The events of the past two days had left me winded, leached of confidence, depleted of self-worth. I had thrown my request at Officer Wilson like a manic actor cleaning out his dressing room so he could retire to obscurity in the unlikeliest of locations—the Ozarks, Bull Shoals. I had passed through that part of the country after I got out of the army. It was the most obscure place I had ever visited, and I was once stationed in Fort Huachuca.

"If he's in there we'll flush him out," Wilson said, but whether to reassure me or himself I could not tell. The capture of Benny would change the dynamic. My word would take precedence over his. I was to be believed. He would undergo a grilling, this man who had been found unconscious in a hole while Pete Larkey stood like Stan Laurel dumping dirt down his collar.

But I did not respond to Wilson's reassurance. I was still recovering from the physical aftereffects of my tree climb. It was not simply the climb, though, but the nerve-shattering shock of Round Two with Benny that made my arms and legs twitch with the reverberation that you see in the hands of dipsomaniacs at the Lemon Tree Lounge.

"How is Mr. Morton doing?" I said. Surely there would be no question now that Morton had not been run down by me.

Wilson looked over and nodded. "I checked on him this morning. The doc says he's going to recover. This was the second trauma his body received during the past six months and he's a bit old to bear up under all that."

"It was my car that fell on him at Mac's Garage."

"I know," Wilson said. He knew everything. I was a yellow flag in his jurisdiction, a hieroglyph that he and his brothers in blue could read like blind men fingering braille.

Police cruisers arrived and stopped on the road. No other cars had passed since we had backed up to the entrance. The county could blast Crestmoor Road off the face of the earth with dynamite and it would have no impact on vehicular stats. I lived in a cracker box at the edge of an infinitely long dead-end road.

"Stay seated, Mr. Larkey, I'll be right back." Wilson opened the door and got out. I looked to see if Coleman was with the arrivals, but no. I assumed he was back at HQ interrogating the taxi driver. This became my new focus. Benny would be lassoed, hauled in, he was already forgotten. What in the hell was the deal with the taxi driver? I wanted to ask Wilson, get the lowdown, scope out the grim dope on that fucker who had hustled me out of one hundred bucks. Christ, barge his way into a man's house and swagger around like a drunk gorilla, demanding answers to questions which, admittedly, he deserved. But I didn't care. He was a bully. An asshole. But what was his status now? What was the deal with the gun?

Wilson spoke to his partners, then came back to the cruiser, got in, and wheeled us around. "What's going to happen now?" I said. I couldn't bear not knowing what was happening. I was not really a part of this thing, a cop, an active member, I was only a stowaway, a hitchhiker, an uninvited guest, but I was there.

"I'm going to drop you off at the station and then return to the woods," he said.

I felt an urge to say, "Stay here, I won't get in the way." And besides, how could a cop leave a scene when things were coming down? How could he resist the urge to ignore procedure and remain at his post in case the shit storm flew? That's what Starsky and Hutch would do. Tackle Benny as he burst from a bush. Pistol-whip the bastard. That's what I would do if I had a gun and a badge. The badge would be requisite, of course. I had seen plenty of movies about corrupt cops—the dark side of the blue line that allows old ladies to dream in peace.

But I didn't say anything. I clung to my perception of myself as a fool and rode in silence. When the police station came into view, I saw three cruisers parked out front and a dozen cops standing by the door. Things were coming down. The APB was in full swing. Homicidal maniac on the loose! Off-duty cops, that's what I saw. They had grabbed their pistol belts off the bedposts, kissed their women goodbye, and said to hell with overtime I'll be home when I get home.

Doubtless, I was wrong. Television does things to me that I probably should not admit to.

"Thank you for your cooperation, Mr. Larkey. I might see you later this evening. Detective Coleman will probably want—"

"A written statement," I said. Christ that felt rude, but Wilson only smiled. We were as one in this scenario. Paperwork was the bane of peacemakers.

"You can go on into his office," Wilson said. "He's waiting for you."

Wilson did know everything. My life was a crude map. I walked toward the front door of the building as Wilson drove away, his siren on, his red lights flashing. Run, Benny, run. The Law is on your tail, you cretinous peanut-brain. Bloodhounds will lick your blood from a ditch if you get cute.

Those were the thoughts I had as I walked toward the group of stern-looking officers standing by the door awaiting their orders. Some of them were sipping from coffee cups. Their world was on red alert. I had the urge to tell them who I was. And who was I? I was the man at the center of the universe. I would never stop being that in my eyes. I tried not to think about it. As far back as I could remember, thinking had not put one goddamn nickel in my pocket. But I would no longer fight it. I would simply accept that which I could not change, and try to get to bed as soon as possible.

as I made my way toward Detective Coleman's office. Cops had always made me nervous, especially at traffic stops, but this was an American response to raw power. Beyond the thin blue line lies chaos. This is the stone wall. Do not cross it. I entered Detective Coleman's office. He was not there. A uniformed man was waiting, and he told me to have a seat, that the detective would be with me soon. He left me alone in there. I wondered if the knife was still in the drawer. They had found the knife and they had found the gun. You cannot hide anything from men like these. That only happens in movies. Crimes do go unsolved, but not crimes by men like me.

The wait was not long, five minutes, then Detective Coleman came into the room and quietly closed the door.

"Thank you for coming here," he said, as though I had a choice. His was the courtesy of kings. He moved around behind his desk and sat down. "I spoke with Officer Wilson. He filled me in on what happened. He said he told you about Benjamin Gruner's escape from the hospital." He smiled. "But then I guess you learned that the hard way."

I nodded. That's how I learn everything.

"Have they caught him yet?" I said.

"Not yet. We will."

He pulled out a desk drawer as if that subject were closed, irrelevant, old news. He withdrew a folder, laid it on his desk, and opened it. There were pages filled with handwriting.

"All right, let me fill you in on the details," he said. "Last night during the incident in the woods, the taxi driver found the gun lying on the road. In all probability it bounced off a tree after you tossed it. He told us that he picked up the flashlight after he knocked you out. When he saw the gun, he picked it up and put the flashlight back on the ground and ran away. It's clear from our investigation that he is not able to identify you as the man who assaulted him outside your house. However, he did believe you were the man who had knocked him unconscious and transported him to the woods. After he radioed for help he opened his trunk and hid the gun under the spare tire."

"Why did he take the gun?" I said.

Coleman frowned and looked down at the witness statement. "He said he was surprised to find his taxi parked in the woods, but he got in and drove out of there. Later on, when he learned that both yourself and Benjamin Gruner were suspects in this incident, he decided to keep the gun hidden in the trunk."

"But why?" I said. "Didn't he know it would be evidence?"

Didn't he think like me? Didn't he watch TV?

"He told me he simply wanted to keep the gun. He said he has a collection of guns. We checked into that. It's true. He has a small cache of rifles, shotguns, pistols. All legal. He has a membership in a target-shooting club. He told me he wanted to make it a part of his collection."

Maybe so, but I could not help feeling that he had a more significant reason.

"Aside from you and Benjamin Gruner," Coleman continued, "he was the only person who could have taken the gun during the time between the assault on yourself and his call for help. But when it became clear that the thirty-eight was a crucial piece of evidence, the driver finally broke down under questioning and told the truth. We searched his taxi and found the gun under the tire."

I did not doubt that the driver wanted to add it to his collection. Imagine finding a pistol used by John Dillinger or Wesley Hardin. What aficionado would give up such a rare find? A handkerchief used to wipe the sweat off Elvis Presley's forehead ends up on a golden pedestal.

241

But no. As far as I was concerned the driver kept the gun because he wanted to see me swing.

"Were Benjamin Gruner's fingerprints on the gun?" I said.

He nodded. "Gruner had handled the gun. We also found your prints as well as those of the taxi driver, but your prints were on the barrel. Do you remember picking it up by the barrel?"

"That's right," I said. "I did do that." But then I wondered— had that been a leading question? Was Detective Coleman helping me? When it came time to talk to the DA, did he want me to say the right thing? Was this a benevolent form of police corruption? A chess master prodding his pupil to make the key move that would lead to victory? Were the two of us sitting on the shady side of the thin blue line? I hoped to Christ we were. I was willing to be led by the nose through the murky and byzantine pathways of The Law in order to put Benny in a lockup for life.

On the other hand, I felt ambivalent about the prick who drove for the Ace Taxicab Service. How could a man do that? Sorry sonofabitch to hide a crucial piece of evidence just to get even with a man who had allowed him to walk into a potential death trap. How could another person be just like me?

"What were you doing in the woods?" Coleman said, bringing me out of my asinine reverie. If I could ignore my mind for the time being and keep my mouth shut on certain issues, I just might find myself sleeping in my own bed that night. I wondered where my brother-in-law was.

"I went there to look for the gun," I admitted. I knew then that my humiliating cheerleader secret would come out. I had climbed the tree to see if the gun was in a bird's nest. It occurred to me that maybe it was a squirrel's nest. It now seemed awfully large and ambitious to have been fashioned by a thing with feathers. Do squirrels build nests? Are they the beavers of the sky? My knowledge of useless facts is pathetically limited.

"What made you think you could find the gun?" he said.

My unbridled ego. What other answer was there? When an amateur gets it into his head that he can out-think the experts, the slapstick commences. "I don't know," I lied. "I guess I just wanted to reenact the moment that I threw the gun to get a better fix on where it might have landed."

But this, in fact, was the truth. It was exactly why I had gone to the woods. I was not insulting the experts in blue. They had come up empty-handed. I was only trying to help in my feeble way. Why did I think that every goddamned thing I said to an authority figure was a lie? It was a question I decided to leave unanswered.

Did they catch Benny the genius? Of course they did. He had fled the forest. He traveled to the far side that I had never visited before, had crossed a field into the nearby township of Belmont, where the APB was in effect. The whole state was on alert. The man was crazy. He thought he was a fox. He had run down my friend Morton and skirted the police before they understood what had happened and who they should be looking for. He had made his slip from the hospital due to the ineptitude of the staff. But why hold that against them? How many criminals does the average nurse find in her charge during a year? A nurse lets him into the john and the next thing she knows the man who envisions himself a Pimpernel is out the window and down the fire escape and off and away. And where does he run? To my house, of course, to find me, to make me suffer, to punish me for turning him into a buffoon. Imagine getting knocked on the back of the head

243

with a shovel. Forget the pain. It was the humiliation that turned his world into a red-hot burning cinder of revenge.

He had broken into my house to hide in wait, only to see me walk down the road from the Motel 6, pass my house, and enter the woods. He thought he was cagey. He exited my house by the back door and entered the woods along the same route that my ex and I once walked in the deluded belief that this would be our Eden for years to come. Perhaps "deluded" is too strong a word. Maybe "hopeful" is the word. We were trying to be happy, make this gift of a forest a part of our home, our lives, to stake our pedestrian claim. It didn't work out. In my experience, things related to hope rarely work out.

Like an animal, Benny crept between the trees, paralleling my advance until I entered the lovers' lane where he watched and bided his time for me to approach the grave where he would make short work of me. Let the police find my body in the very grave that I had dug. The last laugh. How dare I bollix his plans? How dare I expose his ineptitude by coming after him when he had made a run for the taxi driver? I still remember the sound the shovel made when it hit his head. It sounded like this: "conk!" A word from the funny papers. He landed face-down. His nose was bloodied. The police thought I battered his face with the shovel before dragging him to the hole where I intended to bury him alive. His plans had been undone by a man whom he had accused of possessing an inferior intellect.

But who was Benny? He was a nobody. He had served time in prison for robbery, assault, a history of drug use going back to his teens. Christ knows what his childhood was like. A rap sheet a mile long. He had shown up at my house with a companion he had met along the road, Oscar, a doppelganger with a rap sheet of his own, two unemployed losers looking to rob houses to support themselves as they made their way across the land toward their next robbery. A number of unsolved break-ins on their route were attributed to them. Houses robbed. Stores shoplifted. Their antics were caught on security cameras, small packages of food and drink tucked into clothing, leaving the stores hurriedly before the clerks knew what was up. Two-bit crooks feeding themselves with snacks and pop, men without purpose looking for a big score. Criminals. Sociopaths. But to me they were emissaries from the gods. I did not mention this to Detective Coleman. He had enough work on his hands without having to deal with the mind of an unemployed loser who viewed himself as the victim of mythological beings, as had Ulysses and every other Greek who had refused to take responsibility for the mess he had created by taking a chance in terra incognita. Those invisible magicians in the sky have their eyes out for hubris. I was easy pickings.

I sat in a small room at the Crestmoor Police Station and wrote my final witness statement. Backed into a corner, I confessed my real reason for climbing the tree. No use playing hide-and-seek with the gods in blue, the district attorney, a judge, a jury, the people who would be sorting the truth from the clever subterfuge articulated by Benjamin Gruner's defense attorney. Tell it like it was, and hope that as little of my statement as possible would end up in the papers.

I kept the facts to a minimum. I had climbed the tree to see if the gun might have landed up there. I did not disparage the professionalism of the men with badges who had searched the woods, nor their miracle hounds with noses like Hubble telescopes. The details of Benny's hospital escape and subsequent hunt for me emerged after they captured him. He blurted it all out. This did not come as a surprise. There was something infantile about Benny. He came to my house that night to find out if I had identified him to the police in the hit-and-run, and if not, to get rid of me because I could now identify him. He bushwhacked the driver to use his cab to haul my body to the woods. The cabbie had shown up in the wrong place at the right time. "You gotta be ready to make exceptions to rules, see? You gotta be prepared for contingencies, see?" He had seized the moment. It must have made him proud. He was covering all the bases, covering his ass, and moving on. A deranged mop-up. Leave no witnesses. He couldn't wait to describe how clever he was, the finesse he had displayed after running down my poor friend Morton, the slick way he had slipped out of the hospital, the masterful tracking of yours truly like Leatherstocking keeping an eye on a band of Mohicans hiking through the wilds of New England. "See what I did! Aren't I great!" I imagined him saying that to his interrogators.

Doubtless he had no real skills, no talent, could not paint, write symphonies, sculpt in bronze, pen immortal poems. His talent lay in devious means of getting what he wanted, needed, craved, even if it was only revenge. But even at that he was no good. I had thwarted him, and the authorities had caught him in the most banal of circumstances. They found him cringing in a chicken coop in the backyard of a suburban house on the edge of Belmont. How I wished I had been there with a camera. Snap him being dragged out covered with feathers, genius-boy with bird shit on his knees, his palms, his plans. I missed his perp walk. He was transferred in a van from Belmont to Crestmoor, where they locked him in the slammer and brought an end to two of the worst days of my life. I've had other bad days but nothing quite like them. But I got off lucky. The real loser was Morton.

I won't go into the details of the damage done to his body, but it involved cracked bones. He was covered by insurance, so that monstrosity of life was relegated to the background, but his health took a permanent blow. He now walks with a cane. I got over to the hospital after Detective Coleman finished with me. As exhausted as I was, I knew that my physical and mental trauma was a bagatelle as compared to my friend whose bête noire was my green Ford, which I got rid of a few weeks later. I gave it to a junkyard. I requested that they cube it and send it to Goldfinger. The young man at the auto yard did not get my joke. But that was all right. I needed no audience but myself. The gods will never wrestle my hubris to the ground and strangle it.

Prior to that, Officer Wilson drove me to the impound lot where my car sat among rows of other autos with their own sad tales waiting to be told. It was like visiting a dog pound. Not many late-model cars. The rich tended not to get into fixes, and when they did, the fix was in. I popped open the hood and wiggled the cables on my battery for the same reason that all people do things too late. I made a mental note to stop at Apex on the way home and buy a new battery. Sixty bucks. The price of freedom and peace of mind. Cheaper than a psychiatrist.

I drove home and took a shower and did my best to ignore the ghost of poor Oscar, the victim of Benjamin Gruner's contemptible condescension. He had let a man die in his presence. I made a mental note to mention this to the proper authorities when his trial came up. Does a man have a moral imperative to perform the Heimlich Maneuver? There lies a profound question to be debated on talk shows in between commercials for diet crapola.

I drove to County General and made my way up to the second floor and asked if Mr. Morton was available for visitors. The nurse told me I could go into his room. I wondered if this was the same nurse who had made the professional blunder of letting Benny use the john. I supposed not. For some reason,

I thought it would be a young nurse, a recent graduate who was starting out on the long road of human misery, duplicity, hard knocks, moral quandaries, and the devastating fact of human error. For all I knew she had been fired.

I walked down the hallway and paused at Room 222. I will admit it. I laughed inappropriately again, but quietly. I doubted that even Morton would get the joke. He was a reader, not a TV watcher. He did not go to college but he is one of those men who reads Nietzsche and mispronounces the name but knows the material. Self-educated men possess these quirks. Well-read, they have never heard the key words, the names, the concepts pronounced out loud. It gives their conversations an odd tone, as if you were discussing philosophy with an immigrant just off the boat. It's difficult to take seriously people who mispronounce words, but that says more about me than it says about people who know more than I do.

I knocked on the doorsill.

Morton's head moved on the pillow. He was awake.

"Malarkey," he said, his voice ragged from bouts of recent thirst. A full jug of water and an empty glass stood by his bedside. He raised a hand and signaled me toward him with a crooked finger.

"How do you feel?" I said. I was prepared to utter every banality expected of healthy people.

"Alive," he said.

I knew what he meant. I had felt that way before.

I looked up and down his bed. His body was covered by a sheet, his head bandaged, an IV still in his arm. "Thank God for that," I said.

He nodded. For the moment, he seemed willing to concede divine intervention, which is rare among Nietzsche buffs. I stood there trying to think of something to say. What can I do to help you? Can I get you anything? I have no healing powers, but the floral shop sells magazines.

"Did the police find the bastard?" he said.

This caught me off guard. I had been dreading the moment when I would have to explain to him that I did not do this to him, in spite of what he believed. I tried to ease my way through this newly opened door.

"Have you spoken with the police?" I said.

He nodded. "A cop named Coleman. A detective. He told me what happened."

"What did he tell you?" I said.

"He told me that I accused you of hitting me with your car," Morton said. "I don't remember saying that."

The burden left my shoulders like a flock of crows rising ghostlike through the ceiling. I felt lightweight. I would not be going into battle with Morton, pointing out his mistake, trying desperately to explain.

"Do you remember my visit yesterday?"

He shook his head no, then said it: "No."

"I came to see you after I heard about the accident."

"I don't remember anything about yesterday," he said. "The detective told me I had made statements that were erroneous."

"It must have been the drugs," I said.

He smiled. His smile told me that I was a sharp character. That I picked up on things fast. That I couldn't be buffaloed. I decided to let go of yesterday. Yesterday had driven me to the brink of madness. Why did Morton accuse me of hitting him with my car? I had wrestled with this—did Morton have it in for me because my Ford had ruined his leg, cost him his job? Had he been feigning friendship all these months while waiting for the right moment to make his strike, ruin my life, and maybe send me to the hospital? But I had done my time in a hospital. That strike was made the day I was born.

"They caught the bastard," I said. "He stole my car and hit you while you were walking home from the Lemon Tree."

He nodded. "I don't remember much about it. I told the cops things that I don't remember telling them."

"Do you remember the drink we had yesterday?" I said.

"Yes. Your car wouldn't start."

"The man who stole it got it started."

"He must have wiggled the battery cables."

I nodded. There would be a lot to tell Morton after he got out of the hospital and we took our seats together in the bar. I would be the center of attention for nights on end, maybe weeks. That ought to satisfy my insatiable ego. I would feed it scotch and turn it loose. But that was okay because Morton would be the real star of the show, the main character, the victim, he would milk every last detail of the things that had happened to me while he was drugged and unconscious. We would go to Benny's trial together. We would witness a perp walk. We would bring stories clipped from the newspaper and Rudy would tack them to the bulletin board at the Lemon Tree Lounge.

I finally looked Morton square in the eye and worked up the nerve to ask him something that only someone who had been through what he had been through could tell me, a thing that Oscar Easley would never be able to tell me, a thing that I had pondered throughout my encounters with Benny the genius: "Is there an afterlife? Did you see a tunnel, a white light? Did you speak to a guide with wings? Did you review every last incriminating detail of your life? Did you go to that place? Did you see it?"

Morton shook his head no. "I didn't see a thing, Malarkey. It was all darkness. Total darkness. In fact, I don't even remember the darkness. I don't remember anything at all. Just nothingness. Total nothingness. One moment I was walking along the sidewalk in front of my house, and the next moment the world ceased to exist. It was like a boat out of the blue."

I knew then that he was lying. He remembered what he had told the cops. He knew he had fingered me erroneously. He was just embarrassed. He would never have brought up the boat business if he wasn't ashamed of his misinterpretation of the facts. Change the subject. Create a diversion. Make me laugh.

But who among us has never been embarrassed? Who among us has never misinterpreted facts? Who among us has never peered into the abyss and come away red-faced? Cab drivers, garage mechanics, losers, sociopaths, we all make mistakes. We all seek forgiveness. We all realize we should have done things differently. But maybe that's the reason we were born. Maybe that's our purpose in life. To learn how to do things differently. As good a pointless answer as any.

The End

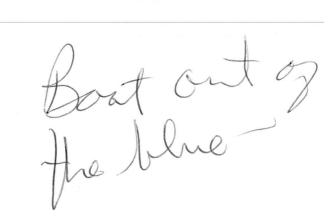